Praise for *The Vicar Vortex*

As hilarious and fantastical as ever, *The Vicar Vortex* takes Tyee Lagoon and its cast of unforgettable characters to a whole new level of dark secrets, paranormal absurdity, and existential threats that will leave the reader in stitches, and in support of dastardly choices. A brilliant finish to the raucous Vicar trilogy.

— PETE MCCORMACK, Oscar nominated filmmaker and author of *Understanding Ken*

Adventure wrapped in metaphysical mystery and served up with contemporary family drama — all while being rip-snorting, laugh-out-loud funny. This is quintessential Canadian mythology.

— ROB BAKER, guitarist of The Tragically Hip

You don't want to stand too close to Tony Vicar, as you know some comic disaster is just around the corner, but you wouldn't dare miss a second of it, either. Vince has revived him here just as Tony himself has brought the dead back to life, and I for one can't look away.

— ALAN DOYLE, singer, songwriter, and author of *Where I Belong*

Praise for *The Vicar's Knickers*

I don't remember the last time I smiled so much while reading a novel. Vince Ditrich's vivid descriptions and colourful characters are the perfect escapism.

— MARTIN CROSBIE, bestselling author of the *My Temporary Life* trilogy

The Vicar's Knickers is a delightful humour-noir novel. Vince Ditrich generously lends his trademark wit and cleverness to the characters of fictional Tyee Lagoon, with laugh-out-loud turns of phrase on every page.

— SARAH CHAUNCEY, author of *P.S. I Love You More Than Tuna*

The greatest sequel since *The Wrath of Khan*, if Tony Vicar was William Shatner.

— GRANT LAWRENCE, author and CBC Radio host

Praise for *The Liquor Vicar*

The Liquor Vicar is an energetic romp through a closet community on the Island, populated by well-drawn characters and strewn with more references to pop culture and euphemisms than you can shake a stick at.

— *Winnipeg Free Press*

Ditrich presents a fresh, gonzo voice in his debut novel, a quirky tale of the down side of life and a promise of redemption in a narrative that is entertaining.

— *Booklist*

The Liquor Vicar is beautiful chaos. Ditrich's characters come alive with all the complexity of a Shakespearean comedy and a uniquely Canadian dry wit. Colourful characters carry this story like a current, moving seamlessly from side-splitting humour to tenderness as it explores our human desire for relevance and purpose.

— MELANIE MARTIN, author of *A Splendid Boy*

THE
VICAR
VORTEX

THE MILDLY CATASTROPHIC
MISADVENTURES OF TONY VICAR

The Liquor Vicar
The Vicar's Knickers
The Vicar Vortex

VINCE R. DITRICH

THE VICAR VORTEX

THE MILDLY
CATASTROPHIC
MISADVENTURES
OF TONY VICAR

DUNDURN
PRESS

Publisher and acquiring editor: Kwame Scott Fraser | Editor: Shannon Whibbs
Cover designer: Laura Boyle
Cover image: cowgirl: 123RF.com/dcart; UFOs: SVGDesigns; Plane: Shutterstock.com/Yaroslav Shkuro; vortex: istock.com/ly86

Library and Archives Canada Cataloguing in Publication

Title: The Vicar vortex / Vince R. Ditrich.
Names: Ditrich, Vince R., 1963- author.
Description: Series statement: The mildly catastrophic misadventures of Tony Vicar ; 3
Identifiers: Canadiana (print) 20230566642 | Canadiana (ebook) 20230566669
| ISBN 9781459747319 (softcover) | ISBN 9781459747333 (EPUB) | ISBN
9781459747326 (PDF)
Classification: LCC PS8607.I87 V52 2024 | DDC C813/.6—dc23

We acknowledge the support of the Canada Council for the Arts and the Ontario Arts Council for our publishing program. We also acknowledge the financial support of the Government of Ontario, through the Ontario Book Publishing Tax Credit and Ontario Creates, and the Government of Canada.

Dundurn Press
1382 Queen Street East
Toronto, Ontario, Canada M4L 1C9
dundurn.com, @dundurnpress

Dedicated to the Three Musketeers
Who will someday be
Three Wise Men:
Ollie, Sparky, Louis

I t was a miracle that the entire building hadn't col-lapsed into a charred ruin. The southwest corner of the old Agincourt Hotel had been burned to nothing, from third-floor roof down to the ground, and the blaze had devoured both shops at street level, as well as the hotel lobby.

But the Vicar's Knickers Pub, the town's centre-piece, located over on the other side of the hotel, still stood and was in surprisingly good shape. The wall that separated pub from hotel lobby was quite heavily fire singed, but other than smoke damage, the rest of the Knickers was standing and in one piece.

For a long time, the entire building was barricaded off, covered by a construction-site fence that blocked the view and left an eyesore in downtown Tyee Lagoon. It took nearly a year and a half to clear the damage and rebuild what was lost.

In the meantime, the stories about Tony Vicar, the entire litany of half truths and rumour that had sprung up before him like a hardened manure ha-ha in a field, heated up to a rolling boil. Several years before, he had become an internet sensation when reports claimed that he had magically brought a dead person back to life at the scene of a car crash. Just like that, Tony Vicar had become famous, although at first his cachet was a bit "niche." Paranormal, woo-woo, comic-relief spooky bits and such.

Members of the media had set upon him like a pack of hounds, absorbed his girlfriend, Jacquie O, into the narrative, too, and then a couple of them had badly overstepped ...

They were real stinkers, those two; muckrakers from Hollywood, deliberately starting a fire in Vicar's hotel, which instantly became an emergency of dire proportions. Vicar had pulled off an impossible rescue of his foster daughter and another baby, and had reported that he'd had, or at least he thought he'd had, paranormal help doing it. Vicar had been guided through the flames by something unreal. A *ghost* ... Or a hallucination. As to which, Vicar wasn't sure.

But he'd got the kids out. It was through a blaze that surely should have killed them, but somehow, he made it out with one kid in his arms, the other stuffed into his shirt. Ann Tenna, his best server, who had been working downstairs when the fire started, had also seen the entity. Her confirmation of his experience made Vicar feel a little less alone, a little less "touched."

After that point, fascination with Vicar and his "magic powers" had no hope of dissipating — long after he was dead and gone, the stories would live on. The tales were exaggerated beyond belief now; Vicar cringed at how they might become full-on nuts after he died and was unable to refute them.

The pair of slimy reporters responsible for the fire had fled back to Hollywood after feeling legal heat coming their way. Truthfully, they more limped than fled ... Vicar and company had gotten their pound of flesh and he hoped the villains' drawn-out attempts at avoiding extradition would someday end in their incarceration. Pretty boys who had done as poorly in Tyee Lagoon as they would face a calamity in prison. Vicar estimated that they both had a *purdy mouth*, and one was even minus a good number of teeth — surely a boon in the Pen.

■ ■ ■

It took a month to remove the fire damage from the remains of the hotel's innards and another seven months to replace it all. The centre and north framework still held firm in the main, but an entire hunk of the building to the south side had had to be rebuilt. This time the builder was much quicker in finishing the hotel rooms and did a rather imaginative job of overhauling what had been left of the lobby, brand new but artfully treated to look antique. The decorating and furnishing took longer still, but things were in pretty good nick as the two-year mark hovered on the horizon. Vicar and Jacquie had finally retired its original name, "Agincourt," and dubbed it "Hotel Valentine," in honour of the day they "took delivery" of their foster daughter, Frankie. She had appeared on their doorstep, from where they did not know.

Valentine was also the name of the ghost that was said to have haunted the old building. If it had ever existed outside Vicar's imagination at all, the spectre had made itself scarce since. Vicar was afraid that he might need to see a psychiatrist or psychic — maybe both. His interactions with the eerie presence had been terrifyingly real.

After the rebuild, no one had mentioned even the slightest ghostly disturbance, though the internet remained rife with ever-escalating speculation. Vicar resigned himself to it. A hotel with a ghost was free advertising in a very big way, like having goats on the roof.

■ ■ ■

At the time of the great fire, some two years before, Vicar was shocked but above all else deeply relieved that he had managed to get baby Frankie and little Wallis out of the third-floor suite alive. As for the rescue efforts by the now wildly famous hotel ghost ... If Valentine had only been an illusion, Vicar would never again be able to trust his eyes and ears.

"He," the ghost, had taken the shape of a young man, who had walked Vicar and the little ones through a roaring, deadly flaming doorway without any ill effects. Jacquie had been certain Vicar had hallucinated the whole rescue, that he had experienced some form of psychosis brought about by ultra-high stress. She had compared it to a ninety-pound woman lifting a car off her child trapped beneath it.

Vicar was left believing Jacquie and his own perceptions at the same time. It was a balancing act that never quite reached equilibrium.

■ ■ ■

Inside the Knickers many months later, only the smell of smoke remained, which had dissipated with time.

The place was a marvel, really. Vicar had spent a colossal amount of money dreaming up and building a pub that was nearly cathedral-like, with a thirty-five-foot-tall ceiling, a giant inglenook on one side, stone seating cut into the floor surrounding it, and a gargantuan, lovingly crafted bar. Vicar's most faithful regulars were presented with small brass plaques attached to the places they preferred to sit, and an instant tradition was born. It was held that, if you were sitting there when they arrived, you surrendered your seat to them. That tradition alone had turned a small handful of regulars into acolytes, some of whom thought of themselves as a *guard of honour* and treated the Knickers almost like holy ground.

The reopening of the Knickers was a surprisingly celebrated affair, right down to the mayor attending.

Vicar hadn't known that Tyee Lagoon even had a mayor, so the guy could have been bullshitting, but whatever. *Hizzoner* was drinking red wine, the cheap stuff that tasted like grape juice mixed with violin bow rosin. Vicar had whispered into the ear of one of his regulars, Chief Hank Wheat, "Is that really the mayor?" as he gestured with his eyes toward the tipsy man with the wine-stained dentures. The Chief just shrugged and replied, "Do we even *have* a mayor?"

However, *Condé Nast Traveler* sent a writer, as did Vancouver and Victoria papers, all the regional publications, and a voluble and thirsty writer from the *Saskatoon Star Phoenix* — hometown of the hotel's ghost, it was claimed. There was also a long lineup of unwanted beggars-on from paranormal websites that had dogged and harried Vicar for years — ever since he was credited with having brought Julie Northrop back to life after the now-famous car wreck on Midden Hill near Tyee Lagoon.

Everyone, *everywhere*, knew the story — and everyone had their own take on it. Those bizarre "takes," often printed in huge, jolly lettering, supported the opinion held by some that logic and common sense no longer were in vogue. In fact, the world had gone to shit so badly that people *demanded* the arcane and magical, or so it seemed. Sheer fluke of timing had hoisted poor Vicar into the stratosphere.

Although the EMT had considered her beyond help, ceased CPR, and called it, Julie Northrop had "come back" after Vicar's stubborn ministrations. That much of the tale was true, although Vicar wasn't sure *why* she had come back. But then paranormal cyber-sleuths had grabbed hold of the story, and it had exploded like a pile of gasoline-soaked autumn leaves. Because of the nature of modern news dissemination, there could be no healthy skepticism about the story. Vicar was, *obviously*, magic. He *obviously* brought people back from the dead. There could be no other *possible* explanation. *Duh, you guys …*

Overpaid movie actors, eagerly watched by fully grown adults in their multitudes, sported tight-fitting leotards, saved the world, and defied physics on a discouragingly regular basis. Somehow, while their heroes hovered, flew, lifted locomotives, and blew up shit with their laser-beam eyeballs, normal folks watched these laughable protagonists with straight faces, and still ended up in the hospital, fallen and fractured, from catching their toe on the doormat. This glaring dissonance was never fully investigated. Vicar knew this phenomenon all too well.

His life had made such a sharp turn in the last few years that he had begun to wonder who he really was. Between the chasm of what he had experienced, what public opinion claimed, and what made sense, lay his story.

PART I

Are you seated comfortably?
Then we'll begin ...

One / More or Less than
Meets the Eye

The view from that high was tremendous. To Tony Vicar's right, he saw the Strait of Georgia, a dark bluish-purple, laid out beneath him in mosaic-like cells, the tideline a margin where colour changed dramatically to a milky aqua green. To his left stood the Beaufort mountain range, imposing, snowcapped, and gleaming in the sun, crowned by clouds that looked like a nicely stiff meringue, brilliant white, a little grey where cloud met mountaintop, and with a base of royal blue. When the sun angle was right, he could even catch a glow of pink tinging the high plumes.

The Merchants' Association of Tyee Lagoon — a tiny, miserly group that sounded much grander than it was — had offered Vicar a free flight in Gunnar Bering's Cessna, in reward for his generosity to the locals: a sightseeing joyride around the gorgeous environs surrounding his hometown. They had had to spring for the fuel, nothing more; even so, there had been some hushed grumbling.

Vicar let a great number of folks hold their club and team meetings in the Vicar's Knickers, on a regular basis, for no fee. Winters here on Vancouver Island were very slow, so getting a few bodies into the pub made a big difference to his bottom line. He had invested in "velvet ropes," which did nothing more than surround little areas within the pub for their events with an uppity-looking, glorified snow-fence. Really it was as pointless as a non-smoking section in a jetliner, but people thought it looked legit and treated those ropes like they were an impenetrable barrier through which non-members might not trespass, nor even listen.

The local Book Club held its monthly meeting there, but that event was a loss because they were all prim teetotalers and brought their own snacks. Vicar could have kicked about that but didn't; they were almost all old ladies and he had a soft spot, even when a couple of them acted supercilious and lofty, bitching about spelling and punctuation on the menu. For a couple of years, Ann Tenna and Beaner Weens, the cook, had been in a low-grade war over authorship of the accursed and often indecipherable chalkboard. They both tended to communicate like trick dogs that use talking foot pedals. Vicar had given up refereeing when he realized how stultifying their arguments had become. The near-brawl that had erupted over the spelling of "Cosmopolitan" was one for the ages. *Kosmopulletin, Cosmapahlitain, Kusmoballintun* ... He'd listened, baffled, his head twisted sideways like a foot-pedal pup.

The sporadically charming Book Club ladies held a raffle every meeting and the prize was usually something knitted or crocheted, and invariably non-essential. Occasionally they made pottery. One of the oblivious ol' gals had actually made and donated a white ceramic elephant statuette. Vicar had snorted audibly and one of their membership glowered at him.

Realizing that the glaring metaphor was invisible to most of these women, Vicar had coughed up a loonie, placing the coin respectfully on the raffle table — just to make nice — and won an oven mitt, made of Phentex or some other ghastly flame accelerant, that instantly snagged a fingernail when he tried it on. The sensation was extraordinarily grating; he'd waited until they departed and thrown it in the trash.

He had found a comfy wingback chair for Mrs. Oliver, one of the nicer ladies, a long-retired school librarian who attended the Book Club's monthly gatherings religiously. He set her chair nearer the ladies' room, at her request, right next to her companion, Mrs. Parker, with space nearby to stow her walker, where it could sit unobtrusively. As customers, Book Clubbers were *el cheapo grande*: long-retired millionaires mostly, but tight enough to squeak. A few even brought their own tea bags and just ordered hot water, but Vicar got a good snicker from his new "walker parking" area and the ten-dollar honorarium they always bestowed upon

VINCE R. DITRICH

him, presented with desultory golf claps, slipped into a dollar-store thank-you card.

In Vancouver, there were establishments that offered valet parking for Ferraris and McLarens. Here ... well, he personally acted as attendant for the Zimmer frames and knew better than to expect a tip.

Vicar had given them back their monthly thank-you card early on and told them to reuse it, knowing how colossally miserly a few of them were — he had heard the minutes of their meetings a dozen times. He wanted to see how far he could push his subtle commentary, and one of the ladies, invariably preoccupied with piddling budgetary issues, had thought it was a splendid idea, and so they'd recycled that same card for a dog's age. Vicar just blinked and pasted on a vague smile, realizing then that subtlety bounces off cheapskates.

The Tyee Lagoon Angling Society, on the other hand, drank like the fish they claimed to catch and perhaps might have done if they didn't get so remarkably drunk every time they met. The whole organization was only an excuse to get pissed up. Their president, a crinkly old scoundrel with the antique-sounding name of Hotchkiss Cooper — known as Hotchy-Coochie — invariably read into the minutes that they had been "overserved" at the previous meeting, and officially censured Vicar, who was not even a member; of course they toasted the censure, making additions and amendments to it, and toasting each of those in turn. They went through this charade every time and laughed uproariously without fail. Vicar would shake his head in bafflement. Hotchy-Coochie was mysteriously eager for this sort of shit, especially for a guy his advanced age — he seemed up for *anything* and had been for decades. Privately, Vicar referred to him as "Enthusula."

Most recently Hotchy-Coochie had declared Vicar a "pusher" and "manipulator of peer pressure," and accused him of wanting, for an unknown and probably nefarious reason, to ply everyone with what they called "the demon rum." Hotchy-Coochie would glance accusingly at Vicar, his nose in the air aristocratically, then turn away in faux-dismay. A rumbling of "hear, hear" always bubbled forth from the gathering, and then of course they drank to that, too.

That old fart hoovered booze like a sink and couldn't have given a rat's arse what anybody thought.

At any rate, it was all in good fun, and Tyee Lagoon needed a dose of that at times — things in this burg were a tad calcified. Vicar had once spent some time sipping coffee on a bench that overlooked the town's four-way stop, agog at the mind-melting malfunctions of the local geriatric drivers as they attempted to run that daunting gauntlet. It was true that the only times Tyee Lagoon had got into the news it was thanks to Vicar, but that was because, without him, the bloody place was as boring as watching creosote drip.

Vicar had matured enough that he could sometimes hide his antipathy toward skinflints — a.k.a., most of the population of Tyee Lagoon — and tried to laugh it off, adding it to the lengthy ledger that recorded his bent reality.

However, the one or two most dominant Book Club ladies lived in a tightly patrolled *irony-free zone*, their stony, disapproving faces the only response to anything light-hearted. Vicar was all too aware that icy disapproval is the safe default response for people who can't understand the most rudimentary joke but have decided their *offended-ness* must look "high status." The little splinter group believed strongly in parliamentary procedure and board governance, and so took such nonsensical reports as Vicar's "overserving" very seriously, dragging the rest of their malleable membership along with them.

Mrs. Morrison, most particularly — a busybody's busybody — seemed to derive purpose from disapproving of, well … *everything*, including things that didn't affect her at all, and in fact, a few things that she had dreamt up. Inevitably dressed up in conspicuous tartan, occasionally looking like the lady on the Export "A" tin — including the goddamn bonnet — she'd pass judgment upon matters like parking (her husband, a thralled marionette, chauffeured her everywhere and manoeuvred torturously to get her as close to her destination as any human could do) or downtown noise (although she lived, she would constantly brag, in the "highly desirable seaside subdivision of Sandringham Mews," a good ten-minute trip from the town centre).

Vicar was certain that she kept book on people who illegally tore the tag off their mattresses, in contravention of its clearly stated injunction. Her most recent bugbear, the "shocking traffic," was now a "daily nuisance." Shocking traffic, to her, was three cars passing in front of her clinically tidy house on the same day. He liked little old ladies a lot, but Mrs. Morrison had really begun to chap his corn-chute.

None of her baloney had the first thing to do with the books she had read, of course, but really, how could she be expected to concentrate on matters literary when surrounded by all this chaos? *And by the way, why don't young people want to work anymore?*

Everyone else seemed to think Vicar was doing a fine job. The Book Club tutted and clucked like five acres of poultry, but still met at the Knickers because the price was right. To Vicar there was a conspicuous correlation between *money cheap* and *kindness cheap*. Margaret Morrison, that self-righteous, disdainful old bat, would know that the Scottish describe cheapness as being "mean." And boy howdy, she was meaner than a scorned mother-in-law — ironically, something she'd never be.

She chronically maintained the spin that her one coddled, adult son just hadn't found the *right one*, as she put it. At one point a few years ago, she had believed she and her dutiful husband would soon become grandparents, but she had been mistaken. Pregnant Kay — Arthur had explained as he served her a cucumber sandwich one teatime — was only a friend. "Mother, you know I'm a confirmed bachelor."

Aloft now for only a few minutes, Gunnar Bering pointed to the two o'clock position and said, "Tyee Lagoon is that way ... Can you make it out?"

Vicar could indeed see it, a vague and smallish footprint near the shoreline. He replied, "Can we fly over it?" He wanted to see his house from the air — also his pub.

"Roger — my pleasure. Here, *you* turn us toward it." The pilot offered control of the aircraft to Vicar, like Grandad allowing one of the kids to steer as the ol' Strato Chief rolled onto the ferry.

Vicar was excited but anxious. He loved the feeling, but as soon as he was in control, he was nearly overpowered by the fear that the little aircraft might tip over, barrel-roll, explode in a ball of fire, disintegrate, eject him, or otherwise defy Bernoulli's principle simply by sensing a newbie was at its controls. When Vicar had first gotten into the little craft, it had looked awfully frail, about as solid as the frame of a motorhome's awning, so he didn't feel very confident. He was required to adjust the heading only by about twenty degrees, but the very thought made him quail, as if the wings were made of gossamer, sure to tear off from such reckless hot-dogging.

"It won't bite you. Just turn a little more. Don't be shy, I've got ya."

"Okay, okay ... Uh, *roger*. Right-O." Vicar was babbling slightly, big headset rattling loosely on his head, trying to hide that his heart was in his throat. But to his surprise, the aircraft turned, and quite gently to boot. *I'm piloting it!*

"'Kay, Tony, now just steer straight toward town. Keep it level. Don't pull back on the yoke. Level, level ..."

Level? Vicar felt instantly as if he was unable to cope with such a deluge of input, and then stopped himself. He'd merely been asked not to wring the controls in a death grip and stay steady. He tried to manage it and relaxed, finally breathing and turning his head to look around.

Vicar noticed Gunnar Berring laugh and wondered if he was remembering his first time at the controls. How nervous had he been?

He revelled in the sensation. Vicar felt his heart soar as he winged above the sea, dancing along the shoreline that lay below, just over his left shoulder, tracing along to maintain his sense of direction and position. He was headed, at a hundred and twenty knots, toward a rendezvous with his hometown.

"We'll be over Tyee Lagoon in a couple of minutes. Steer to the right a bit, and then we'll do a hard left and fly over from the northeast to the southwest."

Vicar was with him now, visualizing the flight path and the manoeuvre, already getting a teensy bit cocky. Man, this was *fun*.

He goggled delightedly at Tyee Lagoon, getting larger and larger in the windscreen. Visibility was unlimited. He turned to Gunnar, about to ask when he should begin his manoeuvre, when the motor stuttered.

He stiffened instantly, his heart rate jumping.

The pilot, well experienced, pored urgently over the control panel. Automatically he retook control of the yoke, but before he could complete a full scan of the dashboard, there was a very loud bang, accompanied by an alarming dislocation of fuselage that bonneted the engine, like a blown hood on an old jalopy. This was followed by a spray and smear of oil that obscured the windscreen.

"We've lost oil pressure … Something let loose in there." Gunnar was tense but not panicky. It was obvious to Vicar that Gunnar couldn't see a thing through the oil slick on his front window; he jiggered around ineffectively with the throttle at the same instant the motor quit entirely.

Suddenly the little airplane was silent, except for the ragged, whistling wind. Choking black smoke filled the cockpit.

Gunnar muttered, "Damn, I think we blew a jug."

Vicar just stared at him uncomprehendingly.

Gunnar instructed Vicar to open the little air vent and made a mayday call over the radio.. Then he briefed Vicar again on how to exit the aircraft once he "got them down."

The pilot craned his neck to get a view of the popped fuselage that had ruined the airworthiness of the little aircraft. "I don't think we can glide back to the airport, Tony. This thing is a falling potato."

Vicar gulped. He feared they'd need to ditch in the drink — after a jolly terrifying death-spiral first, *of course*. Didn't they call that "augering in"? His nice day had become a nightmare and would end in a watery grave momentarily; he swam like a boulder. He looked around for the life jackets.

Gunnar saw what he was doing and jabbed his index finger briefly toward it on the door frame behind him. Then he slapped his palm on the fire extinguisher and looked Vicar directly in the eye.

Vicar nodded quickly to say, "I understand," and then checked his seat belt. They really were headed downstairs — Vicar could feel it in the seat of his pants.

With the top of his head leaning on his door, Gunnar peered through the edge of the windscreen, where there was an inch or so of unobstructed view. He did what he could to keep them aloft, but it was a losing battle. The craft had dropped down to about five hundred feet, but now at least their "feet were dry"; they were finally over land.

The pilot saw a road ahead with no vehicles on it and made the snap decision to attempt an emergency landing on it, quickly reporting his plan over the radio, not even sure if his message had been received.

"I'm going to try to take us down on the road ahead. This might be awfully bumpy, so brace for a hard landing."

Vicar clipped through gritted teeth, "Oh, I'm braced like a mofo, don' choo worry." He was shitting himself with fright.

Out his right-hand window, Vicar could see the treetops and buildings coming closer and closer and realized that they were headed downward to Jersey

Road, the long country lane that started nearly at the water's edge. He felt a surge of hope — the road was straight and nearly always deserted. This was the most nowhere-ish stretch of the most nowhere-ish road in their nowhere-ish town.

Somehow, Gunnar was keeping the wounded craft in the air, keeping the nose up — but not *too* up. Vicar imagined him trying to see the road ahead with the greatest difficulty, estimating his touchdown point, hoping not to bounce on landing and end up inverted in the ditch, desperately wanting to bring the emergency to a quick ending.

They were so close now that Vicar could see the road rushing upward from beneath them. The heavy power lines on the poles beside them made an undulating pattern as they whooshed past, and then suddenly Gunnar yelled, "Oh shit!" in alarm.

A millisecond later, Vicar slammed against his seat belt and felt them shearing downward. He found out only later that their landing gear had got caught up in power lines that crossed the road at an intersection, not visible until too late. They were thrown hard to the right, left wingtip up at a crazy angle, landing gear now gone. They bashed heavily into the ground, the right wing was torn off and exploded in flames, and they slid on their belly into the building that was now in their path, leaving the wing behind in a sheet of fire.

Vicar threw his left forearm across his face and held onto the door handle with his right, bracing for collision with the wall. A vision of Jacquie and Frankie flashed through his mind, and then the hurtling, wrecked Cessna 172 ploughed into the wall, piercing it like a lawn-dart into a cardboard box.

The shock was overwhelming. Vicar felt his upper body pummelled by debris and battered by the collapse of the aircraft's interior. He might have lost consciousness for a moment, but whatever the case, he took a few seconds to come to his senses.

He looked over at Gunnar, who was buried in debris that had fallen through the shattered windscreen. Vicar could barely see him through the litter; he thought he heard a moan and hoped Gunnar might still be alive.

With difficulty he pushed at his door, trying to get out of the broken craft. The hatch was jammed partway shut and his leg didn't seem to want to work. With his shoulder he bashed at it until he, for all intents and purposes, launched himself out of the wreck onto his side, falling onto rubble that cluttered the floor below. The fall should have hurt immensely but Vicar was numb. He smelled burning oil, dust, and aviation fuel. He could see through the jagged tear in the wall that the detached wing was blazing away in the parking lot. He was afraid of an explosion inside but didn't have the strength to lean back into the plane to grab the fire extinguisher — as if that little thing would have done much good, anyway.

Vicar climbed to his feet, using his hands and one good leg, and looked around. The mangled plane's tail was still outdoors, but the smashed cockpit and part of its fuselage were inside the building and had destroyed the entire room with which they'd collided. He did not know where he was, and stumbled over the rubble in his path, discovering in the smoky haze ahead of him a lady in a long gown, lying in the strangest jackknife position on the floor, dead.

Oh, no, we've killed somebody! Steadying himself against a flat surface, he saw ahead of him a man in formal clothes crumpled on his side, not far from the dead lady. He appeared to be dead, too. Vicar couldn't quite put it together. *Dear God, no ... We've smashed into a wedding.*

The room seemed littered with dead. *There are bodies everywhere.* Feeling faint and suddenly nauseated, Vicar hunched over and vomited.

As he upchucked, his thoughts flashed on all the bizarre luck he'd enjoyed for the last several years; all the crazy, almost unbelievable strokes of fortune. If he really did have mystical powers, as everyone was claiming, he hoped they would visit him now. He threw up again, his body writhing like an overplayed accordion.

Someone was pounding at a door, trying to open it, although it was blocked shut with debris and the nose of the wrecked airplane. The propeller had bent back like a couple of flower petals as it bunched up against the far wall, a surreal sight that only added to Vicar's shock. Vicar was stunned at the carnage; his injured thigh was weeping blood profusely and left a thick stain down the length of his leg and onto his shoe. He was close to blacking out but worried about wrecking his new Nikes.

The door cracked a couple of inches. "Is anyone in there?" a voice called.

Vicar merely retched in response.

"We're coming. Hold on!"

Vicar began barfing on his blood-soaked shoes. He collapsed onto one knee, thinking of Gunnar, the pilot. *Save him — he's stuck in there ...* Beside Vicar was yet another body, dead but liveried to the nines, wearing a corsage. Horror washed over him as he imagined having to face the Mother of the Bride. He'd rather face Cerberus at the gates of Hell.

Blood oozed thickly from a gash in his forehead, now flooding his eye, and then he lost focus, everything went dark, and he sank down into the wreckage.

Two / Crash Course

When Jacquie O, formally known as Miss C. Jacqueline O'Neil, had left the prairies as a teenager, she'd had no idea what lay in store for her. Energetic, smart, hard-working, she disguised her less-than-stellar childhood by achieving a great deal, but finances had been lacking. Sure, Mom helped as much as she could, but the years-long ambivalence Jacquie had felt toward Beulah O'Neil was a wet blanket. The first couple of years after she left home, Jacquie had seldom called, leaving her mother feeling abandoned and regretful.

The pair shared a past that had left Jacquie wanting nothing more than to get the hell outta Dodge, find a new place to settle, and forget about her childhood. She managed it but had had to resort to exotic dancing to afford the high cost of living on Vancouver Island.

Jacquie put herself through three years of psych studies at UVic but quit a year short of a degree when her boyfriend was killed riding his bike into town. She shut everything down, moved out of her apartment, and fled to the least metropolitan place she could find: Tyee Lagoon, farther north on Vancouver Island, filled with audiologists; denturists; three shops selling assisted living equipment, but not one that sold computers; an extremely sluggish swarm of octogenarians often partaking in parking capades at the grocery store; and the infamous four-way-stop intersection not far from the grocery store that provided everyone under sixty with hours of entertainment.

Things had somehow worked out for Jacquie, but since meeting Tony Vicar, life had been an adventure inside a hallucination, wrapped in a myth.

▄▄ ▄▄ ▄▄

Vicar had grown up a bit. When he first met Jacquie, he was a free-wheeling bachelor, disorganized, unkempt, unshaven, and prone to flights of fancy better suited to an eleven-year-old. He did not for a moment think Batmobile ownership would be silly or ostentatious, *or wasteful* — and often wondered how he might load one with all his guitars. In the years since he'd first encountered Jacquie while DJ'ing at a wedding in an Elvis costume, his life had turned around remarkably. That night, he'd come within inches of soiling his costume. But by some minor miracle, he had made it to the toilet just in the nick of time, literally and figuratively.

He was older, and now a father — or at least a foster father — to little Frankie. He was owner of the most famous pub on the west coast, and of course everyone you talked to thought he possessed paranormal, almost magical powers; he scoffed at that kind of talk, yet was baffled by things that had happened. It was all a confusing pain in the ass, really.

▬ ▬ ▬

There had *definitely* been a Sumerian way back in antiquity who was the first dude to hear the voice in his head when he sounded out a written word. Something he'd etched in clay. With that kooky sound echoing in his Mesopotamian melon, was he surprised? Did he jump a bit and ask, "Where did that voice come from?" Did he glance around his hut, a little freaked out, looking for a passing ventriloquist? Were there ventriloquists in Mesopotamia?

Why do I feel so weird right now? What is that pain in my leg? I hear beeping; is someone backing up a truck?

Vicar's tunnel vision blurred as a light shone down upon him from above. After a moment or two of disorientation, he arose from unconsciousness and began to run on most of his cylinders. He could tell he was in a hospital bed. The beeping came from a machine beside him that was dripping fluids into his arm through a long, clear hose.

Beside him was his lovely girlfriend, Jacquie O. She looked at him with apprehension, her face radiating concern. He was on dope or something, he could feel it, and so she seemed to be surrounded by a glowing halo as he squinted. It made her look even nicer. He thought she was wearing that tan trench coat he liked so much. He couldn't quite see all the details, but she hadn't even taken it off yet — she must have just arrived. He just lay there for a minute, staring at her, blinking, trying to clear the milky coating that obscured his vision, piecing together how he had gotten here.

As Vicar woke up, Jacquie O put her warm palm on his forehead, like Mom feeling for a fever, offering a loving hand and a soothing touch. Vicar calmed immediately and felt his memory clicking in.

The plane had crashed. *Oh, dear God.* Sheer bedlam.

"Jack ..."

"It's okay, Tony. Everything's okay."

His throat was as dry as a webinar and he nearly gagged. Jacquie reached over quickly and put the end of a straw between his lips. He sucked on cool water with relief.

After a long moment or two, he pulled his head away.

Panting, he explained, "We crashed. The plane. It went down." He cleared his throat roughly.

"Yes, Tony. I know. Everyone knows."

"Gunnar? The pilot ...."

She tilted her head and looked at the door. "Down the hall."

Vicar remembered the crash's aftermath and urgently asked, "How many dead?" His face was apprehensive.

"No one, Tony." She paused. "Thank God. It could have been a catastrophe."

"But there were bodies everywhere ..."

Jacquie looked at him, puzzled for a second, and then realized what he meant.

"Tony, you hit Balmer's Funeral Home."

He looked at her blankly.

"The bodies ... They were, uh, *customers*."

Three / Goat Story

Jacquie gently manoeuvred her car close to the door of the house so that Tony had the shortest distance to hobble after his brief stay at the hospital.

Their home was 411 Sloop Road. It was a sixty-five-year-old Tudor house, tall, roomy, with a tremendous view. Jacquie had inherited it from the late Frankie Hall, a centenarian sweet on her and Vicar both. Mrs Hall, a tiny woman with a spitfire personality had, in the brief time they had known her, steered their lives in a completely different direction. She had an unusually long view of things and had impressive matchmaking skills, too. She also ensured that Jacquie and Vicar would take her beer parlour, her hotel, and her family home after she died. No one had ever been so generous to them. It was clear that she wanted them to be together, for some unknown reason, and her will had come to pass.

They had both been sick at heart at the hotel's near destruction; it felt like a slap in the face to the memory of dear Mrs. Hall. The arson-induced blaze had expanded so rapidly that Vicar had found himself trapped, with two small children in his arms, reconciled to having a flaming doorway become their funeral pyre. Out of the hellish conflagration that should have roasted everyone, a rescuer had come and guided them safely through the flames; this mysterious rescuer then returned to the burning structure. He had been, Vicar thought, an embodiment of Valentine the Ghost, who had until that moment been a black blob or mischievous poltergeist or, more likely, an outright hallucination. Valentine could not exist, but he had appeared again and again, in multiple forms.

The jury was perennially out on the topic. Whatever the truth, had he been an actual human, then he had certainly died a horrible death in the ravenous blaze. There was no surviving that fiery event.

Jacquie could see it on Vicar's face when he mentally grappled with the veracity of Valentine. Not having seen anything to substantiate his spectral existence, she simply tried living with the whole crazy idea, just leaving the whole schmeer in abeyance, so to speak. But at any rate, Jacquie couldn't really spare too much mental energy on it; she had her own ghosts to deal with.

After a week and a half convalescing on the couch, Vicar returned to work; it was too soon but there was work to be done. He shut the light off in his tiny office, made sure the door was locked, and limped into the pub, his leg still tender from the crash. There, to his dread, was the Tuesday Night Tambourine Club, limbering up for another big gathering. And once again, each pupil awaited magical teachings that would show them how to mimic their own death rattle with a plastic percussion instrument; here, again, standing in a semi-circle, deeply non-musical seniors awaited their lesson. And over there, yes, *there*, he spied the goddamn bonehead responsible for this atrocity, a goof who always had some "community activity" going. *Why do civilians always have to get into the act?*

Mr. Organizer-Face had even arranged a minibus for them, which went from the Moose Lodge parking lot to the Knickers' front door, about sixty seconds' drive and unnecessary to civilian tambourine escapades. Vicar glared daggers at the back of his head and gritted his teeth, preparing for an onslaught of clatter.

The guy, Matty Hardy — whom Vicar called "Hardy Boy" — charged his students ten bucks each to come and jangle the soul-crushing noisemakers, and always counted "One, two, ready, *go!*" The whole thing was a mystery, in keeping with the Hardy Boy theme.

One discombobulated klutz wore safety goggles in case she tambourined a bit too close to her own retinas. The gaggle's only synchronization was a sharp intake of breath before a deafening judder of interpretive St.

Vitus Dance, followed by what sounded exactly like a truckload of hubcaps bouncing down a ravine.

▬ ▬ ▬

Merri Crabtree, Tyee Lagoon's purveyor of hot sauces and unbending positivity, had had a choice to make. Either pack it in after the "great fire" or rebuild her hot sauce boutique, named "Hot Thoth," located on the ground floor of the Hotel Valentine, just around the corner from the Vicar's Knickers. She did not need the money or all the endless work, but she felt a drive to be part of the scene that had grown up around Vicar and Jacquie O. Merri was unofficial Town Grandmother. The timing and her proximity made for a seamless dovetail into her new role, showering love on the fostered baby Frankie, and gently teaching Vicar and Jacquie how to parent a newborn. Through them, she missed her dearly departed hubby — Wally, Sr. — just a little less. Through them, she had purpose.

Merri was, to put it gently, "pear shaped," with a notable caboose often sheathed in some sort of tautly stretched Space-Age fabric of pastel hue, but she was chirpy, light on her feet, and inexhaustible, a wellspring of unbridled optimism. No one would go further to please — and no one seemed to have her constitution to take on thankless tasks.

It seemed impossible for her to make a statement without following up with a giggle. It was habitual, a tic, an unconscious effort to ingratiate. All statements were followed by a chuckle, a titter, or an out-of-context tee-hee. Even the mildest comment, "It's overcast today," was worthy of a brief but apologetic schnick. Most people didn't notice it at first, or passed it off as hyper-cheerfulness, but those who knew her well eventually found themselves wondering what the true meaning of her knee-jerk jolliness was all about. The generous Grandma had never, and would never, reveal what propelled it, and may not even have realized how chipper she came across.

■ ■ ■

Wisely skipping tambourine night, Chief Hank Wheat came in early the next day and sat in his customary place beyond the corner of the bar, just under the stairway to the second floor of the Knickers; he watched Vicar pouring from the taps with interest. Wheat was craning his neck, observing closely.

Vicar looked over and called out, "You ever tend bar, Chief?"

The retired Navy Chief Petty Officer — whom Vicar had installed as the honorary "sergeant-at-arms" of the Knickers after Wheat had ejected some ruffians who put their hands upon Jacquie — replied with a smile, "No, lad. But I can open a bottle of beer with anything you've got lying around."

Vicar glanced at the bar, where he kept playing cards, dominoes, and other amusements. He spied a Magic Eight Ball that someone had given him and threw it to the Chief.

Wheat shook his head and grinned. "Okay, okay … *nearly* any object."

"D'ya wanna learn how to pull a pint?"

Hank Wheat stood up immediately and replied, "By all means!"

He strode around the corner of the bar, his giant chest and arms taking up nearly all the space in the pathway, and watched Vicar pour one. Then he tried his hand, with only foam filling the pint glass. A failure … and a waste. He looked at Vicar apologetically, as if he'd accidentally stepped on a puppy.

"Don't worry, Hank," Vicar said, laughing. "It took me a couple of weeks to get it down pat. But it's a skill a man like you should know. Never know when I might need a night off."

Behind them in the kitchen, Ann Tenna and Beaner Weens were going at it in the kitchen; she, hostess and server of the vulcanized tongue, versus he, head cook and an unmitigated outlier desperate to make good. They argued about everything and yelled at each other throughout every shift, Ann the inexhaustible antagonist.

Beaner was incessantly on the defensive and apt to get surly after a few rallies of abuse. He simply couldn't bear up to her onslaught. No one could. People came from miles around to witness the combat, and so the two of them sometimes amped it up for effect. But it was mostly real.

"Goddamn it, Beaner, don't give me shit for not pushing your daily specials. If you could spell, someone might be able to figger out what yer talkin' 'bout."

Accurate yet ironic; her own spelling was severely wanting. She pointed at the chalkboard and said, "What the fuck is *Oof Poshay*?"

"Poached eggs."

"What's wrong with saying 'poached eggs'? Jesus, what's wrong with 'ham sandwich'? Everybody's heard of 'ham.'"

"Cuz people don't always want ham."

Ann Tenna stared at him for a second, brought up short by the glaring flaw in her argument but unwilling to back down. She shook her head tersely, blurting, "Well, fuck them!" and stormed out of the kitchen.

━ ━ ━

It was awfully early to have a customer who was over the line when he entered the Knickers. There was something wrong; either he'd had a wretched morning, or he was not psychologically stable. Whatever the case, his vibe sprayed the pub like dark, sticky paint.

He was loud and obnoxious, especially to the people who were eating, attempting to have a civilized, though somewhat early-bird dinner — a demographic tradition. He looked like a bit of a greaseball, with dark, threatening eyes. He sat alone but yelled numerous times, almost like hiccups of anger spurting forth, and then wobbled up to the bar, which Vicar was tending, and began to complain about his beer. Vicar, very much wanting to avoid an altercation — since most of his clientele at that moment were about a thousand years old, gumming on their cod and chips, and easily startled — immediately offered him a replacement, *on the house, of course.* He said it again to make sure this unpredictable customer had no reason to take offence. The guy grudgingly accepted the replacement and took a large, spilly swig right at the bar while Vicar shot a quick glance at Chief Wheat, who instantly snapped to and went on guard, ready to leap into any potential fray.

Chief Wheat was the man who protected these premises as a point of honour. No one would be allowed to sully this sanctified pinting cathedral, his true and beloved local, his church of happy tidings. He had his name on one of the dedicated plaques: "Chief Hank Wheat — Sergeant-at-Arms."

"Skunk. It tastes like a goddamn skunk!"

The guy was worryingly angry. Heaven only knew what inner demon was stabbing him with a pitchfork. His eyes were black as coals, emanating antagonism.

Vicar very calmly asked if he might be allowed to smell the pint for the odour of skunk, a possible sign of old, beyond-its-shelf-life beer. The guy held his glass up for Vicar and then shoved it upward violently, splashing Vicar and submerging his nose.

Within a heartbeat, Chief Petty Officer Hank Wheat, Royal Canadian Navy, retired, was beside him. He gingerly took the pint sleeve from the guy's hand and set it down in front of Vicar, then offered his hand in greeting. The guy took his hand in an automatic response, not even thinking about his actions. Wheat, his forearms the size of fence posts, squeezed his hand ever harder until the guy's knees buckled, and then gently waltzed him to the exit door, all the while whispering soothingly, "Your time here is over, laddie. Go home and don't come back. It will not be safe for you to return. I think you get my meaning. Go home, go home."

The guy, in tremendous pain, couldn't even speak. He merely gasped and quietly obeyed. His darkness switched off. He had met someone who could not be intimidated.

Almost no one in the pub noticed the scene, it was done so quietly.

As the door clicked shut behind him and Chief Wheat turned back to face Vicar at the bar, Vicar gave him a faux-military salute.

Wheat's huge voice retorted, "Don't salute me, Vicar! I worked for a living!" Chief Wheat's face was red, but his grin was wide.

■ ■ ■

Serena was back, free from her legal peril, the charges against her for kidnapping Jacquie O dismissed due to a technicality. She quietly skulked around Tyee Lagoon letting her kooky wheels turn. She had never been right in the head and things weren't improving. Her attraction to Tony Vicar had now become an obsession, a fixation. No one had ever made her feel the feels she had felt on the fateful evening when the cops had finally took her away. She now hungered for that feeling again. Vicar would come with her and *do the right thing*. She knew that about him. *Vicar* always *does the right thing*. She would get her baby back, and she would bag him, too. Then they'd live their best lives.

If she had to kill to get her wish, so be it. It was beyond Serena to imagine a bereaved Vicar, falsely accused of paternity, heartbroken and forever a widower, shattered, unwilling to stand beside her while her hands dripped with Jacquie's blood. When speed bumps like that popped up on the road to her irrational fantasy, she just spun a new and more satisfactory illusion.

Four / The Geneva Convention

A few days later, as Jacquie hung up the phone, she screwed up her face as if she'd just swallowed a wheelbarrow full of lemons. *Attention all hands: She's incoming.*

"Tony ... Tony ... Beulah alert! Hide everything. Say nothing!"

Vicar, just in the other room, called out, "What? Is your mom coming for a visit?"

Jacquie made a hissing, growling sound. "She's coming next weekend and she plans to stay for *weeks.*"

Vicar liked Beulah O'Neil a lot. She had visited a number of times, the first occasion being after baby Frankie arrived. She instantly lit up the place like a cheery fire that might go wildcat at any moment, stayed tipsy for the duration, but was generally fun. She also cooked incessantly while swilling what she called "cooking wine." Things like salad and fried chicken did not need cooking wine, but Vicar, having spent half his life slightly "refreshed," was at peace with high-volume raconteurs with drink in hand. What a character, but the tension between Jacquie and dear Beulah was constantly on display. He couldn't quite figure it.

Even with the massive news nearly two years ago that they had suddenly taken delivery of a newborn babe out of the blue, Jacquie had left Beulah in the dark about it for a couple of weeks. Vicar had pointed out that there were already plenty of news reports about the unusual event, and she'd really be on the shit-list if Mother heard about it third hand from some gossipy website that overflowed with inaccuracies and dark innuendo.

He knew mothers and daughters usually had a thing, but this seemed so uncharacteristic of Jacquie. They'd always been stiff, uncomfortable toward one another. Jacquie did put in an effort to stay on good terms, phoning as frequently as she could stomach it, but the tension had really escalated since the arrival of the baby. Clearly, Jacquie didn't want any parenting advice from her mother, even though she herself seemed to have grown up a perfectly solid citizen. Jacquie was nothing if not reliable, pragmatic, logical. Even cheerful, at times — at least with other people.

He knew her patience with him was beginning to wane. He just dismissed it. Without him, her life would be excruciatingly normal, boring as rat-shite. To the grand and exalted table of relationships, he brought *variety*, something she *clearly* had failed to fully appreciate.

She hadn't failed, but Vicar sometimes couldn't delineate between *variety* and *lunacy*. The large pumpkin catapult he had installed on the master bedroom deck for Hallowe'en observances was an excellent example. In no way was it as charming and fun as he had expected, and using it for watermelon salvoes in the summer proved far too expensive. *Those things used to be a dime a dozen ...*

All the same, Vicar thought they'd have some non-weaponized fun while Beulah was visiting. The last couple of visits she had shown so much enthusiasm toward Frankie, had pitched in with babysitting, and had cooked delicious food from morning till night. Vicar couldn't see a downside.

"She can stay as long as she wants, as far as I'm concerned."

"Thank God you are not the only one concerned," Jacquie shot back.

Vicar considered prying into the guts of her issues with Beulah but thought better of it for the moment. It would become just more baggage strewn in his path. He was finding the road to be awfully cluttered these days.

■ ■ ■

It wasn't just Tambourine Club that disturbed the peace at the pub. A group of ersatz dancers calling themselves the Tyee Happy Cloggers had practised once at the Knickers. *But only once.* In their clunky shoes, they'd lurched as if stomping on tarantulas hallucinated during the DTs. Vicar couldn't hack the racket of their arbitrary convulsions and had had to kibosh it. He was determined to do it gently — they were nice people, "community minded," always up to some unnecessary crap involving fundraisers, bazaars, or borrowing other people's flatbeds or boats or bingo machines. Oh Jesus, the fricking blizzard of raffle tickets they spread. It made Vicar imagine driving at a hundred miles an hour through a field of dandelions gone to seed. To Vicar, they needed to get a life — but one of the Cloggers, Fire Hall Gordy, had a prosthetic leg, so if nothing else, they had a gimmick.

"Look, uhh … it's just too loud." Vaguely he'd swept his arm toward his beer-drinking patrons on the other side of the bar; most were staring glumly at the tacky stompers in their midst. Vicar hoped that his true thoughts didn't shine through. Yes, they were shockingly loud, but then again, a big rock show is loud, too. But the Cloggers sucked ass. They carried with them a hodgepodge of electrical relics that amplified obnoxious fiddle tunes, while the "caller" bellowed the instructions into her microphone.

The pack of wobbly volunteers were badgered though the steps of their feature piece, which they hoped would be a jewel in the crown of the Tyee Lagoon Canada Day parade; they practised for months and months, prodded by the caller's promptings in some sub-dialect of hoser Esperanto.

Every July 1 since 1980, precisely from 9:00 to 9:07 a.m., they had clogged their way down two blocks, a few hundred feet, escorting a prehistoric fire engine that lamely squirted water out of its little nozzle like an old man with a giant prostate.

Their practice that evening was the worst sound Vicar had ever heard, and for God's sake, he had once witnessed his buddy Farley, soused as a rat and starkers, dry-humping a light standard beside the Turbo Station while joyfully yell-singing along to a Jann Arden song blaring on their outdoor speaker. At least Farley had *meant* to be insensitive. The Cloggers, however, were oblivious to the emotional and spiritual harm they perpetrated with their spasmodic flailing. He thought of grape stompers after a hit of acid. It was supposed to be for fun, but to Vicar it was about as entertaining as watching his hotel burn down.

There had been no human remains found in the wreckage of the hotel after the fire, and Vicar said he was certain there had been no one else up there, just the sleeping children in the one and only near-finished "show suite." There had been nowhere else to house a tenant, a guest, a sneak, or a squatter without it being obvious. Jacquie hoped he was right — the fear of having left someone behind in that conflagration was a horror too awful to contemplate.

Tony had reported that the ghost wore only one sock, of an argyle pattern. This matched a sock that he had discovered months before, filled with a couple hundred bucks in old-issue cash and tucked into the bottom of the closet wall in room 222. How Tony could be so certain of it, she did not know; people in life-and-death situations do and see weird things, fixate on little details. Jacquie had learned in university that eye-witness statements are often wildly inaccurate. *Just look at Ray and his flying saucer stories.*

One thing she could do was cut through the bullshit and get to the black and white of it. She had a lifetime's experience with that. *Somebody* had to show some skepticism in this clown car of beer and bangers.

Jacquie also knew she had kept Tony's feet on the ground by example. He was an artistic type, a bit un-moored, too often way the hell out there. She never said it out loud, but she sometimes wished she could just *let go*, dream wildly like Tony did, even when the result was another fallen soufflé in an oven of unrealistic visions. Jacquie saw herself as the anchor. An anchor's job is to settle in the mud.

▬ ▬ ▬

Across town, as she lay on her motel room bed, Serena thought through her plan again and again. She just couldn't think of a way to get her baby and Vicar all in one go. It would have to happen in two parts. Baby first, then use her as bait to get to Vicar next. *Get in his head and then get him in bed.*

The only thing that could scotch that plan was his girlfriend — that cow, Jacquie.

Serena absently changed channels on the TV, from national news to incredibly local news. Oh dear, footage of children weeping over a missing dog ... She felt nothing except annoyance.

Yet she wanted her baby back now; she hadn't before, but it had become a tool in her machinations. Jacquie was scrappy — Serena had already learned that to her detriment — so she'd have to kill her to achieve her aims, and any plan to off Jacquie would have to be quick and violent. She glanced at her belongings, lying in an untidy pattern surrounding her suitcase, which, she realized, contained nothing that could be used as a deadly weapon. She was not strong enough to strangle Jacquie with a G-string, and anyway, that'd take far too long. Wearing one was only for show, and briefly.

Cracking that evil slut on the head was too unreliable. She could miss and cause all kinds of yelping and hollering. A knife ... She needed a knife — to the throat. Grisly, but then there would be no obstacle on the path to her desires, and the sooner she did the deed, the sooner she could get her hooks into Vicar. Serena wouldn't just barge in and hogtie him, no, no — she'd respect a certain period of mourning. A couple of weeks, perhaps. *I mean, really, how long would he miss that bitch?*

■ ■ ■

Distracted with housework and feeling out-to-lunch, Vicar stared dumbly at the TV droning in the background, where reports were, as usual, grim and getting grimmer every hour. This week they had managed to turn a cruise ship run aground into a mini-series. Someone had died, you see. Almost certainly a jammer unrelated to the grounding. The ship was brimming with the elderly — it was bound to happen, accident-at-sea or not. The whole thing was stupid yet engrossing. It had cost the network a fortune to get their earnest interviewers, with great hair and perfect teeth, to the site of the "catastrophe," so they felt around for anything they could grab hold of to fill the news cycle. *How did it feel when you heard that your ex-husband's third cousin was aboard the* Oceanic Duchess, *Mrs. Blatyap?* Then they filled the rest of the hour with commercials featuring badly strummed ukulele and some sonofabitch whistling out of tune. Whistling for catheters ... it all made him want to infarct on a boat.

But if you scrolled down the network's website, you bumped into jarringly unrelated shite — gossip dressed as important news — about singers' greatest regrets, actors' hardest roles, and Vicar's astounding paranormal powers. He grumbled to himself, wondering how it was that a world balanced at the precipice of war, pandemic, pestilence, flood, and drought could spend so much time wondering about him. *Damn, I'm a big deal.* He smirked as he vacuumed the bedroom rug, shirtless but sporting a remarkably regrettable disco sweatpant.

Vicar carefully glanced around the room for Frankie, who sometimes hid under the bed, "like a kitty." Neither Vicar nor Jacquie knew that she was Serena's biological daughter; though invisible to them, her bad mojo was still in the air, lingering like a cloud of corrosive gas hanging over a battlefield. Even Serena's lawyer and the courts had not been aware of her pregnancy or the secret birth of Frankie in a chilly motel room — she had hidden it so well and dispensed with baby so quickly.

Ironically, this was one nugget of information that the media had *not* uncovered, the only possible tidbit that Jacquie and Vicar would ever have found useful blaring forth from the *National Sputum* or the *Truthfully Truthlike News Substitute Network* ... or whatever in the feck those assholes called themselves.

Frankie was the result of an assignation between Serena and some guy whose name she could not remember, but she could have found out had she not thrown away his wallet after her sticky fingers emptied it of money. The whole thing had merely been a tactical shag on the night of her release on bail. Serena merely did what she had to do ... she just needed some cash.

When the Crown Councillor called to advise that Serena had waltzed out of the court room scot free, had escaped justice due to a technicality — it had taken too long to bring her case to court — Vicar and Jacquie both braced but knew not what they were bracing for.

Five / Black Hole and Tweed

"You're most welcome. Thanks for coming to visit the Vicar's Knickers." He spoke very clearly and the superfans grinned and shook hands enthusiastically. Vicar had a smile pasted to his face but no American Sign Language whatsoever. He kicked himself; he could say *hello* and *goodbye* in many languages now, even Japanese, yet he couldn't even say *thanks* in ASL. He was embarrassed. Unacceptable. If anyone needed to learn how to communicate through sign language, it was a worn-out rock guitarist with self-inflicted hearing loss. How else was he going to communicate with his equally deaf band?

The pair took pictures and looked at the merchandise booth. They settled on the now-famous tighty-whitey underwear Vicar had designed, the backside proudly emblazoned with *The Vicar's Knickers*, within a large maple leaf, surrounded by fir trees, a salmon, an orca, and a bear. It was all for touristic consumption.

The locals always told their friends from far away about the local wildlife, the amazing fauna of Vancouver Island. But if truth were told, Vicar's tighty-whities ought to have featured crap-filled seagulls, entitled deer, and *Rattus norvegicus*, the dreadful rodents that could find a quarter-inch gap under any door and be dining lavishly in your pantry within the hour. Like vagrant hillbillies, they always brought the whole family along. The other animals did cameo appearances when the spirit moved them.

Vicar had been going to get some felt pennants made up, too, but couldn't locate a manufacturer. Apparently, souvenir pennants were no longer much of a thing. At any rate, he was unable to keep fleeting ideas like that in mind for more than a flash. He had to grit his teeth and focus in order to remember to *eat* some days, and even a single paparazzo on the street sent him bouncing about on a tangent like one of the "super-balls" he used to buy at the old confectionary. The last time someone had come a-skulking around the hotel with cameras and an ulterior motive, the results had been nearly fatal: Vicar had discovered within himself a protective fury that he did not know he possessed. It had terrified him. He never believed himself capable of murder, but on that night of the hotel fire, he could practically taste it. He knew that, pushed just a step more, he could have unleashed death on a couple of slimy bastards. He was glad things had turned out the way they had. Prison would have cut into his publican lifestyle a wee tad.

He was so famous in certain circles that it boggled his mind; he constantly saw photographs of himself and Jacquie featured in gossip magazines that printed made-up stories, which had begun with fake romance bullshit, but had now graduated to tales about "Vicar the Clone," who had been placed on Earth by "Hitler's Time-Travelling Nazi Scientists." No matter what Vicar and Jacquie's response, the stories seemed to multiply like the decapitated heads of a Hydra.

Yet, he found himself standing at the door of the Knickers nearly every day, waving to the timid who hovered outside the pub as if they weren't worthy of simply walking in and ordering a pint. They travelled from literally all over the world. South-East Asia, Russia, every European country, Tasmania, Argentina, and one couple — surely in their sixties, hauling multiple cameras — from Ulaanbaatar, Mongolia. They had no English but bought a lot of Knickers-logo–bedecked underwear. He imagined Mongolian friends and family presented with them, wondering what possible utility the undies would provide way out on the arid steppe. The goofy things would end up on the head of a nomadic horseman — after all, they were a popular hat here — after a pint or two.

Vicar showing himself like he did, waving them over with open arms, seemed to represent great significance to many of his visitors. But Vicar was not trying to *summon his people*. He just didn't want everyone hanging around in front of Western Stationers on the other side of the street, which the extra-timid types often did. Mr and Mrs. Tincknell got pissed when their entrance was blocked and, since the hotel fire, had eyed Vicar with a flinty glare.

■ ▬ ▬

Merri Crabtree was one of those people who constantly got invitations to weddings — often, the nuptials of couples she barely knew, probably the grandkids of her many friends. This was the downside to being so sociable. And, oh fiddlesticks, it cost a fortune. Toasters were no longer the standard gift, and even if they were, a really good one cost more than had an entire year's college tuition when she was nineteen.

"My mother's coming for a visit again, Merri." Jacquie shared it as if confessing her secret pain. Mother Beulah had anointed herself Frankie's "grandmother." Merri Crabtree, however, had spent so much time with Frankie that she thought of *herself* as honorary grandmother. Her own grandson, Wallis, along with his mom and dad, had moved farther away and she saw much less of them than she preferred. Merri felt a twinge at Jacquie's news … this *usurper* was going to waltz in, get all kinds of baby time, and be treated like a celebrity.

Merri had met Beulah once before and had not approved of what she'd seen. Pleasant enough, but a bit sloppy when she drank. Beulah had come to pick up Frankie from Hot Thoth, smelling of alcohol. *You really shouldn't be sucking back cocktails when you're in charge of a baby. This isn't the 1960s.* Merri tried but failed to hide her antipathy.

"Do you remember how to care for a baby through the fog?" Merri had asked archly.

Beulah looked back at her and said, "Well, *lah-de-dah* … Happily, I don't have to peer back through the mists of antiquity like *some*."

There was no doubt that she was attractive for her age, but Merri couldn't imagine how Beulah remained so well preserved. Maybe it wasn't gin she was guzzling, but formaldehyde. Merri wasn't one for jealousy, but a little venom slipped out. Yet, as ever, she covered it up.

She looked at herself in the mirror, Jacquie standing behind her, and said dejectedly, "My God, I look like a giant pile of snow." The crisp white outfit she wore magnified her plumpness. As ever, she followed her quip with that titter, her habitual leading laugh, unwilling to her core to leave anyone wondering if she were being something other than perky.

Jacquie replied, "Well … Maybe you can put on something darker, to reduce your silhouette."

At that, Merri slumped. "Jacqueline, I would have to wear a dress made from a black hole to reduce my silhouette enough."

Jacquie burst out laughing. She looked at Merri with affection. "No one really cares what you look like. It's your character that wins them over, every time."

Merri retorted, "Yes, I know. I've always been the one with all the character — never the gorgeous leading lady, like you." She smiled. "I have so much character it's running out my arse."

Jacquie instantly began cackling at Merri's rare use of such an "off-colour" word. *Sweet mother of pearl, she is so straight!*

Merri continued, "Yet another reason to wear something dark — in case I have a character leak in the middle of the toast to the bride."

— ▬ ▬ ▬

Steven Leigh was Tyee Lagoon's only lawyer. He was tweedy and responsible, vanilla, but the very soul of reason. He felt like a sponge for the anxieties of the town, an ink-stained father confessor, an un-knotter of tangled arguments, C-list celebrity judge of pointless pissing contests, and the owner of an antique notary stamp that could bludgeon even the stubbornest deadbeat dad into coughing up child support. He'd been in the same office for a quarter-century and was bored half to tears.

The most excitement he'd had in a long time had been Frankie Hall's will, where she'd finally named her beneficiaries as "Anthony Louis Vicar" and "Caoilfhoinn Jacqueline O'Neil." He'd been instrumental in the cause and then witnessed the after-effects. Simply remarkable.

The young pair had required his services multiple times since then. He was happy to do it. His association with Vicar and O'Neil had resulted in an upsurge in profile that really brought in business. And at any rate, he was touched by their desire to adopt little Frankie. He and Vera had missed out on children, so he was particularly sensitive to their plight — being so in love with the child but living in constant fear that a biological family member might suddenly arise from the muck and steal her away. He sympathized and was working assiduously to move their adoption ahead as quickly as he could. He was doing it all pro bono, bless him, and worried it might well be for naught — but at least seeing someone doing *something* would give the young couple a sense of peace, however small.

He had bugger-all else to do with his time than work. He was suddenly a bachelor — or, more precisely, a widower. The house was empty and dark when he came home. Vera's death had not been a shock, but it had left him empty.

Taking his huge boat out alone was no fun and all his pals had moved away, gotten busy with their grandchildren, or croaked. What a strange stage of life; he heard the tocsin sounding in the distance but could still plausibly blame it on tinnitus.

His hair had been thinning since his twenties and he now sported a classic, horseshoe-shaped white-collar tonsure. He needed larger pants every year and was simply not in the mode of looking for "hook-ups"; that didn't sound like an apt description for finding a date. It was closer to what a tow truck did. His lumbar couldn't take *that* kind of punishment.

- - -

Jacquie found herself short tempered and prickly as Beulah's arrival neared. She wore a mask of smouldering anger for an unknown reason.

"You're awfully bloody snippy, Jacquie," Vicar said, hoping to cool her jets.

"Ummm, howzabout fucking off, Vicar," she snapped. Vicar was shocked and withdrew from the room, his confused tail between his legs.

That night she slept in the guest room, too cranky and too embarrassed by her own behaviour to lie beside Tony. Tomorrow would be a new day.

Finally, asleep after tossing and turning for hours, she had a dream, a Technicolor scene, unusually vivid.

She was being chased, but her legs were not co-operating. She tried to scream at an unseen foe behind her, frightened but uncertain why. Jacquie knew she was dreaming, yet her awareness didn't stop it from continuing.

Jacquie found herself in the Knickers, but it was not quite the place she knew so well — the layout was strange and constantly shifting, the ceiling was open to the sky, and she saw threatening clouds gathering. She worried about rain flooding their gorgeous pub.

Very suddenly, from within the swirling clouds came a ladder lowering into the centre of the Knickers. Escorting it were flying animals — a bear and a cougar, both with wings. So eerie, almost sickening. Someone was on the ladder, and after a few moments she recognized Frankie Hall, the long-dead woman who had been so kind to her and to Tony, too.

Frankie Hall spoke, "Beware the mother. Be careful, my dear. Beware."

And then the ladder upon which she stood was smoothly pulled back to the heavens, suddenly dark and glittering with stars.

Jacquie woke suddenly, overheated, the bedding a little damp. She rose from the guest bed, went to the master bedroom, and crawled in with Vicar, spooning with him for comfort. Vicar very lovingly ceased snoring for almost twenty seconds.

■ ■ ■

Serena presented herself for inspection in the mirror and was satisfied with what she saw — a wig and clothing that made her look well put together, but not so glamorous that it made her memorable. Blending in was her goal on this mission. She was surprised she had pulled it off, as she usually tried to tart herself up like a movie star on the red carpet. This time, however, her look was a short, practical hairdo, chestnut brown to go with her eyes and skin tone, an upmarket shirt and jacket, a knock-off Coach bag, and plain black tights under fashionable boots — stylish heel, but not her normal ultra-high, bitchy fetish footwear.

She changed her posture, consciously ceased her signature siren's strut, and almost meekly shuffled into the Vicar's Knickers. *It feels weird to walk like this.*

She opened the door and the trademark smell of a pub greeted her; flat beer dregs and fried food hit her nostrils. The scene changed instantly from the breezy, sunny day outdoors to the cool dimness within.

Dishes clinked and the sounds of a twangy guitar wafted around. Serena stood a moment to let her eyes adjust to the darkness and then checked out the Knickers.

■ ■ ■

Vicar was in his little office on the phone, on hold yet again with the food supplier as they puzzled through the complexities of ground beef delivery. He couldn't bear it. He just wanted to make the order from a website and then receive the goods a few days later. But, because Jacquie was such a stickler about food quality, he almost always had to get on the blower with them and customize the order. *Customization is where shit goes sideways, every time.* He tried to shake off that old-man suspicion that "they" were trying to edge everyone out of individuality. *A conspiracy!* At any rate, Jacquie would not bend, and Vicar could not understand. He just wanted things to be simple. It was just another burr under his saddle.

He had gritted his teeth and mentally prepared for a long wait with its attendant ghastly music, fished out of some unemployed simian composer's desktop recycling bin. Even giants like Air Canada used cheap hold music performed by a roomful of underpaid chimps on a million keyboards, subtly indicating that you'd be waiting for an infinite amount of time. But fortunately, this time the phone was silent during the wait.

Yet he could not fully escape the audio aggravation. From the pub, he could hear a nasal cow-individual singing rhapsodically about dental hygiene products and bathroom fixtures. No doubt he would someday be a judge on *Dancing with the Steers*. For now, his song simply floated about. Vicar pulled the phone away from his ear momentarily to be sure the words were as insipid as he feared. They were. Earlier in the morning he had overheard, with great revulsion, a singer discovering the rhyming potential of the words "think" and "drink." Aspirational, probably — he surely couldn't do both.

Vicar stood up partway, about to hang up the phone, and then thought better of it. Instead, he yelled over his shoulder, "Annie, turn off that shit! This is supposed to be a civilized establishment."

Ann Tenna yelled back, "I like it. Bite me!"

Vicar plopped back down in defeat. *Of course* she liked it — it went with her hairdo. Annie was beyond discipline and far too valuable to the establishment to get pissy with over a yodelling cowpoke. At any rate, he wanted to take care of this extra-lean hamburger issue on the phone before stumbling into a new beef with her.

▬ ▬ ▬

Across the room, Serena pricked up her ears and felt a little flutter in her heart as she heard the voice of *her Vicar*.

■ ■ ■

Jacquie was bothered by her recent dream and had thought about it all day. She tried to replay it as accurately as possible, but dreams were chimeras, changing as they dissolved.

One thing that stuck in her mind was the voice of Frankie Hall saying "beware the mother." She tried to parse it, find its hidden meaning. It had to be about *her* mother, Beulah. But no, that couldn't be it. *Could it?* Not finding an immediate interpretation, she deliberately pushed the thought away so she could get on with the day.

■ ■ ■

"Just you?" Ann Tenna asked the lady standing next to the hostess desk near the entryway.

Serena cleared her throat and pitched her voice up a few notes to sound as submissive as possible. "Yes, just me — for lunch."

Ann Tenna, in a disastrous control-top pant of powder blue and an A-line blouse that recalled tenting in the bush, just replied, "Follow me." She looked back at Serena, sizing her up. *All these rich bitches look the same.*

"Can I sit here?" Serena wanted to be able to see the whole bar and the office door beside it, from where Vicar's voice had come.

"Oh, shit, yeah. Anybody joinin' you? No? No friends, huh?" She laughed pleasantly but felt little sympathy for this attractive young woman who was all alone. If *she'd*-a been blessed with those looks at that age, she'd-a bin bustin' dinks off purt 'n' near every day. But she finally had her man, Ross Poutine. Rough as the pothole-strewn road he lived on but a man of his word, with a steely handshake and no nonsense. Ever. Like, *ever*.

Serena smiled wanly and pretended to peruse the new daily special printout, using it as a shield of sorts, to keep her face hidden.

What do boring women drink at lunch time? Serena was a fish out of water in her disguise. Tea — caffeine free, of course. Weak, with lots of milk and sugar. And some flavourless meal with no garlic. She decided that in order to really sell her disguise, she'd ask some fussy question about organic cilantro.

As she sipped the tea, Serena cased the joint thoroughly, checking out the stairs, bathrooms, and especially exit doors. She still wasn't sure what her play would be, but she'd need to do a little surveillance, just to make sure it was even possible to get "their" baby back. It had become *their* baby, exactly when she couldn't recall. She had decided she wanted the little girl back somewhat out of the blue and, as ever, she wanted Vicar for her own. The baby was a tactical move, but now she simply wanted it back. Vicar was the main target. They could take care of the baby together after they set up housekeeping. It would be *their* daughter, as if he had immaculately conceived her at great distance, hurling his magical seed through the ether. Heisting the baby seemed the only sure way to coax him. Once Vicar was near, she would abscond with him. She'd figure out the forever-after later.

Though her plan had not yet coalesced, one thing seemed certain: the baby was the key, and she would *definitely* fail in trying to get her back the legal way. She'd been through so much with the law. Her past was too checkered, her reputation a ruin, her record too long, and her stability questionable to anyone in a position of authority. *They are all corrupt bastards.*

She had almost never come out on the winning side when she faced officialdom, although getting off the hook recently was an exception, and maybe a *sign*, a sign that her plan was *meant to be*. She passionately believed she had a special destiny. She grasped at it like a drummer scrabbling for the last beer.

Serena was certain that everyone in the government — she pronounced it "guv-mint" — were unfeeling pricks, every single one of them, and more than a few of them had gotten a bit rapey with her. Reptiles, all. Yet even she had to admit that she'd overstepped this time. People do not react well to a mother who abandons her child.

So, Serena refused to seek legal means to get her baby back. She appeared at times to rage in anger about all of it, but in fact she was simply too embarrassed to admit what she had done. She had been in a total panic and believed she had nowhere else to turn. And anyway, it left her with a connection to Vicar — in her mind, an invisible but permanent bond.

Because she had never asked anyone expert in these things, not wanting a single soul to know the truth, she was oblivious that the laws would almost certainly grant her custody of her abandoned daughter, immediately. Blood nearly always trumped good Samaritans. It was the way of the world.

Serena, alert but acting nonchalant, heard a phone banged down firmly, a muffled profanity, and then Tony Vicar strode out of a door that was just down a little hallway, beside the bar. Her heart skipped a beat as she gazed at him piercingly with one eye, the other hidden behind the menu. The slight grey at his temples and on his chin aroused her.

Vicar spent two seconds surveying his customers, his eyes skipping past Serena in the distance without seeming to recognize her hidden face in the dim light. He spoke quietly for a few moments to Ann Tenna, jotted a note on a clipboard attached to the wall, then headed out the front door.

Serena waited until Ann Tenna had left, then reached into her purse, plopped money down, and quickly departed toward her car.

■ ■ ■

Ann returned to take her lunch order and saw twenty bucks tucked under her half-finished tea.

Where did she go? She briefly squinted in confusion then put the money into her apron, moving along to cheerfully abuse the next lucky customer. *Good tipper, though.*

▬ ▬ ▬

In Littleton, Colorado, two sisters named Debbie and Dawna both had the same dream. It was of a tiny, elderly woman, speaking in a croaky voice, warning them to "beware the mother." The psychic sisters had shared dreams before, but this one was heavy with urgency, as if they were responsible for delivering a message to a person and location unknown, to stave off great danger. They had no idea where it fit, who it applied to, or when they might need to deliver it, but it had a very special feel to it. A *texture*, almost, that was signature. They would know who this was for if they ever felt it again.

Six / Bottles, Cans, Mooses

Farley Rea was Vicar's old buddy. Harmless, sweet, eager, frequently unemployed, and one of the world's worst bass players, he had entered his thirties still unconcerned about his future or the yawning gap in his *plan*. He had a personality that bashfully whispered, "I am Beta," and constantly looked to Vicar for guidance and reassurance. At that moment he had −$36.48 in his bank account, but a beer stein filled with coins and a $500 overdraft. Everything was copacetic.

His hair was a long, tangled mop, almost always crowned by a toque. He knew it annoyed Vicar, who constantly razzed him about wearing it indoors, or in the summertime. "For fucksakes, Farley ... Where's the snowstorm?" Vicar would say it with exasperation, while obliviously wearing a faded, shrunken T-shirt emblazoned with "King Crimson, Massey Hall '71."

Farley had amassed a pretty large collection of toques and wore them proudly in a rare display of disregard for the wants of Vicar. Sometimes he wandered around his tiny basement suite, naked, but with one sitting merrily on his head. He could really zone out sometimes.

■ ▬ ▬

Beaner Weens, head cook at the Vicar's Knickers, verbal duelling partner of Ann Tenna, and infamous character known for collecting bottles, cans, and golf balls while disguised as a moose, had by some unknown manner transformed himself into a popular guest on various paranormal podcasts. It earned him dozens of dollars. It was true that he had been near the centre of events when the Agincourt Hotel had been burned down by arsonistic reporters a couple of years ago, and the tale did, legitimately, involve him driving Vicar's huge old Cadillac while disguised as a moose, with a spitting-mad, muckraking journalist rolling around in its trunk. But after a couple of years of telling the same story, he began to embroider the tale, making himself more important, creeping closer to a starring role, and earning himself a much higher profile.

He was now too well known to harvest abandoned golf balls at the links — everyone was hip to his moose costume. But he still picked bottles, timed to coincide with the weekly recycling schedule. He had bought a dinged and rusty truck and retired his moose costume but mounted its head on the grille of the pickup. He always arrived just before the guy in the big industrial recycling truck and tried to scoop him.

A long-retired sign painter had slopped lettering on his doors that read *BEANER'S BOTTLES* in big cursive font, and below, an afterthought in small print, Beaner himself had used a Sharpie to add *& Cans*. His penmanship was atrocious.

Much of the citizenry of Tyee Lagoon did gather their bottles (*and cans*) for Beaner as he drove by each week. Like Vicar, he had helped put Tyee Lagoon on the map, at least a little, and so, suddenly, everyone became generous. Yes, there were still dour cheapskates who hoarded their recyclables like buried treasure, but at least no fancy ladies now tried to bend broomsticks over his head for raiding their blue bins.

At this point, he could stop nearly anywhere to collect his bounty — constantly gregarious and cheerful, his conversational skills topping out at the "high-school-dropout-people-person" level, but always uber-buoyant. He dearly loved having his own little side hustle.

It was remarkable to watch him puttering down the roads in his moose-mobile, his ancient tape deck howling the old Croce number about time and bottles and other wistful emotions unrelated to recycling. It was his theme song, played loud and proud.

In times past, kids would listen for the ice cream man's jolly music. Now those same people, decades older, perked up their much deafer ears for the sound of the distorted tape deck of Beaner Weens, who would gladly take the empties stowed on their porches and decks.

Unfortunately, it hadn't worked out to get Vicar to record a custom version of his theme song "for advertising purposes." Beaner had explained that he wanted it to go, "I'll save you time, gimme bottles." Vicar, thinking it was a joke, and in a mischievous mood, had sat down with a microphone and an old boom box while badly fingerpicking his six-string. He lampooned, "If I could save farts in a bottle." After a well-timed comedic pause, he'd added, "And cans."

Beaner didn't see the humour in Vicar's satirical take and didn't know any other musicians, so just gave up. At any rate, he had fantasized about Bryan Adams doing it. Hell, Lagoon Hardware repair department had once written a letter to him. They'd wondered how much it would cost for him to do a cool version of "Can't Stop This Lawnmower We Started." They never heard back, *but y'know, he's real busy.*

— — —

Once Cosmic Ray returned from his years wandering the desert, Vicar gave up on the countless throw-together duos he'd mounted with Farley. Vicar, always on the lookout for gigs for his group, Hospital Fish — featuring Cosmic Ray on drums — was unwilling to admit the glaringly obvious: that they had collapsed under their own ponderously pompous weight again and again; he threw himself against the gate holding him back with pathetic tenacity. Vicar began exploring alternate ways to get in front of audiences. And anyway,

Farley and Ray needed money, so Vicar justified accepting awful engagements by convincing himself that he was doing it for a noble cause: the financial solvency of his pals.

He knew that his celebrity was enough to draw a few folks to a gig, but no one could attend a show they'd never heard about. *It is all about advertising, man. Gotta get a buzz going.* Vicar worried so much about *buzz* that he was blind to the red flags of an incoming nightmare.

Enter the Turbo Station. They had remodelled: a new countertop and possibly a new coffee maker, the burned-out bulbs were replaced in the sign, and there was a new sink to replace the old one that someone had sheared off the wall during a drunken faceplant. The tile in the men's room was still chipped and grimy, but, really, *what more do you want?*

The boss of the station had engineered a so-called "grand reopening," a shoddy affair, having put his every ounce of artistic zazz into "publicity." That is, he'd put *Grand Reopening* on the sign, and below it, *Band*. That band, never once mentioned in print, would be Hospital Fish, recommended to the boss by a random motorist filling his tank. The boss, as artsy as a bag of wet compost, simply went with the recommendation without question.

Vicar took the booking and, after a gruelling negotiation, had wrested a hundred and sixty bucks for two hours — and two free pops each from the vending machine. The Turbo manager warily watched the expenses climb up and up and up … This band's fee would crimp his budget, dammit. He had arranged an ad in the ol'

Tyee Firestarter newspaper, which cost over eighty bucks after GST!

He was mollified a bit when the nondescript, postage stamp–sized ad in Thursday's edition read *Turbo, New Sink, Orchestra*. Seemed classy! He glanced up at his big revolving sign in concern and said to his young cashier, "Do we have enough letters to spell *Orchestra*?" It sounded fancy, so he thought they ought to match the advert. She glanced at the box containing the letters and replied, "Uhhhhh …"

"Just try, will you? I gotta order some parts."

The teenager went up the tall ladder, scared shitless at the height of her wobbly perch. Dutifully she took down *BAND* and started assembling *ORCHESTRA*. One good wind blast from a passing semitruck buffeted her enough that she bailed on the job after *O, R, C*. The sign now read:

GRAND REOPENING

ORC

When the boss came out of his cramped office and clicked off the light switch with the patina of filthy finger-stains surrounding it, he looked up and blurted out, "What in blue blazes is *that*?"

His young cashier teared up and blubbered, "I almost got blown off."

He looked at the sign again, then back at her, and then downward at the floor. After a pause, he said, "Ah, th' hell with it. I'll go buy one of those blow-up killer whales at the Lagoon Hardware and put it beside the band. Orchestra. Orc. Whatevs."

The young girl, relieved to have gotten off the hook, glanced up at the baffling sign and back down at her birdbrained boss, wondering why *she* was the one making fifteen bucks an hour.

Seven / Oh Brother, Mother

Beulah O'Neil was driving her daughter crazy. She wouldn't shut up, couldn't hold her opinions, and never simply left it alone. She chafed and offended and was bloody hilarious to anyone lucky enough not to live with her.

Vicar thought she was a card, and Beulah seemed to like him. But Jacquie O's shoulders were up in aggravation at the very mention of her name. Her mother said the most inappropriate things, at high volume, in public, and if anyone was insulted, she invariably fell back upon, "I was only joking." Beulah was a cheery, sex-starved social menace who got away with blue murder again and again.

She was in Tyee Lagoon to see her daughter, maybe give her the gears a little — *to keep her honest.* She was also looking forward to seeing Tony Vicar. Nice fellow, a little old for Jacqueline, but a good sport. He liked to laugh.

But most of all she was there to see her "granddaughter," Frankie. Granted, Frankie was only the *foster* daughter of Tony and Jacqueline, but there was no point in quibbling about details when there was a baby involved. Babies needed love. And care. But mostly protection.

What she'd heard about the destruction of the Agincourt Hotel gave her confidence that Vicar was up to the task. Walking through fire seemed a clear demonstration of his commitment.

Vicar wasn't exactly a looker, but he was by no means JoJo the Dog-Faced Boy. He had a hint of grey at the temples and on the chin, where he was cultivating a variety of facial stubble that looked, to her, like a crop plowed under. Jacquie always seemed to go for old farts. If Vicar would just wear some clothes that weren't from a lost-and-found bin, he might manage to be a little better turned out. But she knew that her husband had been a bit of a style-impaired slob, too. The best he'd ever looked was in his casket.

■ ■ ■

The last time Beulah had visited Tyee Lagoon, she had said to Jacquie, "You need to eat more. You're wasting away." She had stayed slim but curvaceous for a woman her age and was more than happy to obliquely draw attention to the fact, especially when there were gentlemen around to compliment her.

This time, while enjoying too many pre-dinner cocktails, she said, very loudly, "Jacquie, you're getting a fat ass!" as the latter bent over to help Frankie, who was playing on the floor.

Vicar snorted and grimaced. Jacquie's face contorted and she stormed away, furious. Beulah had an unerring knack for finding her soft targets, and drinking high-falutin cocktails seemed to remove her filters. Beulah could sometimes morph into a "frenemy."

Vicar watched Jacquie depart and said, "Well, that went over like a fart in a spacesuit." Beulah's rhetorical stiletto stabbed unpredictably; he did not approve, but as ever he tried to take her as she was — not attempting to change her. That wasn't a thing a guy did, really.

So, he cautiously chuckled, but needed to intercede before a mother-daughter donnybrook broke out. He needn't have worried: Jacquie's normal response to the flagrant hurling of verbal hand grenades was the silent treatment. Beulah had been banished to Coventry so many times she had a *pied-à-terre* there. It was almost as if she preferred awkward silence.

Vicar said quietly, "Jacquie has been working really hard the last couple of years. You might cut her some slack. She does the work of three, y'know." His tone was good-humoured, but he reflected on Jacquie learning to mother a newborn baby with no prep — quite literally in one urgent swoop on a blizzardy night. To say it required some emotional resiliency was putting it mildly. All the while she ran the front end of a busy pub, and lived with *him*, surely a challenge unto itself.

Vicar was still oblivious to a lot — blind to his shoddy deportment, his semi-cooperative Chachi-from-

Happy-Days hairdo, his psychotic impatience with customer service agents who talked like twelve-year-olds, his inflexible opinions on music, food, history, and the noxious spread of general stupidity. But through all that, he was acutely aware of how much Jacquie brought to his life. He had never, not in his wildest youthful fantasies, imagined that he'd end up with a woman as smart, capable, or beautiful.

Beulah responded dismissively, "Oh, well, maybe … But you mustn't get too mushy with Jacqueline. You don't want her becoming one of those women who is constantly in tears over every little thing … It can't all just be oolong and scented candles."

Vicar looked away for a moment, feeling that her statement held subtext but unable to unravel its meaning. He tried to remember one single moment where Jacquie had expected to be treated like an ornament; fact was, she was a gorgeous tomboy.

Beulah had lived through some dreadfully tough times and so had a callused soul. She had been a widow raising a daughter on meagre financial resources in a grim environment; it had been tough for her to manage. She had long ago ceased wringing her hands over small potatoes, and too often *called 'em like she saw 'em* with cutting, charade-bashing honesty.

But Vicar had never known Jacquie to be irresponsibly emo, either. Under stresses that were almost otherworldly, she had held up remarkably well, and she had steadied him again and again.

"She looks damn fine to me," Vicar said, with finality.

Beulah, a pensive look in her eye, patted his hand and replied, "I hope you always think that, dear."

■ ■ ■

After the hotel fire two years before, Ross Poutine had spent weeks grumbling and growling while he cleaned up the remnants of his new liquor store. Before it was even completed, everything had been destroyed, including most of the lobby to his one side and Hot Thoth to his other.

Poutine's real last name, McFaddish, was never used. Poutine himself never said it out loud except for in official circumstances, like renewing his driving licence. He had been nicknamed "Poutine" decades ago, fair and square, and he would never consider relinquishing that unique and now famous moniker. Shit, since all that spooky Vicar stuff had started a few years ago, he sometimes got *fan letters*, usually addressed to *Ross Poutine, General Delivery, Tyee Lagoon, BC, Canada*. One wuz a racy pitcher of some nekkid chick that he looked at just a bit too long and then chucked out before Annie could catch wind of it.

Poutine was owner of the only liquor store in town, which made him a VIP. He had been in Tyee Lagoon since the 1970s, coming west from Montreal. Some clever smartass, no one remembered who, had called him Ross Poutine because he was from Quebec, the only place you could find such mushy, goopy ambrosia back then, but also because, for reasons unknown, Ross smelled like a goat — a lot like Grigori Rasputin, the mad Russian monk. All these years later, people genuinely wanted to get close to him just to briefly get a sniff, but in the early days, his goaty scent had been considerably concentrated and notably unpopular. In fact, it was a real date killer and had reduced his social life to jiggering with cars, head down in the engine compartment, ass crack up and proud.

Back then, even the roughest gals wouldn't touch him with a ten-foot pole. Not even Gladys "Glad Ass" Loesche, her arm tattooed *DADDY*, stringy, mud-coloured hair, and a darned impressive moustache for a girl, accented by a random sampling of teeth. Her *S*'s were notably uneven when she told him that he "thmelled like a futtin' goat."

Oh, he had tried, dousing himself in everything from Roman Brio to 'Lectric Shave, but he always reeked of a hobo's Tensor bandage. Eventually he gave up and let the bouquet waft freely.

It wasn't an exaggeration to call the Knickers a unique venue — maybe even a glorious one. It was for one and all, and as majestic as you could get without being uppity. In order to assure the clientele would be people of good cheer, the Knickers had, owing to Ann Tenna, morphed into a place with food service that was highly critical of its customers. The topsy-turvy arrangement was a tremendous draw. Vicar was deathly allergic to fussy cheapskates with delusions of aristocracy. The type of people who'd go to a restaurant and then piss and moan about the "uninspired" mignonette drizzle on their overpriced oysters had come to the *wrooooong* place, and his opinion was supported wholeheartedly by his staff.

Head server Ann Tenna, outrageous and salty "barmaid" and Ross Poutine's one and only love interest, swept her eyes across the place and zeroed in on one reckless diner who was pushing her plate aside, screwing up her face in a look of revulsion. Ann marched over, as was her style, and barked out, "What's wrong with your grub?"

The whole pub was primed for it, except this lady, who had either not been informed or believed herself above criticism. Ann Tenna's schtick was not only bawdy, but deafening — hilarious to most and a terrible offence to others. To her, complaints about the food were no longer a thing. Customer *abuse* was now *de rigueur* and inexplicably popular.

After all, Annie knew that the food was of the finest quality. Jacquie saw to that with tenacity. The cooking was done by Beaner Weens, who had become a regular Captain Bligh in the galley. His assistants lived in terror of fucking up. Her own inimitable service was superb, *of course*.

Ann Tenna grabbed a hunk of sausage from the lady's plate and jammed it crudely into her yap, chewing at it until chunks came flying out everywhere. The woman recoiled in disgust.

Ann turned to face the entire clientele of the pub and yelled, "Tastes fine to me!" It sounded like "Tah ine ooee." She swallowed like a starving wolf and said, a little quieter, "What's your problem with it, princess?"

The woman turned beet red and shrank in her seat as if just thrown onto a stage, completely naked. She had never once been challenged in her judgment, so she was at a loss for sound, never mind words. She was, after all, one of *those* "I pay your wages" ass clowns, as if ordering bangers and mash made her a co-owner of the fucking joint.

The rest of the place burst out into raucous laughter, some customers applauding. A man sitting next to the woman — her husband, it seemed — wore a look of nirvana-like pleasure; he had been fantasizing about this for a while.

It wasn't an ambush. There were signs posted at the door: a photo of Ann Tenna, wretched hairdo and sardonic grin, warning in bold font, *Complain Wisely*. Most people had heard what to expect and just enjoyed the broad but generally good-natured comedy. But Annie would pounce even when she liked you. God help the people who rubbed her the wrong way.

The fuss-budget in question shrank down in her seat until she was almost invisible to everyone. Her husband left Ann Tenna a hundred-dollar tip.

— — —

They had been a raucous group, mostly harmless but getting louder by the minute. Jacquie O was on duty, keeping a close eye on their hijinks. She had been doing this job long enough to have honed a sense of when things were about to go sideways; she had always been unusually gifted at sensing brewing trouble.

Suddenly, a huge explosion of laughter arose, followed by a reckless clatter of mugs and glasses. One man shot up out of his chair, pint in hand, and emptied it over the head of his friend, who gasped in shock.

Before Vicar could even react, Jacquie was on the guy. He was easily a foot taller, but she roughly grabbed him by the lapel, dragged him to the door, and violently flung it open. He was laughing until he saw her face, drawn taut and bloodless. She pushed him bodily into the street and shrieked, "Don't you *ever* do that again!"

The room fell silent.

Vicar watched the whole thing, left in mystified shock.

Jacquie turned to face the hushed crowd, put her chin up defiantly, and marched out of sight.

Eight / Secret Chimp

The Denver-based production office for *Extra-Large Mediums of Littleton*, which aired Thursdays at 9 p.m. on the Panorama Paranormal Network, had a research department consisting of two or three people whose lives were spent online, occasionally dashing off to a coffee shop for a break, only to stare at their mobile phones while waiting for chai tea lattes.

One of them had been following the crazy and ongoing story of Tony Vicar, that weird Canadian *Liquor Vicar*, for some time. An alert popped onto his screen and he clicked on it, while gorging awkwardly on an exploding pastry and attempting to make the walk signal.

It said something about "The Liquor Vicar" and more details on the "hotel fire" and, more to the point, had a rundown on its reopening. Very interesting. He knew the producers were hot to stay on top of this story — they had discussed it in planning meetings several times. This might be the right timing. He quickly read the brief story on his phone.

The tall young man ran across Colfax Avenue and got back to the office as quickly as he could, to dredge up more information. If this was what it seemed to be, then the Extra-Large Mediums would want to know about it right away.

Five minutes into his research, he said, "Jackpot," and pressed the speed dial to the executive producer.

Sitting in a booth at Mesopotamia — an upstart exotic restaurant on Jersey Road trying its luck with "dining and dancing" and that Vicar had nicknamed "Mezzo-ptomania" — he tried to ignore Pat Horrigan, the evening's entertainment, smearing through dismal arrangements of show tunes on an ancient organ. He'd known Horrigan for years and had once had the misfortune to sit in with his band, Horrigan's Heroes. Vicar, in denial about too often being the source of it, was seldom in the mood for crap music.

A slurry of macerated melody came dribbling out of Horrigan's keyboard of "real imitation woodgrain" until a modulation intervened, at which point he lost the plot and was reduced to making the sound of doomed cattle being swept off train tracks. Vicar's teeth were immediately set on edge. All that was missing was some shoe-less, patchouli-ponging cocksplat randomly slapping at his "Canadian Folk Congas." Horrigan's disheartening rendition of Bobby Darrin sputtered along, with Vicar muttering, "Oh joy … It's 'Mack the Spork.'"

He was sitting beside Beulah O'Neil, with Jacquie seated across the table and Frankie in a high chair at the end. Beulah beckoned the waiter over and held up her empty glass, her third so far, while staring holes in his pants. She waved it inches from the baby's head and requested another gin and Dubonnet.

"Mom …" Jacquie's tone sounded a warning.

"Oh, stop, Jacqueline. You're driving me sane," she yucked. "It's what the Queen used to drink," as if that rendered the booze harmless as a newborn's tears.

Jacquie immediately thought, *She's going Royal — fasten your seat belts*, and then replied, "She didn't have four of them before the main course."

Beulah, unconcerned, just blew her off with a smirky shrug.

Vicar was already bracing for an escalation; this wasn't the place for a brawl. He shot Jacquie a look, hoping she'd make a tactical withdrawal, and tried to move the conversation along.

"Oh, yes, that's right. Beulah, you really were a fan of Her Majesty, weren't you?" He said it with pre-emptive unctuousness and Beulah responded with satisfaction.

Jacquie pursed her lips, knowing she'd been out-manoeuvred for the time being. She held her tongue. They were, after all, in a restaurant.

Slightly wobbly, Beulah purred huskily, "I was a great admirer of the Queen." It came out "uhmirer." "I'd like to think she'd-a liked me, too." She shook her head, nose up, as if to imply that mere happenstance had prevented a royal friendship.

Jacquie contorted her face, looking about to spit up.

Beulah shot back with an offended look, her cheeks a little flushed from the gin.

Vicar had heard some of Beulah's set-piece stories before and prepared for a repeat. He'd grit his teeth through it. Anything to avoid another mother-daughter clawing. Strangely, for someone as steady as Jacquie, she would swiftly become a dog snapping at bacon if her mom stepped over "the line." Vicar remained quiet about seeing both sides of the dynamic. Jacquie's line shifted an awful lot.

■ ■ ■

Back at home, Jacquie had had enough of her mother and went off to bed. Vicar stayed up and chatted with Beulah.

Beulah was well into her cups now, a frightening quantity of "Queen's Cocktail" rumbling around in her belly. It lubricated her conversation.

"… I was crazy about Marv. He was such a good-looking boy."

Vicar asked, "How old were you guys when you met?"

Beulah scrunched one eye shut, attempting to recall. "He was twenty-two. I was barely seventeen."

Vicar replied, "Wow. Jacquie said you were a teenager, but I had no idea you were *that* young. Why did you get married at that age?"

"He knocked me up," she said bluntly.

"So, you had Jacquie when you were …?"

"Seventeen, almost eighteen. It was a total screw-up. I was still in high school. All that went for shit … But I made the best of it. I made him promise to go to school, get a degree or a diploma so he could take care of us."

"Did he?" Vicar had never heard a lot about Jacquie's dad. She was unusually tight-lipped about him. A cloud came over her when he asked, and he knew her well enough to not poke the bear over certain issues.

"Well …" Beulah paused and wobbled slightly. "He tried to go to college for auto mechanics, but he dropped out. He was gorgeous but not very bright, to tell you the truth. If he'd lived, I think I would have left him eventually." She remembered the despair that had come over her when she realized he couldn't really read or write very well.

"So, heart attack took him? Maybe the stresses of crummy jobs and a young family?"

"Heart attack, all right. And a giant stroke along with it." She hiccupped and resumed. "After he dropped out of college, he started drinking. Drinking heavily." She slurred, sounding like she'd said "hawily."

"Mmmm."

"And he smoked like a frickin' chimney, too." She used her left hand to drunkenly mime smoking a cigarette. "And I know he got into cocaine. Always wiggling his jaw like Lancelot Link."

"Lancelot Link?"

"Yeah, *Secret Chimp*. You know …"

Vicar did *not* know. How obscure must a reference be if even *he* didn't recognize it? He continued, "I guess you couldn't convince him to get help, huh?"

"Help? *Help?*" She was suddenly animated. "He needed a punch in the nose, that bastard. The more booze and dope he took, the more abusive he got. He was a *monster.*"

She stared out the window where the half moon shone.

She continued, "Lost his looks. Left us broke. He yelled at me, slapped me around, made me feel worthless. He slapped Jacquie, too. Many times. Random backhands; he even kicked her. I can only imagine the damage it's done. I prayed that he'd drive off a cliff and die. No damn cliffs in Regina, though." She cracked a sickly grin.

Vicar didn't know they'd both been physically abused, and his hackles went up instantly. "What a tragic story, Mum." He called her that sympathetically, feeling a closeness to her well up, obscuring his discomfort at talking about such issues with his blotto mother-in-law. *Goddamn, if I'd witnessed that, I'd have stopped it in one second.*

Beulah, on the couch with Vicar, leaned over and gently put her head on his shoulder. The silence was long and heavy. She sniffed. She began speaking in a raspy whisper now.

"He was standing in the living room, drinking rye right outta the bottle." She went silent for a few moments. "Gets this funny look on his face and then collapses on the floor. Sorta just sinks down."

Vicar knew she was replaying the scene. His head was turned toward hers, and he reached out to hold her hand.

"Had a jammer right there, right on the carpet. But he managed to set the whiskey down without spilling a drop."

Vicar could envision it and imagined the despair that must have settled over her at that moment. "So, they couldn't save him, huh?"

She seemed to sober up a little, and her voice pitched down. "I didn't call for help for hours. I just sat there like a rabbit in front of a snake. That killed him, and, and ... I wanted him to die."

Vicar breathed in deeply, trying to accept her heart-breaking story calmly. There was silence for a few long beats and then Beulah continued.

"Turnabout is fair play, right? Don't you think?" She was looking for support now, her eyes pleading slightly. "He abused us, I ignored him in his moment of need. Jacquie saw it. She knows what happened. She blames me, I know — thinks I'm a *murderer* ... but she's never said a peep about it."

"Never? No discussion at all?" Vicar was skeptical.

Beulah turned her head away uncomfortably and shook her head. "No. She just shut down."

Vicar sat there a few moments, trying to absorb the story. Jacquie seemed so normal, so in control ... Yet there were triggers that made her cloud over and storm away. Not often, but it had happened enough that he knew better than to go there again.

He kissed Beulah on the cheek and retired wordlessly to bed, his mind turning over the story as he protectively wrapped his arm around Jacquie.

■ ■ ■

It was getting real now. Serena drove to a sporting goods shop at a mall, miles away, and bought an ominous foot-long Buck knife that, in her small hands, looked like a machete. She fondled six or seven different knives while the clerk watched her, wondering why a woman who looked more like a runway model needed something like that. It was as practical in her hands as a Shriner's costume scimitar.

"Oh, it's for my boyfriend. He hunts."

"Mmm … Well, it's a good choice. That one will help him fight off a bear."

Serena looked at him, impressed. "Really?"

"Well, ah, yeah, I guess … If you could get close enough without being eaten first."

She looked at it again, stroked it sensually, and then said, "I'll take it."

■ ■ ■

Little Jacquie had heard Mommy and Daddy fighting again. Daddy was crashing around, slamming things in the kitchen. She cowered under her quilt and prayed that it would stop, just stop — oh please stop.

And then it did. With a suddenness that was unusual

for nights like this, everything went silent. No grumbling, no storming around, no sounds of Mommy crying. Jacquie knew the patterns like a mind reader.

After a long time, she climbed out of her bed — clad in her pink flannel nightie to fend off the wintry Saskatchewan night — and crept out of her room. Just outside her door was a railing where she often looked down into the living room; she could sometimes sneak out and watch TV from up there, if she was quiet.

From her high vantage point, she saw Daddy, crumpled on the greenish shag rug, the front of his pants dark and pee stained. The sight of it made her tummy hurt. Beside him was Mommy, sitting with her legs crossed, on a vinyl-covered, high-back kitchen chair of burnt orange and brown, looking down at Daddy silently. She wiggled her foot like that only when she was upset. Mommy took a glug from the bottle, stared at it for a moment, and then poured out the rest on Daddy's head.

Jacquie began to whimper, shaking as if she were freezing, and Beulah's eyes flashed upward at the sound. She leaped up the stairs, and, blubbering uncontrollably, held Jacquie.

Jacquie was utterly traumatized; she couldn't feel her extremities. In her mind she saw only a dark tunnel — had already backed away from the sight and slammed a door shut. She promised herself she would never think of it again. Never. It was all just a bad dream. She felt the small covering of protection she'd known tear loose and fly away, a tarpaulin in a hurricane. She rocked back and forth, dazed, and felt the heat from Mommy's quaking body, was squeezed by her panicky embrace, and felt her own heart disengage from the world. She was on her own now.

She pushed Mommy away and shuffled back to her room. The cave where this secret now lived was already buried — buried forever, under a thousand tons of rock. Mommy kept chanting, "I've killed him, I've killed him." Without turning around, Jacquie, instinctively revising her own history for the sake of survival, muttered numbly to her mommy, "No you didn't," and shut the door.

Nine / Wise Balthazar

Farley Rea needed a new place to live. The basement suite he'd been in for a couple of years had flooded so badly that nearly all his belongings had been destroyed. Even some of his toques ... Septic backup. *Shitty*.

Luckily, his bass guitars and collection of speaker cabinets were stored at Tony's house. But his furniture, a slapdash collection of dead-dog-tired IKEA crapola, was done. The fates had taken care of what Farley ought to have done himself years and years ago. Never more would the hex wrench emerge from the junk drawer.

By coincidence, his bandmate and old pal, "Cosmic" Ray McCullough, also needed new digs. He had been crashing on couches and crouching under the floorboards of partially finished basements for over two years. He seemed merrily unaware of the sometimes-desperate conditions under which he lived. At one point, he had spent a month in a motorhome, in the dead of winter, the rains pummelling the roof of the leaky vehicle like the wrath of one of his vengeful avant-garde gods. Even he, never worried about reputations or the niceties of respectable society, had to agree that he was headed toward total isolation.

Of course, his main concern was "the vibe" of the place where he hung his hat — or, more precisely, his crocheted Rasta tam. His dreads were long and accentuated his height, which was well over six feet. Handsome, with dark skin and soulful eyes, and when clad in the McCullough tartan, he made the ladies swoon. He had discovered years ago the power of a kilt — to date, he had yet to meet a woman who didn't enjoy 'em. But he was almost never interested in "dating" — unless he could find someone fascinated by herbalism, smudging, meditation, and sitar music. Shoes were optional. There had been a few who'd met the requirements, but they never seemed to own a car. Neither did he.

One frizzy-haired vegetarian gal from Sointula, up north and inaccessible on Malcolm Island, who some-times drove a giant 1880s steampunk bicycle, "dated" him by mailing diet-supplement circulars and political pamphlets warning about the imminent collapse of Capitalism. She copied all of it on something she had discovered at an estate sale, a "Gestetner."

So ... Antique copier: check. Giant, squeaky penny farthing: check. Slightly chipped collectible plates from the Bradford Exchange, including John Wayne holding a Winchester rifle: check. Six chickens and an overindulged pet cow named "Joan Baez," after her favourite singer: check. And as an added attraction, soul-congealing porcelain dolls that petrified absolutely everyone who saw them: *check*. *But no car*. All the same, Ray had to tip his hat — he had never heard of a cow named Joan.

Whereas Farley followed Tony Vicar around like a puppy, Cosmic Ray was more likely to march to the beat of his own drum; bongos, bodhrán, or shamanic hand drum. Hell, maybe a hollow log in a boggy fen. It depended on the day — or, as one might guess, the "vibe."

Someone had suggested once again renting the infamous "Bachelor Pad," the residence he had shared with Vicar and Farley in years past, but Ray wouldn't even consider it. The place had been little better than an abandoned warren ready to be overtaken by a passing badger.

Too much upsetting stuff had happened to him there. He had quit the band, he had been awash with guilt about it, and he was certain he'd been taken away by the flight crew of a UFO.

Farley's "Douche Bassoon" bong and some hash, probably from Pakistan or that dank shit from the lady on Quadra Island — a person weird enough that even Ray was cautious of her — might have added to the effect. Yet, no matter how many times Ray went over the memory, he was sure it was true. Plus, they'd visited him again, many times. He communicated with them, *telepathically maybe?*, and sometimes after he did, they'd show up and check on him.

When Ray had guardedly recalled the events and the fear surrounding his first visit to the saucer, Farley listened quietly. Ray had dug deep and revealed the story that he'd kept bottled up for years. He spoke with painful honesty about the trauma.

Farley waited for Ray to stop talking and then cheerily said, "Cool." Pivoting, he asked, "Do you think I should learn how to dance hip hop?"

Ray just closed his eyes and said, "Sure, brother. Sure."

■ ■ ■

Vicar mentioned to Jacquie O that Farley had been forced out of his sodden basement suite and Cosmic Ray had finally concluded that he needed a real place to live. He had cautiously agreed to pair up with Farley, but they had not been able to find a rental that was affordable — or even fit for human habitation.

"Do you have any ideas?" Vicar was leaning against the kitchen counter.

Jacquie replied, "You know, I might have one connection ..." Her friend Ronnie had a large old farmhouse and rented out part of it.

She called right away. "Ronnie, do you still rent out your house?"

"Yeah, I do," Ronnie replied. "In fact, my tenants just left. You lookin'?"

"No, Tony has friends who need a place."

"A couple?"

Jacquie burst out laughing. "Yes, a couple of weirdos."

Ronnie replied cheerfully, "My people!"

"Uh, I should be clear … They're … uh … *musicians* … Ish."

"Oh God, Jacquie, what are you trying to do to me?" She sounded aghast while laughing.

"Ronnie, I gotta be honest … They need work, but they're gentle souls. Can they just come see the place and then you can check them out?"

■ ■ ■

Jacquie took Ray and Farley over to meet Ronnie. Farley emerged from Jacquie's Jetta, signature stringy hair under an appalling toque unwisely salvaged from the basement-suite flood of liquid *scheisse*. In a glance, Ronnie put him down as someone who would bring a pet ferret along on a visit to an old-folks' home. He was followed by Ray, who unfolded his long legs from the small vehicle. Ronnie was attracted to tall men, and this one met the classic description of tall, dark, and handsome. She was surprised to feel a twinge when she saw his dreadlocks. *Mmm, interesting.*

He was dressed like a rubby, but she could see his broad shoulders under an old T-shirt. His hands, even from twenty feet away, were huge, his fingers long and graceful — not the stubby meathooks of most of her suitors. *Hands tell you so much about a man …* She felt mild annoyance when Farley blocked the view of him.

Cosmic Ray's paternal great-grandparents had moved from Jamaica to Halifax before the Second World War, and as a result, neither he nor his parents had any vestige of a Jamaican accent, and Ray lacked anything in the way of Caribbean presentation. Save the tam, he was a total homeboy, as Canadian as overpriced cellphone contracts, and had a soft voice that occasionally drifted into full-on hoser. He spoke in disjointed tangents about his "spiritual life," delivered cryptically and providing a damp squib to conversation.

A stranger had once pleasantly offered "Man, it's hot out here."

The Cosmic response: "The sun is, like, uh, *flame*; the dharma of flame is to, like, *burn*." He had read that nugget in a pamphlet.

Ray's offering of small talk had been disturbing to the ramrod-straight local, a guy who sometimes thought ketchup was too spicy; he'd slowly retreated backward, fake-laughing with fake agreeableness, hoping to flee for the hills ASAP, as soon as he was out of this hippie's reach. Ray just stared with a flat expression, unaware that he came across as a serial killer when he blurted out shit like that at the bottle depot.

Ronnie Balthazar, on the other hand, was a cowgirl, not easily startled, confident as an empress, and owner of a little farm. Her bank account was healthy. She loved horses and lavished attention on them; she claimed to have a secret mental connection with her beloved animals. She owned four and wanted more. Communication with Ray, therefore, would not be dissimilar.

Tall, with a lovely figure and known to wear tight Levi's or jodhpurs, she never lacked male attention; nor did she shrink from it. She and Jacquie represented one hundred percent of Tyee Lagoon's strategic reserve of *Island Girl* glamour.

Farley had never lived in a place with a proper paint job, never mind a dishwasher and a double sink, so he was sold at first glance. Cosmic Ray, able to readily accept far, far worse conditions, was fine with the place but had to admit that there was some electricity coming off this Ronnie lady. Her aura was *hot*: rich, flaming purples and reds; tendrils of yellow and orange. She kept going on and on about the place — details about the electrical upgrade and the new fridge, just to keep the conversation going. Coupla times she blocked the exit, slinging out her hip and brushing her long hair away from her neck. Plus, she kept touching his arm and giggling.

Ray wasn't used to normal people easily warming to him, so he mumbled tentatively, "You have a colourful aura."

She tittered nervously, to her own surprise, and asked, "You can see auras?" She'd heard of it, but the reports were usually from sources rather unreliable.

"Oh yeah, I see auras. And I do reiki. Mebbe you wanna session?" His prime but modest source of income was this kind of stuff. He was constantly on the lookout for potential clients.

She imagined those great big hands so close to her body and felt a little quiver. "Oh, I've always wanted to try that! Perhaps after you two move in, we can have regular sessions." She hung on the word "regular" for just a bit too long.

Ray and Farley glanced at each other, relieved but slightly mystified. *What, no credit check?* Looking on, Jacquie could see what was happening and didn't quite believe her eyes. Ray was the very last person on Earth she'd thought Ronnie would be interested in. She knew that opposites attracted, but *Jaysus* ...

Ten / Overheated

On the couch, munching on a slice of pizza and watching TV, Vicar wiped his mouth on his sleeve and kept at Jacquie, who was being unusually stubborn.

"I don't know why you won't talk about it, Jack ... your mom told me everything."

Jacquie shot Vicar a look of betrayal. "She's full of shit. Don't believe a word she says."

"Honey, she admitted that she left your dad on the carpet to die — she said she was too stunned to react. Frightened stiff, I guess."

"Really," Jacquie replied venomously.

"That's what she told me." Vicar raised his brow and shrugged.

A dam broke inside Jacquie. She raised her voice, saying, "Did she mention that she poured out the bottle of whiskey all over his head? Or that she watched him for God knows how long? Just sat there staring at him, savouring the moment. She was overjoyed when he had the heart attack. *Overjoyed.* Everything since then has been crocodile tears. For years it's been *poor, pitiful Beulah. Fetch her another gin and Dubonnet.* Well, go drink with one of the high-society dukes or viscounts that live in *Regina*, oh sainted piss-tank Mother ..." Jacquie looked fierce yet vulnerable.

Vicar went silent and gathered his thoughts before saying, "She told me that he was violent, dangerous. She said ... umm, she said that he slapped you around, too."

Jacquie turned to stone and looked away.

"Jack?"

Silence.

"Jacquie? Honey?"

"I. DO. NOT. WANT. TO. TALK. ABOUT. IT." She slapped her hand on the couch to emphasize each word.

"But you were *just* talking about it." He knew that pointing out contradictions in her statements could be dangerous.

Clearly, a direct discussion was going to come up dry. He mentally flipped a coin, thinking a little humour might change the tone of things; he changed tack. Jarringly and with maximum tactical inappropriateness, he taunted, "If you don't fess up, I'll do it. I swear I'll do it, Jack."

She shot him a vicious look. "I am not joking." He wouldn't! *That's beyond cruel.*

But Vicar's eyes were wide in a mock threat.

Jacquie stormed out of the room.

That was his cue. Vicar jumped up and gave chase, whistling "It's a Small World After All." The punishing earworm would stick with her the entire day. She ran up the stairs to the bedroom, moaning *AAA-aaa-AAA-aaa* to block out the sound of the pernicious melody, clapping her hands over her ears.

He heard the bedroom door slam as she kicked it shut behind her. It was a crappy prank, but he needed to keep her from going dark. That had always been *his* domain.

＿ ＿ ＿

There were several Wikipedia pages related to Vicar and the Knickers Pub. The pub website used a photograph of the entrance taken from Dumfries Street, where the mansard roof could be seen poking above the building, which Wikipedia had poached. That much was at least factual.

The listing about Jacquie was vague and filled with unsubstantiated crap, almost none of it true, and they even misspelled her real first name, Caoilfhoinn — pronounced, as they noted, *Key-Linn* or *Que-Linn*. Their chosen spelling was "Coalfinn," which to Vicar could only be interpreted as "Coal Finn," not a great first name for such a babe. Sounded a bit industrial, really.

His own Wikipedia entry featured a spectacularly awful photo of him playing guitar in some rundown dump, obviously contributed by some shaky drunk. It contained a list of references thirty entries long, almost all from gossip publications, where not one solid fact was included, other than that he was indeed a bipedal humanoid, currently alive, and from "Tyee Lagoon, Canada." It had obviously been written by an American, as they seemed allergic to including the province when referring to Canadian locations. Also never mentioned by them, but implied, was "a frigid unappetizing wasteland filled with moose." He thought of Beaner, back in the day, bedecked in his moose-y bottle-picking disguise, and ruefully had to give them that much.

The references linked to stories that were so outrageous it made Vicar squirm in his seat. Shocking. He couldn't fight it. He just had to suck it up, turn the other cheek, but also prepare to repel boarders. He'd already learned that lesson all too well.

■ ■ ■

Ronnie could see Cosmic Ray from her high bedroom window. He was bringing a laundry basket into the house, along with an armload of ill-assorted junk. *Everything those two own is junk.* She spied a pile by the gate, featuring a cheap electric fan sticking out of it, listing like the Tower of Pisa. Today Ray was wearing regular adult clothes, nothing shamanic, magick, or pseudo-religious. Just torn up Levi's and T-shirt. *By God, he looks delicious in those jeans.*

She could hear the washing machine lid being opened and closed several times. Then a voice came from the basement, "Uhh ... Ronnie ... I can't make the washing machine work ..."

She found herself quickly going toward Ray's voice, just a little too excited for her own comfort, but loving the strange role reversal of being the pursuer for a rare change.

Ray stood at the bottom of the stairs, leaning on the handrail. "Can you show me how to use this thing, please?"

"I just have a load in the dryer, Ray, but I can help you start the washer."

She showed Ray how to put in the soap and fabric softener, and set the temperature, all while bending over just a little too provocatively. Ray was feeling the effects, his throat now dry and his eyes slightly hypnotized.

As before, she stood too close to him, touched his arm and put her palm on his chest. It was getting awfully hot in the laundry room. Ronnie bent over like a yoga instructor and retrieved her clothes from the dryer. Underwear. More specifically, G-strings, scanty and alluring. She began to fold them, play with them, while Ray began to quake.

The *coup de grâce* occurred when she finally held the undies up against her pants and pretended to model them; at that point, normally Zen and imperturbable Cosmic Ray snapped like a rubber band, grabbed her by the waist and lifted her onto the washing machine, the pair suddenly pawing at each other like bears in a Dumpster.

Farley walked into the house and down the stairs only to discover, there, right before his eyes, his buddy, jeans around his ankles, and his landlady bare-assed naked, having a threesome with Lady Kenmore. It sounded like cats in a sack, but they were clearly enjoying themselves. Farley beat a hasty but silent retreat before any kind of spin-cycle freak could commence.

- - -

Ronnie had not realized how *into* it she was going to be. Something about Cosmic Ray gave her the whips and jingles. When she broke it down, nothing about him really worked for her. Chatting was a chore. Their paths in life were utterly different, their basic philosophies opposite.

When she got close to him, she became as randy as hell. She couldn't remember the last time she'd met a man who hit her in that primal spot and her adventurousness escalated to heretofore unknown heights.

To her own surprise, she began to cook up scenarios, role-play, costumes, long-hidden fantasies. The logical part of her realized that she'd never last with Cosmic Ray. There *was* a reason people called him "Cosmic," after all, and she knew his eccentricities would eventually drive her away. His insane UFO business was so far out it was all she could do to let him talk about it without being rude. In the meantime, she kept a straight face by fixating on his tight ass. For now, she was going to ride that stallion like a teenager drives a stolen car.

Ronnie had a vintage dress with crinolines that she had worn to a costume ball years before, and she had stumbled upon a long, purple-velvet frock coat in downtown Victoria. She found an old-fashioned naval cocked hat at Roberta's Hats as well, and decided that Ray would wear it and the coat — and maybe some boots — but nothing else. It was doubtful that he had a cutlass or sabre; that was not the sword *Lady Ryder* was interested in, anyway.

Cosmic Ray was unable to act the part and had to be coached to speak like the fantasy pirate she called "Poldark." He managed to squawk out "Arrrr, Billie," having heard it somewhere before (and not realizing its connection to frozen fish sticks) — and then scooped up Ronnie like a bag of sphagnum moss, chucking her unceremoniously upon her large bed. She moaned something along the lines of "Run me through, Captain Poldark!" and then the rest was mostly sound effects and a bed frame in distress. It held together for the duration, but the mar it left on the wall would require professional repair and a few knowing looks from the drywall guy.

■ ■ ■

Over at Ross Poutine's liquor store with the barren-sounding name of "Liquor," he strode around the place as pleased as punch. He had thought he was King Shit of Turd Island now that he had so many square feet to spread out in, a full-on walk-in cooler, all new plumbing and electrical, and two public washrooms. There was even a place with a counter and a sink where he could do wine-tasting events. Had he mentioned the small fridge beneath the counter where you could put the cheese?

He hosted one wine event where an attendee went on about not wanting Limburger cheese with her wine. Her crinkled nose sensed something dastardly in the air. Limburger! Taleggio? Some regrettable, *stanky* variety of Chevre? There had been no offending cheese at all, but rather Ross Poutine, who had been wandering around behind the wine tasters, watching with interest while wearing a three-day-old shirt.

In the early days of the rebuild, Ross Poutine had at one point bitched to Jacquie O, digging in his heels about not wanting any "inferior decorator" screwin' around in his shop. Jacquie had thought it was an attack upon her superior capability, especially in colour selection. She had, after all, been at him incessantly through not only the rebuild, but throughout the first interior design, long before the hotel fire.

Then she remembered how outrageously he scrambled the English language. She was never quite sure if he was doing it on purpose or if he was just that out of touch with his tongue.

Poutine was situated next door to Merri Crabtree's Hot Thoth, and although an infamously crotchety man, he really liked her. How could he not appreciate someone who made his custom hot sauce? He nipped out of Liquor and walked the few steps to her door at Hot Thoth, the bells inside tinkling loudly.

"Merri! Y'got my hot sauce order ready?" He was yelling at high volume in the tiny shop, barely bigger than a master bedroom. Poutine tended to be awfully loud at times, adding to his "charm."

Merri came bustling into the front from the rear kitchen area. Her voice was deliberately quiet, in hopes of muting his enthusiastic bellow by example.

"Hi, Ross. No, I have the peppers on order, but it might be a day or two more." She dreaded making his specially ordered acidic death condiment, so powerful it could take rusty lug nuts off wheels. It had a proven record of leaving people in agony; happily, some of them deserved it.

"Well, when you git that jug o' Dumpster Fire ready, gimme a ring." Ah, yes. Dumpster Fire, his very own name for his very own recipe that surely to heavens must contribute to his appalling goatiness. Under his harsh exterior, Poutine was a warm and wonderful man, but best appreciated at a distance.

"I will, Ross." She wasn't much in the mood for being yelled at, even when it was from an oblivious but friendly hog-caller. Or perhaps more precisely, a goat-caller.

Poutine headed back to work at Liquor. As he left, he felt yet another wave of delight at the place, to him the very hot spot of Tyee Lagoon. His '66 Chevelle, Annie, and Liquor were his world. He yelled over his shoulder, "Hey, Merri, Annie picked you up a big bag of that Abridged Mix-chure youze like so much."

"Thank you, dear." Merri just smiled and gently shook her head.

PART II

Intermission: Go to the bathroom and fetch more snacks while you're up.

Eleven / Extra-Large Mediums

The Extra-Large Mediums of Littleton were two sisters, Debbie and Dawna, now television stars, and self-proclaimed psychics. At any rate, one *would* have to self-proclaim. It wasn't as if you could get a diploma in ESP and Mediumship at the nearest community college.

Based in Colorado, the pair of them were indeed extra large, a fact they played up to the maximum. They were constantly snacking on camera. It became part of their onscreen formula; they often shot scenes in restaurants that offered "devilishly delicious snacks," and used catchphrases like "don't talk to demons with your mouth full." One could, after all, be misunderstood, and everyone knows a demon doesn't politely ask, "Pardon me?" The line was always followed by a jolly high-five. There were T-shirts.

One early investigation had required power tools to rescue them from a dark cellar, all while they freaked out about the creaks coming from the woodwork — they pronounced them shrieks of spirits that needed to be guided "to the other side." But really, what woodwork wouldn't shriek if you were attacking it with a reciprocating saw? Then, cut in the dessert scene, a close-up of a mile-high banana cream pie, the psychic pair leering at it like stalkers peeking from behind a bush. At the sight of it, they'd emanate sounds that were alarmingly close to orgasmic.

So popular was a first-season onscreen salvation by firefighters with hydraulic tools that they force-fitted climactic scenes into subsequent episodes that involved rescuers of one sort or another, often moustachioed, always handsome and, of course, selflessly noble. The pair had found a way to conflate their love of food with their affection for hunky rescuers. Nearly every episode somehow managed to discover these rescuers shirtless, playing basketball, or polishing their ... fire engines. The sisters referred to them as "my brawny cinnamon bun" or "Punkin' Pie"; one handsome young firefighter, whose nametag read *FF Scott Pepper* and who had high cheekbones, a strong jawline, and wavy locks, had earned a few extra highlights in one episode. They'd instantly dubbed him "Peppermint Biscotti."

It had been their season two finale; yummy Biscotti-boy was shown rappelling down a cliffside above a high cave — a haunted one, of course. The hunkily hunky hunk was dressed in nothing but a skin-tight T-shirt and form-fitting tactical pants, armed with a can-do attitude, six-pack abs, and a bag of fancy donuts. The donuts kept the psychic sisters occupied as he surveyed the emergency with his handsome, crinkly eyes. Dawna's attention was split between the gourmet baked goods and his fantastic bulge. The show was ludicrous, called "tone deaf" by screaming cognoscenti, and yet was the number one show on the Panorama Paranormal Network for the third straight year.

The program that the Extra-Large Mediums had dethroned from the number-one position on the network was a stabby-stabby-cut-cut docco series that featured mass slaughterers from the UK, France, or any country that was not the USA, really. It was called *Killing with an Accent* and had been tremendously popular. Exotic dialects and speech patterns made stone-cold murder ever so much sexier, or so it seemed. The sisters had learned a lesson from them. In order to compete, a gimmick was required.

So, it had become integral to the format of *The Extra-Large Mediums of Littleton* that local first responders be used, to give a sense of colour and variety to every show. Each episode was in a different location, so it provided endless variation. And of course, it was cheaper. Every new set-up needed "unpaid assistants" from search-and-rescue or the fire department, or occasionally police. They had hoped to someday capture a SWAT team in action. Yes, a SWAT team. But getting special weapons and tactics teams to show up for ghost reports was no easy task.

As nervy as it seemed, they had cooked up a scheme that would surely get them one. A single panicky phone call was all that it required. The SWAT team quickly arrived at the basement of an office complex of their hometown of Denver, in hopes of disarming a hostage-taker reported to be wielding a huge "sword or machete." It had not been communicated to them that the hostage-taker in question was the ghost of a Civil War Southern colonel, possibly turned poltergeist, and very much a figment of imaginative scriptwriters.

Though it had begun with good intentions, there was very little real about the Extra-Large Mediums' reality show now. Yawning gaps in the storylines seldom mattered, either. No one bothered to clear up the glaring discrepancy of Southern colonels haunting the modern office structures in Denver, except to say that one of the hostages was from Richmond, Virginia. The colonel must have attached himself to her by some mystical means. *Well, sure …*

Because they had been, to put it kindly, "inaccurately informed" of the situation, the SWAT squad had made a snap decision to storm the room in which they believed hostages were being held. A nutjob with a sword was no match for six officers with semi-automatic weapons in a lightning attack, after all.

A battering ram took the door off its hinges and the small, heavily armed platoon came running into a large area filled with rolling cameras and klieg lights. It would be accurate to describe the ensuing moments of panic and screaming as "chaotic and confusing." But every moment was caught on camera and manipulated in post-production in such a way that some viewers honestly thought they had witnessed a spirit vanquished by the law.

Presumably, you could now legitimately call the cops after a ghost sighting, so any strange noise was blamed on a spook or a goblin. An appalling precedent had been set. Summoning the local *gendarme* would be like calling out for your mommy after a bad dream.

There were threats of fines or charges, and the viewership of the show soared ever higher. So did junk 911 calls about hauntings in nearly every North American town and city. Thanks to *The Extra-Large Mediums of Littleton*, it was remarkable how "paranormal" wind gusts and roving raccoons had become.

▬ ▬ ▬

Ronnie stared absently at the television as the Extra-Large Mediums of Littleton were pulled out of an attic by a couple of gorgeous firefighters and felt an idea blink to life. *Cosmic Ray's Fire Rescue*, mmm ... She glanced up at the access hatch in her ceiling that led to her own dusty attic, where, incidentally, all her surplus clothing was gathering cobwebs.

She would eagerly play a damsel in distress for a jolly formidable shagging. She summoned Ray from the basement as she compiled a honey-do list.

She called out loudly from the top of the stairs, "Ray, honey ... I smell smoke ..."

■ ■ ■

After dealing with the Steven Leigh Law Office for some years now, Vicar had started referring to him as Steven "Leigh-*gal*," erupting in gut-busting laughter as he entertained Jacquie with plot lines for an imaginary TV show. His sidekick would be some vivacious paralegal named Paris ... *Paris Tweed* ... with thick-framed glasses and a bun in her hair, ever dutiful as the pair heroically parallel-parked within a block of the courthouse, on only the second swipe. He could just see those tan, pleated chinos stretched to bursting as Steven roundhouse-kicked documents all over the block-and-a-half of "downtown" Tyee Lagoon. Vicar lifted his leg and kicked around the living room, yelping, "*Objection!*" The sight of him in his misshapen tricot Stanfields while attempting to look like a Kung Fu master was ridiculous, and Jacquie cackled uproariously. Vicar, getting into it, spin-kicking and nearly wiping out the vase on the end table, liked Steven but couldn't imagine a person drawing inside the lines as he so unquestioningly did.

He glanced at himself in the hallway mirror, thinking that he looked *dashing*.

■ ■ ■

Steven had a fat envelope full of adoption paperwork for Jacquie and Vicar and ducked into Hot Thoth to see if Merri knew where they were; he breathed in the wafting, exotic aromas and smiled. She had done such a nice job of rebuilding after the fire — the place looked great and smelled even better.

"Oh, they're not in right now, Mr. Leigh. But I know they'll be back. Their daughter's here." She put her index finger up in a shush and nodded toward Frankie, napping in the little vestibule on a cot. Merri shook her shoulders in a silent giggle.

"I haven't seen her in months. Look how big she's getting," he whispered. He leaned over the counter and admired the angelic, sleeping face pouting cutely, her blanket kicked aside.

"… And talking up a storm," Merri tittered.

"We never had kids. I missed out on all that good stuff." He was regretful but said it so lightly.

Merri took note of that — Mr. Leigh was someone sensitive about other people's feelings.

"Oh, it's a lot of work. Joyful, but exhausting." She snickered apologetically, a vaguely seasick look on her face.

Merri found herself checking this guy out, although she'd never admit to being so deliberate, so brazen. Such a good conversationalist, though, and a widower, to boot. She rebuked herself for daring to be presumptuous, but she was just so lonely now — it occasionally got the better of her.

He chatted amiably, "If I were smart, I'd spend more time on my boat. I have a great big one down at the marina, but I just haven't felt the urge. Vera and I used to have so much fun on it …" He trailed off, embarrassed to be so revealing and to have smothered the nice tone of their chat.

Merri was not thrown off by mention of his late wife. "A boat! Oh my, Wally and I lived on a boat in Eleuthera for a few years." She mercifully skipped her set-piece saga on the shocking expense of owning a yacht.

"Eleuthera? I have such fond memories of it. I spent a couple of weeks there many years ago." He thought of the wild escapade he'd had with that sweet lass from the Gulf Coast. My God, they'd even done some *heavy petting*. But Merri ... Wally. Husband. *Damn* ...

"Well, that's a coincidence indeed." Merri felt the little twinge of interest inside her ratchet up a notch or two. "It was such a shame that Wally, *my late husband*, died so suddenly." She threw that little nugget out as gracefully as trying to recreate a fart with your shoe on the doormat. She heard Frankie's soother hit the floor, yet again, and glanced back to see it lying in the middle of the narrow hallway. She seemed to spend half her time picking it up and rinsing it off.

There was an awkward pause, Steven staring nervously at the corner of the shop, seeing a yawning crack of opportunity, not knowing if he should take the shot — and then he blurted, "I'm going to take my boat out for a little tour sometime soon. Why don't you act as my first mate when I take 'er out?" He turned and looked up at the sky as if already predicting the weather. He was fairly certain it was charming to do that, but he was terribly out of practice.

Demurely, Merri turned away, blushing like a schoolgirl, until she noticed that Frankie was again sucking on the soother, the blanket now tucked up under her chin. Not possible. *What in the world?*

She turned back to Steven, astonished, and caught herself before freaking out. She didn't want this handsome gentleman to write her off before their first boat ride.

Back in Denver, at the production office of *The Extra-Large Mediums of Littleton*, Debbie and Dawna sat at a small conference table.

"Debbie, have you looked over this stuff on that Liquor Vicar guy?"

Dawna replied, "Yeah, talk about a *continuing story*. There's so much publicity surrounding him, I think it's a no-brainer."

"He's quoted as saying there's been no paranormal activity since the renovation of that hotel."

"Well, that's never stopped us before." She was referring to their practice of manipulating events to look paranormal, even when the place was as dead as a statistics lecture. In fact, the pressure to deliver had become so intense that they had no other option but to fiddle with outcomes. It kept them on top of the ratings, but had eroded their sense of mission, which had been genuine back in the day. They really *had* helped solve murders and disappearances. Now, they snacked and faked.

"So, we're a *go*, then," Dawna said. "Okay, let's find a good restaurant in that town."

— — —

"So, what's this I hear — that you're sweet on our lawyer, Merri?" Vicar had a twinkle in his eye.

Shocked, Merri responded, "Why, that's nonsense. I simply agreed to go for a boat ride with him sometime."

"Word on the street has you hot and heavy with him, Mer."

The look on her face was as if she'd been slapped. "You! Out!" She pointed at the door, violently pumping her *finger bayonet*, ejecting Vicar, who was laughing.

As he walked back to the pub entrance around the corner, he thought about his long, tortured experience with rumour and insinuation. The phenomenon was a shock to neophytes, and he had just treated her like people treated him. Suddenly his offhand teasing didn't feel very amusing at all.

— — —

Slumped in his soft chair, close to a cheery fire, the convalescing pilot, Gunnar Bering, drifted pleasantly through the afternoon on painkillers, feeling quite fine for the time being. He stared at the flames licking against the stove's glass door and thought of the crash. He couldn't understand it; he was a solid pilot, decades of experience, but crashing into a parking lot and blasting through a brick wall? He should not have survived.

Sure, he was banged up terribly, from his smashed cheekbone to a busted tibia, and a few other painful whangs to boot. But he had lived. And Vicar had lived, too. No one had died. *No one.* Vicar had received some painful deep lacerations, but he could have limped away from the wrecked craft, even though he had apparently blacked out and had to be carted off to the hospital.

Gunnar knew all too well that death was the usual result of uncontrolled crashes — it was nearly impossible to believe this kind of luck, if you could call crashing a plane into a funeral home *luck*. In his cotton-mouthed, numbed state, he savoured the off-kilter irony of it all.

He had always liked Tony Vicar, an eccentric but big-hearted fella, but had never put much stock in the weird stories attributed to him: the magic powers, the ghostly friendships, the gossip-rag bullshit. But, by God, there had to be something going on. Gunnar simply could not explain their survival without factoring in divine intervention. *Well, some kinda intervention ...*

Twelve / Turbo Bust

Beulah was sharing her breakfast with Frankie in the high chair. Frankie in turn was distributing scrambled egg and toast in a splatter pattern around her. Vicar saw the ketchup way over on the window and thought the place looked like a crime scene. How did a toddler heave food that far?

Jacquie noticed him checking out the ketchup, caught his attention, and then flicked her gaze over to the kitchen sink, raising her eyebrows eloquently. Vicar knew what to do and shuffled over to get a dishrag. He was well trained.

Frankie was talking chirpily and Nana Beulah was chatting back enthusiastically, just a little too loud, repeating everything she said, cackling and mugging, a bit much for this ungodly hour but happy and loving.

Beulah asked, "Who is the boss?"

Frankie pointed to Jacquie, who smiled.

"Who is the most fun?"

She pointed to Beulah and said, "Nana!"

"And ... Who is Mr. Stinky Bum?"

Frankie's eyes lit up as she jabbed her finger toward Vicar, accidentally flinging more ketchup. "*Daddy!*"

Daddy ... He melted instantly, awash in a feeling better than any other. He had never even conceived of love like this. On its heels came the shadow, the worry, *the fear*. In their private moments, both Vicar and Jacquie felt it and had been afraid to even speak of it out loud.

The powers-that-be could still take her away from them ... It really chafed that they had to wait while some faceless government ministry, in its majestic wisdom, decided whether *they* were worthy of parenting Frankie instead of a biological mother or father who had abandoned her on a doorstep in a blizzard — wrapped in nothing but a tattered blanket and stuffed inside a beer box.

How long would it be before they could move the paperwork along to legally adopt her? This state of limbo was tough to bear. Jacquie also resented the red tape, but seldom said anything.

They were the ones who had stepped up; *they* were the ones who had unquestioningly taken care of a baby who would have died without their instant emergency response. Because they wanted Frankie permanently, they'd keep a sock in their cake holes about the endless paperwork and the indignity. They'd jump through the hoops, but it really didn't feel fair.

Beulah wiped Frankie's face and hands and set her down on the floor. Frankie headed right to a stuffed animal and gathered it up, chatting with it, petting it, talking to it like they talked to her. Vicar watched her for a few moments, and then turned to his forensic janitorial duties. He had to hurry up; he had a big gig today.

━━ ━━ ━━

Tyee Lagoon's Hospital Fish arrived at the Turbo Station, knowing not what kind of set-up would await them. Vicar, the visionary leader of the sublime art-rock power triangle, imagined a custom-built stage, small but just enough for him and Farley and Ray, perhaps tucked into the corner of the property — under the big sign. They'd be highly visible and a draw to everyone who passed by. A curiosity impossible to ignore.

The Grand Reopening was upon them, and they had even gotten together to go over everything. The trio had rehearsed in an unusually focused manner. In fact, an entire *portion*, perhaps up to thirty percent of their performance, might be remembered accurately and performed properly.

The boss of the Turbo Station, on the other hand, had not spent even one second worrying about what his "orchestra" was going to need, where they'd be, or what they thought. He was already breaking the bank with the fee. *You gotta guitar, you gotta voice. What more do you need?*

The huge, borrowed box truck, on loan from Tyee Furniture because they didn't deliver on Sundays and Farley used to work there, rolled into the station with Vicar at the helm, buggering around with the stalks in an attempt to put on the windshield wipers, and rubber-necking the lot to see where the stage was.

What greeted the trio was one dismal string of streamers hanging limply from the corner of the canopy over the gas pumps, and an irritating inflatable tube man waving madly next to the far entrance. Other than that, there was nothing, save for a couple of cars in for repair, one raised up on yellow jacks and minus a back tire. The outdoor speaker scratchily prickled out an old song by The Who. Vicar, feeling unease building, closed one eye like a smoker getting an eyeful of his own noxiousness.

"Is this the right place?" He knew it was, but it seemed the only thing to say at that moment.

Farley, confused, replied, "This is the only gas sta-tion in town."

Vicar raised his eyebrows, acutely aware of the fact, and slid out of the cab of the box truck. He felt a twinge of pain in his thigh when he landed, which made him think of Gunnar Bering, who he had heard was still in recovery — which made him think of the airplane crash, which made him think of bad things, which made him feel snake-bit. *More layers than a Mexican bean dip.*

He entered the station and saw a man behind the counter. It was the slightly hostile-looking boss, who immediately piped up, "You guys the orchestra?"

Vicar had filled up his Peugeot here a thousand times, but the guy didn't show even a flicker of recognition.

Vicar ignored the grandiloquent designation and replied simply, "Yup." He turned to survey the parking lot outside and said in a friendly tone, "Where's the stage? We'll move the truck closer to it."

"Stage?"

"Yeah, and the PA and lights."

"The *what*?" The guy looked annoyed. Did this guy think he was Elvis or something?

"The stage and the PA, the speakers — y'know, so we can be heard?"

"No one said anything about speakers, buddy."

Vicar, instantly stressed, blurted, "But I faxed you our *technical rider* weeks ago!" Riders were big league, man, and that was how Vicar rolled. So big league, in fact, that he hadn't even called back to confirm — he'd just presumed his demands would be met.

"You … faxed …? We haven't had a fax machine for years."

Vicar found himself near panic in an instant. He had found the number in a twenty-year-old phone book, the one that had for years held up one side the BarcaLounger he'd found in the alley. Even the threadbare Turbo Station had progressed to email by now. He knew this was going to be a shit show. He swore at himself about the damned fax machine.

"Well … Where did you expect us to play?" His question was half challenge.

"Anywhere you want in the lot. Not in here. We gotta hear the customers. You can walk around, if you want."

Vicar had a sudden nightmarish vision of Ray, his nineteen-piece drum kit surrounding him, moving to different locations on the pavement after every song, with Farley shouldering his gigantic bass speakers into place right beside him. A calamitous buffet of wretchedness was about to be served.

Vicar hoped they could, maybe, just maybe, set up in the rock garden over in the corner. Ray's drum kit could be on the sidewalk just behind it. It would mean that all the automobile traffic racing around the corner would have to pass inches from Ray's back. But ... *the gig must go on.*

With heartbreaking but predictable suddenness, the sky opened up and the rain began to come down in earnest, scotching any plan to perform in the parking lot. Bracing himself, Vicar bounded out of the gas station and said to the guys, with as much false bravado as he could muster, "Ahhh, guys ... turns out there was a little miscommunication. This is an *acoustic* show. No PA. No lights."

Farley was wordless. Ray said dryly, "I guess you're gonna hafta sing louder." His eyes broadcast his sinking feeling: *not again ...*

Vicar, hiding his dread, smoothly said, "No prob. We're gonna do all *instrumentals.*"

Yes, his imposing, thematically deep art-rock trio would somehow, he prayed, turn on a dime and miraculously sound as innocuous as *Kenny fucking G.*

Cosmic Ray, highly dubious, asked drily, "Are we going to try 'The Torture Pits of the Death Monks of Gehenna' with no vocals?"

They all knew it just wouldn't sound the same without the agonized, reverberating shrieks of the eternally damned.

■ ■ ■

A half-hour later, Vicar, soaking wet from moving equipment out of the truck in the downpour, had managed to string an extension cord from the auto service bay to his amplifier, into which both he and Farley were plugged. The sound produced was horrific, but Vicar was desperate to achieve even the lowliest, stopgap jury-rig, and kept silently chanting, *never again, never again, never again.*

The drum equipment was set up straddling the gas pump island, Ray having refused to simply play maracas or something. He felt naked without his massive drum kit, and even when pared down to a more modest size, it blocked access to the gas pumps.

The boss of the Turbo, already aggravated by the "orchestra" and its "outrageous demands," was mad as a bull about the drums blocking the way. Ray dutifully moved his floor tom away until the guy disappeared back indoors, and then put it back in place. He did this several times, his eyes fixed on the station's interior.

The miserable trio began playing and were instantly commanded to quiet down, the unhappy boss man leaning out the door to bark his complaint, regretting having hired such a bunch of unkempt bozos. He looked at Farley, stringy hair topped by a rain-soaked toque emblazoned with a peace sign, pure hippie shit, and twitched slightly as he thought, *That ain't music ... Sounds like they need a new alternator.* He was a man whose life revolved around his mundane job, hockey on TV, and fishing for steelhead. He was one of the only people in Tyee Lagoon who had never heard anything about Tony Vicar or his legend, though Vicar stood right before his eyes.

Acting against his own instincts, Vicar said quietly to Ray, "Can you switch to brushes instead of sticks?" He just wanted to get this show over with and avoid any permanent damage to his already limping band.

Cosmic Ray McCullough, barbed by the harshness of the boss and depressed by the hopeless situation, and in a rare show of annoyance, snipped, "Brother, do you really think I use brushes in Hospital Fish? Mebbe you can switch to a ukulele?" Posed as a question, it was a rebuke, a million-watt light of truth shining upon the folly of their situation.

Vicar leaned back in surprise. However mild Ray's tone, he hadn't heard him say a biting word in years. Clearly, he was pissed, and Vicar realized that accepting this gig had been stupid of him. In one bumbled decision he might lose all the ground he'd gained with Ray. He'd quit once when Vicar had been too cranky; now he might quit because Vicar had been too accommodating. Pathologically unable to admit the pointlessness of an art-rock trio playing seven-minute-long original pieces of awfulness, requested by no one, ever, Vicar gritted his teeth and plodded on.

Ray, now having vented, backed down a little and played his snare drum with his bare hand and grabbed the nearby squeegee with his right, reaching over to clean the side window of the car parked next to him, all the while playing almost silently. He shot Vicar a look that was a mix of slapstick and venom. Vicar began filling with unease. In that moment, he saw in Ray a bit of himself, back in the days before Jacquie and the Knickers — the old, cranky Vicar, persistently huddling under a black cloud. At least back then, he'd started his days disappointed and didn't have to wade through this stressful optimism shit.

Two Dungeons & Dragons types stumbled by, with undistinguished hairstyles and pallid skin, there hoping to find Tolkienesque Orcs, as advertised on the big revolving sign. One craned his neck up toward it, and then back at the decidedly non–Middle Earth rock band before him. Disappointed, the pair shuffled away, probably back to Mom's basement.

A woman briefly did the Twist and grinned while filling her tank. As she pulled away, she yelled out her window to Vicar, "Hey, you guys aren't too bad!" She threw coins from her departing vehicle.

Vicar dodged the incoming dimes and yelled back to her, "Great. I'm glad we're not *too* bad." Anguish cascaded down upon him.

Mighty Hospital Fish, Tyee Lagoon's premiere *prog* ensemble, now dutiful buskers for the amusement of bewildered motorists, started another song. Ray remained prickly but gamely attempted to play quietly; in truth he wanted to throw his bass drum through the front window of the gas station.

Tragic timing occurred as another motorist came wending into the lot, manoeuvring egregiously, revealing his rotten driving skills as he tried to get his car pointing the right way to access his gas tank. Cautiously, he crept toward the pump just behind Ray. Herky-jerky in the first place and distracted by all the impediments in his path, he accidentally lurched forward and bashed into Ray's illicitly positioned floor tom, which, in the driver's defence, was something of a surprise in an automobile refuelling context. The smack by the car's bumper sent the floor tom skittering into the paper-towel dispenser, where it ricocheted to a clattering halt upon Vicar's guitar, perched on a rickety stand.

As day follows night, his prized Gibson Les Paul on its stand fell forward, off the concrete island, and plummeted face first onto the ground. Vicar watched its neck shear off, decapitated in slow motion, providing a sickening *per-twang* as it landed.

After years of failing to keep going if someone played a clam, Farley decided on this day to finally do just that. He acted as if everything was hunky-dory. He may, in fact, have been mesmerized by the sight of the nearby Bacon Cheddar Ranch Doritos, his beloved

"Triangles of Joy," tantalizing but unreachable through the big window before him.

Ray, on the other hand, leaped up, truly furious for the first time in years, and kicked the bumper of the offending car. Then he pushed over some of his drums in a display of abject masochism, a low-rent Keith Moon losing his marbles in a petrol forecourt, while Farley thumped away obliviously on his old Ricky, just like Geddy's.

Vicar felt something boil up — a long-hidden frustration that was triggered into rage. Though it wasn't thought out, Vicar sympathized with Ray; after a schemozzle of this magnitude, his anger was justified, at least a little bit. Ray stormed off down the road on foot and Vicar knew his drummer had quit, again. Horrified at the thought of abandonment and all that wasted effort, he began his own epic meltdown. Vicar slid the acoustic guitar off his shoulder, raised it high above his head like a battle-axe, and smashed it to death on the gas pump behind him.

The boss of the Turbo Station was well entertained by the destruction and snorted when Vicar's guitar exploded into splinters, roaring, "Now that's more like it!" He'd check the pump for damage later, but for now ...

A guitar neck with flaccid strings hanging from it in his hand, an anguished Vicar stood limply, now spent of fury, feeling like a little boy who had just wet himself in class. *Goddamn it, another exploded guitar.*

Its splinters and shards had become a monument to another Hospital Fish gig. Their equipment was in ruins and their biggest failure yet had brought everything to a floundering but perhaps merciful halt. They had bumbled into many weird situations, but this one … *well, Jesus.*

Farley finally stopped playing, confusion in his eyes. After a time, he muttered obliviously, *"Maaaaaan …* uhm. Can I still get a free pop?"

Thirteen / Ray of Light

By the time Cosmic Ray had cooled down, he had walked all the way home. Plunking himself down into a chair, he hung his head. He was ashamed at his own selfish behaviour, but he just couldn't go on playing in Hospital Fish, a combination of Rush, Yes, and humiliation. The band felt silly ... In fact, it was bloody stupid and would have been twenty years behind the curve twenty years ago. Even he recognized this, a man who could put up with nearly any outlandish behaviour; he knew how depressed Vicar would be when he broke the news.

Ray wandered to his bedroom and looked at his meagre belongings. He wished he still had the old promo photo they had taken, a classic black-and-white 8 × 10 glossy, the three of them so young, wearing a hodgepodge of costumes, Vicar in karate jammies, trying to look "studly." He remembered Farley following the photographer's directions, hanging his mouth open in a graceless attempt to come across as sexy, and then Vicar's mom bursting out laughing, asking if he was catching flies.

What was the allure of it to Vicar, who seemed so overly enthusiastic about his band that hailed from the middle of nowhere? Ray, like all of them, used to be all in, but he had been young; then his outlook had changed years ago when he met the UFO people. Ray's mind wandered as he thumbed one of his healing crystal books, colourfully illustrated, which had cost him only a dollar at a used book shop in Santa Fe, New Mexico. It had been extremely useful and was now dog eared.

He had rejoined the band, when he came back from his self-imposed exile in the Southwestern desert, only to make peace with the boys. He had felt so bad about abandoning them. Abandonment was, to Ray, a poisonous mix of coldness and cowardice. He hated it and hated even more that he'd acted in such a dishonourable way. He had come back to make amends, but he hadn't dreamt things would get this silly again, and so quickly. Now he wondered why he hadn't seen this coming.

Vicar's plate, Ray could see, was obviously full. He was a father and loved Frankie, everyone could see it; he had Jacquie — she was just amazing ... so together, so cool. He owned the best pub anyone had ever seen. He was world famous already.

Ray had simply not been bitten by the music bug in the same grasping manner that Vicar had. It was an addiction, maybe ... Vicar appeared to suffer bouts of depression and self-medicated using not drugs but rock shows as his painkiller.

Ray would absolutely never, ever, ever say it out loud, but Vicar could get like a fanatical keener about the band, like a guy who'd spend thirty agonizing years researching the Beatles' every bowel movement during the recording of *The White Album*. He took Hospital Fish so seriously that it had to be a sickness.

Why not just play once in a while for the laughs, and maybe even play songs that the audience *liked*? Was that so much to ask? *That* lesson had been served to them again and again, but never seemed to stick. It *could* have been fun.

And there was Ronnie to contend with. His feelings for her were strong, passionate, but he was certain that she didn't connect with him where *she* really needed a connection. So together, yet blind to the other side. Ronnie was confident she was *all that* and more, and no one had ever challenged her supremacy; she'd spent so much of her life in the driver's seat that she didn't have the first idea how to enjoy being chauffeured.

He'd observed it many times before: unusually beautiful people allowed to proceed through life untested. It almost always ended badly. *Ronnie has no idea how badly she needs me.* Cosmic Ray was in love, but the feeling was so unfamiliar to him that he misread it as a magical mission.

He would explain his journey to her; maybe she would join him. It was lonely work, seeing things that no one else could begin to imagine.

■ ■ ■

Steven "Leigh-*gal*" sat on Merri's couch and sipped at a coffee with triple cream and triple sugar — a confection, really; a pancreatic super-blaster pick-me-up — and listened to Merri's merry tale.

"And so you see," she was embarrassed already, "little Wally — he was named after his grandfather, my late husband. Umm, he had been playing with his toys ... Oh dear, he has so many of them, Steven ..." She looked briefly into his eyes. "... And, well, *somehow*, he got a little Lego tire stuck on his, umm, well, on his *winkie-doo*."

Steven started laughing despite his determination not to lose decorum, slightly worried he might be insulting her. He already knew her well enough to have understood her basic philosophy that *neither children nor dogs ever need criticism*. He gave those subjects a wide berth. But then Merri began howling. She repeated "stuck on his winkie-doo" two or three times as tears came down her cheeks.

As the laughter subsided, she muttered, "I don't think you'll have to worry about that problem, Steven."

He looked at her, surprised. They both blushed.

nn Tenna passed the phone to Vicar, who was standing around, staring at a sheet of paper within a sheaf of papers, tacked together into a book of papers, all in spreadsheet form, all nauseating to him. He would never get used to all the paperwork. It was all so boringly normal, square, soul sucking. It was almost as bad as adoption paperwork. He liked just tending bar, but in his current state of mind, he'd rather be sharing a hole with a groundhog — with his luck, it would be February second and every camera in Christendom would be there to record his misery for posterity.

On the phone was a young fast-talker who identified herself as a producer for *The Extra-Large Mediums of Littleton*.

Once she stopped long enough to take a breath, Vicar jumped in with, "Oh, I hate to tell you, but since our rebuild — after the big fire — there hasn't been a single sighting of 'Valentine.' I'm afraid he has scrammed."

"Debbie and Dawna still think it would be a very lively place for an investigation. They want to spend a couple of days there, taking some readings, doing a few interviews. It *totally* boosts the profile of the places that we've done episodes at."

Vicar immediately felt flags go up as he cringed at her clunky wording and auctioneer-speed pitch. The last thing he wanted was more false advertising, and he was very cautious about entering into agreements with people who wouldn't let him get a word in edgewise. Nothing but hassles could result — extra hassles he did not need.

He gently skipped over how ridiculous he thought the show was, though it could be *amusing-while-drunk*, like funny home videos where Dad gets a bocce ball in the nuts. How come *they* could have a network show, but Hospital Fish never could get a record deal? Vicar had no idea what was on "the radio," but bitched about it constantly. He was stuck living in an era where radio was king, and disco still sucked. In fact, he sometimes listened to an ancient "found" eight-track player and the three K-Tel cartridges that had been lying next to it at the dump; that time, he'd brought more home than he had discarded. His fave cartridge was *101 Saxes Play Bossa Nova!!*

He responded, "I'm cautious about turning up the volume on all this paranormal stuff that seems to follow me around. It's a private issue. I don't really like talking about it — and your bosses might be disappointed because … I honestly don't know if it's real or imagined." He cleared his throat and continued, "I'm probably not the right guy for your show — which I've seen, by the way …"

His half-assed explanation was mostly true, but he did not mention that it wasn't just all the "paranormal" stuff that was the big obstacle course; now, your average Monday was challenge enough.

Running a pub had, at its outset, seemed *romantic* — these days, Vicar woke up in the middle of the night, concerned about running out of serviettes.

Add math, online forms that never seem to work on the first try, and incessant requests for donations by *everyone*, it seemed, it had all gotten as appealing as unclogging a garbage disposal with his bare hands: another of the shit jobs he had to do. Every business in Tyee Lagoon was peppered with charity requests; he decided that he'd donate to only kids' charities and events — he was a softie for "little ones," after all, and lavishly sponsored the Tyee Lagoon Vicars baseball team.

Word got out; he was inundated by countless requests for kids' stuff. He decided that he'd have to push back the line and limit it to "sick" kids, although it bothered him a great deal. Suddenly every kid with a wart or head lice needed a fucking fundraiser. The pub was going broke being charitable. He said to Jacquie, "That's it … From now on, only kids with their heads blown off in a war zone." Jacquie had stared at him and shaken her head. It had to be bad if Tony was saying no to children.

Vicar thought he'd made up his mind and just wanted to get off the phone. The talky producer, on the other hand, knew how well the reluctant but honest ones came across on shows like theirs. Slick self-promoters stunk to high heaven, but these confused types generally read as authentic, and the audience could sense it. Plus, it provided a great contrast to the psychic sisters' shenanigans. The young producer ran conversational rings around Vicar until she ran out of ideas. Then she repeated it all again, but even faster. Finally, she offered money. Money to film on location, in the hotel and pub.

"*How much* did you say?" Vicar's jaw was slack. He could visualize the pub's bank account rising into the black for a month or two. It'd partially make up for the tubs of cash he'd donated, that was for sure. Vicar would never admit it if asked, but his imagination, in a horrible habit, flashed for a millisecond on buying a Höfner bass, *for that true McCartney sound*. Then he pushed the idea aside. He needed a Beatle bass like this young producer needed more syllables between breaths.

He cleared his throat and replied, "Uhh, in that case ..."

So, the deal was struck, and Vicar spent the next several hours rehearsing how he'd break it to Jacquie.

"… Anyhoo … it's a fat payday, and they'll only be here a couple of days. We can do it once and never again."

Jacquie looked at Vicar wordlessly, her eyes smouldering with anger. Tony had not only done what they had both pledged never, ever to do, but he had made the decision without her input. It felt to Jacquie like something Mother would pull off, and that was miles out of bounds.

■ ■ ■

Ray had filled the basement with a choking cloud of incense that made Farley flee like a cheapskate when the bar tab arrives. He had never really liked the smell of it, but after a wretched hangover he had once suffered after a night of calamari and ouzo, he experienced something akin to PTSD when getting a whiff. He departed with great haste.

Ray was really trying to get his ducks in a row and had concluded that he and Ronnie needed to get closer, to be *connected*. Hospital Fish had obscured his vision, had taken up too much of his mental space. Now it was gone; he looked toward the future. All the clarity he had mustered to compose his grand speech to Ronnie abandoned him now, and he reverted to type.

"… So, you see … Time is so, so, uh, y'know, *short* here on Earth. We really have to make the, make the … uhh, ah, uh, like, the *best* of it." He simply could not be eloquent. Around Ronnie he was always nervous, and when he got that way, he babbled in disjointed tranches of gobbledygook.

"Folks … uhh … *people* who, like, y'know, uh, really *like* each other, uh, kinda need to come, uh, y'know, *together*. You know, *spiritually*." It was like listening to a skipping CD.

His quicksand of filler words did not help to communicate his feelings. Ray fell back into grasping at cogency; Ronnie's eyes were clear and magnetic and seemed to peer right through him. It made his throat dry and his groin active.

Ronnie had sat through a good, solid five minutes of his painful, halting emotional outpouring. "Ray, Ray, Ray, pah-rup-pah-pum-pum … I get it — *I get it*. You like me, you really, really like me. I'll dress up like Sally Field in a nun's habit. Now put on the fireman's outfit, climb that fricking ladder, and bang me like a drum."

Ray looked at the floor, slightly dejected, but got a boner anyway. She might never commune with his soul, but in the meantime, she could connect with his nether regions and that would do.

Vicar was amazed by the amount of gear required to film a network TV show, even a piss-assed little paranormal program like *The Extra-Large Mediums of Littleton*.

The producers came early in the morning and began scoping out angles and shots and set-ups, and generally presuming first and apologizing later. It left everyone at the Knickers a bit on edge.

They had rental vans filled with equipment and strung miles of electrical wires throughout the hotel. How they intended it to appear antique and intimate, Vicar didn't know, because it looked like the album cover of *Who Are You*, cables lying in piles near anvil cases and metal stands.

Debbie and Dawna entered the Knickers and took it in. From the TV perspective, it was ideal. Lots of light, lots of character. The vibe was … unique.

But when they left the pub and entered the lobby, that vibe changed radically. There was a shift, a kind of visual wobble. The whole place was restive.

"Did you feel that?" Dawna stared straight ahead but spoke to her sister, a pace or two behind.

"I sure did. Remember it?"

"Yeah, I remember, but the feeling is so, so …"

"Yeah … *so* …"

One of the major issues the production team of the *XLML* had been unable to fully resolve before their arrival was casting first responders to appear as Hunky Rescuers. Comm with the police and fire services had been spotty at best.

Debbie and Dawna very much took point on any Hunky Rescuer decisions and waited to interview a few hopefuls in a room at the Hotel Valentine, its furniture arranged to look office-like. They moved out the beds and brought in some banquet tables, draped in heavy cloth, which they sat behind as if on an expert panel, bringing their great knowledge to bear upon the supplicants before them as they chomped on giant Rice Krispie squares.

Hailing from distant Colorado, the entire outfit had absolutely no idea what a Vancouver Island Volunteer Fire Department was apt to deliver for their on-camera needs. They were used to big-city, body-proud athletic types with unnaturally clean garages and giant pickup trucks.

What they got was a ragtag collection of paunchy men, all sporting colossal walrus moustaches and ball-caps. Their extra-extra-large T-shirts displayed slogans like *WTF ... Where's the food?* Dawna, in particular, was disappointed; half her enjoyment was the hunks.

The only guy they interviewed who didn't have a gigantic waistline was a taciturn old character everyone referred to simply as "Fire Hall Gordy." He was the fire hall's unofficial spokesperson and "PR advisor." He had, in fact, been the guy who had failed to respond to the production staff's multiple queries about wrangling firefighting volunteers for a role in the episode they were about to film. He didn't recognize the number, called it "spam," because he'd heard his granddaughter use the word. He actually liked Spam quite a lot. Fried. Picked up a taste for it in Hawaii one Christmas. He couldn't quite grasp the connection between one of his fave snacks and bullshit phone calls.

For a public relations contact, Gordy was notably weak on relating things to the public and was certain the internet had been invented specifically to bedevil him. He was seventy-four years old and owned a fifteen-year-old flip phone that hadn't been able to text for years; he hadn't ever quite figured out how to use it, anyways. "'Parently, ya got the whole *goddamn* public library at yer *goddamn* fingertips, but it cuts out every time you try to order a *goddamn* pizza." The texting function died after he chucked it against the wall. Alphanumerics were not his friend and he could never find his glasses, anyway. At any rate, there was no way that ancient brick was going to access a "goddamn" public library.

He bemoaned the loss of pay phones, even though Tyee Lagoon had only ever had a couple of them; in his advisory capacity, he often suggested imaginative methods of public relations along the lines of, "Maybe we should get on the blower and raise the newspaper. It worked for the Cloggers."

Gordy had lost a leg in a tree-falling accident decades before and wore a prosthetic replacement. He barely even noticed it anymore, although he joked about how he didn't need to diet to lose a few pounds. He could just remove a limb. *Ewww* ... Rich ladies from Vancouver didn't laugh, but his pals sure did.

He was dressed in jeans and his only shirt with buttons, the blue one, and Debbie and Dawna didn't even notice his prosthetic leg. They settled for him immediately, knowing the sexy "fire hunk" *thing* might have to become "elderly-but-noble rescuer" in this episode. At these volunteer wages, it was the best they could do. The only other camera-friendly option was Hayley Constanz, the Mountie the locals called Con-Con, a six-foot-tall woman not one bit interested in being anyone's "cinnamon bun."

■ ■ ■

Who to interview? Tony Vicar, of course — that was obvious — and his girlfriend, Jacquie O, but there were others who were a part of the scene, too.

With just a bit of poking around, they'd heard about Beaner Weens. They tracked him down easily — he was, after all, just downstairs in the kitchen at the Knickers, looking a treat in his houndstooth trousers and gravy-slathered chef's jacket that read *BEANER* in flowy embroidery. The psychics were always willing to befriend a cook.

Since starting up Beaner's Bottles (& Cans), their willing interviewee was alive to any opportunity for publicity and suggested, quite without subtlety, filming him standing in front of his moose-mobile. They went along with it, capturing footage of Beaner, chest puffed out, head wagging back and forth all proud and shit, posing with a decapitated costume moose head and grinning smugly like some asshole strumming a guitar in an erectile dysfunction commercial.

Being a show about psychics, Beaner thought they'd be asking about "Valentine the Ghost," now as notable as the Knickers Pub and nearly as well known as Vicar himself. But the questioning started with Vicar.

"Can you tell us a little about your boss, Tony Vicar?"

Like every unskilled storyteller, he started his response with a long, "So …" and then stared heavenward for a moment. "Nice guy. Umm, but he's got powers. Real powers. Kinda spooky …" His pronunciation was odd: *powahs*.

He lurched inarticulately through backstory jumbled with adventurous tales of Vicar, told with a massive dollop of artistic licence — a.k.a. bullshit — making sure to mention the dangers of bottles (and cans) with wasps inside them (he used gloves and a finely honed instinct, he stated for the record). This would be cut from the segment, but they let him blab on for a while. But more to the point, he had seen Vicar bring a dead lady back to life — fascinating, and what they wanted to hear about, except he had *not* seen it, and had not even known Vicar then. He went on to claim that he had gone with Vicar to help rescue children from a burning hotel. He had not done that, either; he had been three floors down at the time, saving his own arse.

Beaner was canny enough to keep up with the Vicar stories online and occasionally added a little detail to his versions of the story that fell in line with the freshest gossip and innuendo.

"Seems like everything goes right for Tony and his friends. I don't think you want to be his *enemy*." Beaner drew out the word for maximum drama. It was true that a couple of Vicar's "enemies" had ended up suffering, but that was an exception. But Beaner's take gave the stories verisimilitude — a word he had never heard. He clearly understood the concept, though. He digressed into unabashedly bogus tales loosely based on situations he knew nothing about.

His out-to-lunch innocence had evolved over the last few years — Beaner was still relatively harmless, but he put himself ever closer to the centre of events. He told himself, and he believed, that it was all in an effort not to steal the limelight, but to hype his bottle (and cans) business. He was such an odd man.

The interviewing producer said, "Can you describe some of these so-called 'spooky' powers?"

Beaner immediately warmed to his subject, putting his arm out in a gesture of grandiosity that urged the listener to imagine a wondrous scene. "Well, y'know, when he was in the burning hotel, he put out the flames with his *mind*. He just waved his arms and the fire went out. That's how he got through that doorway and saved the kids."

"You saw him put out the fire? With his mind?"

"Oh, shit, yeah," Beaner lied. "He did it. I'll bet he can start frickin' fires, too." He conjured a scenario, a "horrah" movie scene. His strange accent made him sound foreign, or maybe just like he had a mouthful of overcooked vegetables; his point of origin was impossible to place. Wherever he was from, it wasn't here.

Beaner had been born in the UK but grew up on Vancouver Island. His parents had spoken with a Mancunian accent and they could certainly posh it up, they said, but "only if needs be." But after his youth on Vancouver Island, doing crap jobs, picking bottles, and becoming expert at lying around, Beaner had begun to talk like the night manager of a Barbary Coast whorehouse.

He had learned much from Ann Tenna, who could curse the paint off a battleship; the pair of them used blue-streak lingo as part of their schtick at the Knickers. People came simply to hear them snipe at each other in their guttural, lowball Canuck way. But once Beaner turned it on, he couldn't shut it off.

The interviewer glanced at the elapsed time on his phone — this windbag was finally getting interesting, *keep 'er rolling*. He clicked a button, leaving a timing marker that would help him locate the good part in post-production.

Beaner was on a roll. He could sense their interest warming as he bullshat to the max. For a microsecond, his inner voice told him not to say anything too screwy — Vicar was still his boss, after all. But then he looked at the camera and the far-too-earnest interviewer who was listening to him with deep, penetrating curiosity, a situation that beckoned him like catnip, and thought, "*Fuck it*." Beaner Weens had always dreamed of being first banana.

Sixteen / Vicar's Interview

The production company was led astray by someone mentioning that Farley Rea was Vicar's best friend. In a way he was, but more precisely, he was a mascot; Vicar truly loved the guy, but he was not of the highest wattage. Plus, he smoked so much pot that his brain just sort of floated slightly above the surface, like a waterlogged deadhead near a log boom — barely visible above the surface and occasionally a real hazard if you wanted to move quickly.

He sat in the pub, eyeing up the taps. He didn't have enough cash on him to buy a pint. "Hey, youze guys at least gonna give me a beer?"

The pub was closed for business and no one was manning the bar, but they managed to find a can of American light beer in one of their coolers.

Farley cracked it and screwed his face up in disgust. "Ugh. Jesus. This tastes like the pee of somebody drinkin' real beer."

The production crew just stared, appalled at the oblivious ingrate before them.

"Mr. Rea, how long have you known Tony Vicar?"

"Ahhh, since school. Long time. Hey, d'ya think y' could gimme a ride back home after this?"

The production assistant's eyes widened, and then he said patiently, "Mmm. Sure. I'm sure we can get you home."

"Cool."

"Back to how long you've known Mr. Vicar."

"Like I said, since school. You guys got any snacks? I'm fucking *starving*."

The producer dropped his head and stared at his shoes for a moment. "Joe, get him a sandwich, will you? ... Back during your schooldays, did Mr. Vicar show any hints of paranormal capabilities? Any signs at all of what was to come?"

"Nope. Uhh, I uzh-lee like mustard on my samwich ..."

A look of bemusement passed over the producer's face and he said, "Mr. Rea, that'll be all. Thanks very much for your help."

"Huh? That's it?"

"Yes. That's it."

"Can I still get that samwich?"

"Yes."

"Cool." *Nailed it.*

■ ■ ■

Vicar sat in a wingback chair from the pub, repositioned so that the capacious inglenook was shown burning cheerily behind him. He had a mic on his lapel, and one over his head. The crew fussed with the lighting like von Sternberg capturing the butterfly under Dietrich's nose. Vicar refused makeup. Jacquie intervened.

"Tony, use some makeup."

"I don't want any makeup, Jack." He thought it was fey.

She was surprised by this and tried a new tack. "Honey, think of yourself as Gene Simmons. He always wears makeup."

He paused, eyes twinkling, and said to the makeup artist, "Do you have any rouge?"

■ ■ ■

Taping began, Vicar now with Pagliacci's bright red cheeks, as the interviewer started his questioning:

"How long have you had secret paranormal powers?"

Vicar stared at him and responded with resistance, "I don't have any." Something about the overconfident production assistant annoyed him; Vicar wasn't about to bare his soul to some pushy asshat whose gaze was constantly glued to his phone.

Awkward silence.

"Well, how do you explain all the remarkable events that are attributed to you?"

Vicar wore a bewildered look and shrugged. "I can't."

Asshatticus maximus looked at his phone again. Did he have prepared questions on it, or was he just admiring some other idiot's photos of this morning's over-priced avocado toast?

"You can't explain any of it, Mr. Vicar?"

"Nope."

Great ... First the clown makeup and now the one-word responses. Could he possibly come across as more belligerent? This guy's a total dud. The producer asking the questions decided to take a verbal swing at Vicar, to punch through his defences.

"Is there *anything* paranormal about you?" He said it snidely, like a way-too-popular girl in high school.

"I dunno." Vicar looked blank.

Jacquie watched from behind the camera with concern. She became apprehensive, feeling the tension from the TV crew.

The interviewer decided to tactically "lose patience." "So, it's reasonable to think you're perpetrating a fraud for publicity purposes." It was not a question.

"Listen, you pushy prick," Vicar snapped, "are you just here to do a hit piece?" He knew about that kind of journalist all too well and had sent one of them to hospital to enjoy a few weeks of traction. Vicar would have been well pleased to slug this guy and glared at his omnipresent mobile phone. "You ever heard of a pencil and paper?"

Jacquie began to rise from her chair in case she needed to intercede.

There came a pacifying voice echoing from the background: the Extra-Large Mediums themselves.

"Maybe we should take over the interview, guys."

— — —

Vicar had cooled down after Jacquie gently reminded him of how hard it was to take him seriously dressed as a Red Skelton painting, emitting laconic grunts in response to questions from a paying customer, all the while asking herself why she was trying to fix a situation she had never wanted in the first place.

With her help, Vicar reluctantly removed the circles of rouge on his cheeks and resumed the interview, this time much more co-operatively, but very much on edge. At least no one was staring at their phone like a mindless, regurgitating automaton. *Doing things purely for the dough is always dangerous*, he thought. His relationship with money was fraught and always had been.

"Well, I'm sure you know that there was a very active something-or-other in here at one time. I guess you could call it a ghost. We named him 'Valentine.' I saw him — well, at least I thought I saw him. Several times. Mostly in the hotel, but once right here in the pub." Vicar pointed to the little booth over to his side.

"What did he look like?"

"Well …" Vicar paused, and his eyes flicked around as he recalled his sightings of the spirit. "Usually he …

umm, 'it,' was a black blob. Like a black hole wandering around, kinda shaped like a person. It's weird. But …"

Debbie and Dawna leaned in.

Vicar was not only forthcoming now; he was digging deep. They tried to hide their excitement and remained impassive, keeping the tone low and intimate.

Jacquie watched and thought that they might or might not have been genuine mediums, whatever that meant, but they knew how to make people spill their guts.

Vicar continued, "But when he came during the fire, he was a man, a young man. Short hair. I remember an old-fashioned checked shirt and one missing sock."

"Did he communicate with you?" It was Debbie with the question this time.

"Umm. Yeah. But he wasn't talking *per se*. I heard him but I don't think his lips moved. It was like a dream …"

"Did he help you get out of the blaze?"

"Yes — yes, he did. I still can't understand what happened. He just walked us through the flames, and I didn't feel a thing. We should have burned to death instantly."

"Mr. Vicar, your friend Beaner Weens claims that you can start and put out fires with your mind."

Vicar was startled. "*Beaner* said that? Oh, for God's sake. How would he know?" Vicar was annoyed. "He wasn't even around, he knows nothing. He is so full of shit."

"Are you denying it?"

"Yes, I'm denying it. Who in the hell could possibly do *that*?"

"Someone pyrokinetic, obviously." They looked at him in challenge, both with completely straight faces.

He stared back at them as if they were street preachers, screaming threats of damnation at passing dog-walkers.

Vicar shot Jacquie a look, in the background. He was deeply curious about what he'd experienced but this kind of jarring abracadabra yap was a total turnoff. He suspected now where the episode was headed and felt regret flooding through him. In one question, they'd gone from detectives to fools. So had he.

Next thing you knew, they'd start cooking up a casserole of pseudo-religious crap, like Ray. Every superstition put in a blender of every religion in order to make a smoothie of drivel.

He reached to his shirt and unclipped the little microphone and stood up. "I think we're done."

Debbie responded by saying, "Dawna and I had a shared dream, Mr. Vicar. Shared dreams are very rare. A little old lady on a ladder came down from the sky and warned us both that *someone* should 'beware the mother.' *Beware the mother*, Mr. Vicar ... Does that mean anything to you? We think it does."

Vicar looked at them, impatient and not of a mood to connect any fanciful dots, and left the pub. As he departed, he shook his head and thought about how wide a strip he would take off Beaner's hide.

Jacquie, rather than going after him, sat frozen in the corner, shocked.

After a few beats she cleared her throat and said to the sisters, "You had a dream about a lady on a ladder?"

"Yes. We both had the dream on the same night. Probably at the same time."

"Uhh ... did it take place in this pub?"

The sisters glanced at each other, surprised. "Yes, yes it did."

"Were there flying animals in the dream?"

Now the psychic sisters were the ones who were shocked. "Yes, there were."

Jacquie simply silently sat in the corner, her lips pursed thoughtfully.

"Uhh, it had a certain energy, a *feel* ..." Dawna added.

Debbie followed up, "And as soon as we walked into the Knickers," she gestured around her, "we could sense it again. The dream was meant for Tony Vicar."

Jacquie looked upward, thinking of how vivid and crystal clear the same dream had been in her own mind, and mumbled, "Maybe."

■ ■ ■

At Ronnie's urging, Cosmic Ray had hesitantly ambled to the volunteer fire hall and talked to one of the firefighters, who was sipping a coffee.

"Umm ... So, yeah. We're gonna do this video. Ahhh, *music video*. So, we need t' borrow some props."

There was no video shoot; there would never be one. He was pretty sure there'd never be another gig for the blighted and benighted Hospital Fish; he was the group's principal cause of collapse, yet again. Guilty regret barbed him.

The firefighter had heard about Hospital Fish, knew a good bit about Vicar, and had even been one of the guys attending the plane crash, and was more than happy to lend Ray a turnout coat and a helmet for an ill-defined scene in an "art-rock music video." Ray, no liar and far too uncomfortable to simply admit that he needed the costume to help put out the fire in Ronnie's lady parts, barely managed to croak out his request. But he was propelled by his groin and Ronnie's needs. If she wanted to be "rescued," he'd rescue her all right. Rescue her firmly and for a long, long time.

From Vicar, Ray borrowed an extension ladder that had been stored behind the shed in the backyard — and that required Ronnie's big pickup truck to transport.

Ray departed Ronnie's place, driving the pickup in halting spurts and grinding gears, Ronnie wincing as she heard him go, playing a metallic tune with her heretofore perfectly functional transmission.

■ ■ ■

The pub, quiet of all ghostly reports for many months, sat unoccupied at nine o'clock in the morning, except for Beaner Weens, prepping the daily special in the kitchen. He had earbuds stuffed into his skull as he listened to a podcast featuring him, talking about Vicar and Valentine the Ghost, recorded some weeks ago but only recently available. It sounded so cool. He was quite happy about the publicity.

As he chopped carrots, he did not at first hear a stack of bowls rattling. After a moment or two, they settled. But then the utensil rack behind him began to sway, the ladles and slotted spoons rocking back and forth noticeably. Beaner kept chopping, immersed delightedly in the sound of his own voice through the 'phones.

It took a rapid toggling of the overhead lights and a flying frying pan to get his attention. And once it did, he ran like a frightened doe directly toward his rattletrap pickup truck with the moose-head hood ornament and vintage tape deck. Had the engine enough power to burn out, it would have left a strip of rubber all the way home.

"Well, it's probably for the best. I was going to give him so much shit he'd have probably quit anyway." Vicar absorbed the news but was slightly distracted by Ann Tenna's distressing hairdo.

Beaner had fled, terrified, and couldn't imagine even walking past the hotel now. He had been hiding at home, twitching. The Knickers was without a head cook and everyone was sluicing around in the muck of an incipient panic.

Vicar, distracted and overloaded, was irked at yet another irritation, another unwelcome surprise that seemed to be a major feature of running a pub. So typical, so standard, so *normal*. Normalcy was going to make him puke.

Ann Tenna looked unhappy and piped up, "Who else could I ever train to do the job properly?"

Vicar looked at her quizzically for a moment, realizing she meant all the byplay, the schtick.

"You mean you do all that on purpose? I thought it was your natural charm."

"Oh, lick me, Vicar. Me 'n' Beaner gotta *thing*. You think I dunno how good it is for the Knickers?"

Vicar was silenced, moved but embarrassed. He loved her schtick, but he regretted not being able to financially reward her for the massive draw she had become. *Beaner, too, I guess.* Once again, money peeked around the corner and stuck its tongue out at him.

"Tony, I'm gonna get Beaner back. I'll go see him."

■ ■ ■

Ross Poutine had gone over every square inch of Ann's 1950 Chevy half-ton; he had focused his attention like a Jack Russell terrier trying to retrieve a ball from under a couch. The vehicle that had been her nemesis was now a gleaming showpiece with the innards of a Swiss watch.

In it, she rumbled toward Beaner's place up on Royal Mountain, determined to convince him to be brave. Ha ha. He was the biggest pussy, but she'd lie to him. Men would believe *anything* if you smoothed their feathers, those big, adorable goobers.

■ ■ ■

Beaner was still rattled. "You should have seen it. A flying pan — I mean, a *frying* pan went past my head. It could have killed me." His lip quivered.

"Yeah, but it din't. And it ain't going to."

Beaner looked at Ann incredulously. "How do you know? You got some kinda secret phone line to his hideout?"

"Beenie-Boy, I seen him. I seen him with my own two eyes. He is the one that got Vicar through the fire. Him 'n' th' kids."

"Bullshit." Beaner could tell she was going to try to coax him back and he was determined to have none of it. She might as well try to get him to swim in a swamp full of reptiles.

"He fuckin' waved at me, Beenie-Bottom. Vicar was holding the kids, him holdin' Vicar's arm. He. Waved. At. Me." She laser-focused her eyes. "And I'm here to tell the tale. He ain't got no bad intenshuns. I think he might be a perteck-ter."

"Protector? Are you bloody *joking*?" That kind of talk was so outlandish that he recoiled at the thought. "That din't feel like protection to me, Annie. I am not going back there, *ever*."

"I heard whatcha said to the puh-sy-kicks. You were makin' yerself sound like some kinda movie star. I *was* there — you wuz out in the street, shitting yerself. Mebbe the ghost is giving you hell for lying."

Beaner looked away in discomfort, busted for bullshitting but totally unwilling to accept the idea of being scolded by an incorporeal poltergeist.

He finally spoke. "Well, all the more reason to stay away from that creepy old dump."

"Listen to me, you little chickenshit. You put on your chef's costume and get in my truck, or I'll kick your girly-man ass all the way there." Her steely eyes would brook no disobedience.

Beaner looked at her, measuring his fear of the ghost versus his fear of Ann Tenna. After a few heartbeats, his shoulders slumped, and he headed toward the door where his sticky, grease-spattered anti-slip shoes lay. He reached down and put them on.

■ ■ ■

Beulah had gotten into the gin again and was feeling jolly. She heard the bell and steered herself toward the front door.

It was Merri and her gentleman friend. What was his name again? Sammy, Soupy, Smithrite? No … Steven.

"Oh, hello!" Her greeting was way over the top. "Come in, come in! Can I offer you a refreshment? I was just enjoying one myself."

Merri managed to stay chirpy, even though she thought that this woman babysitting while day-drinking was an abomination. Beulah's yardarm was an early riser.

"Oh, no, but thank you! A tidge early for us." Merri managed to chuckle, as usual, and as ever for an unknown reason.

Steven glanced at her, thinking it might not be early for *him*, but he didn't dare contradict Merri when she was being judge-y. That'd be a tactical error of epic proportions.

Merri continued, "I just bought some tea while Steve and I were in Victoria, and I wanted to drop a little of it off for Jacquie."

"Oh, how lovely of you!" Beulah enthused blowsily. "You went to all that trouble. It's such a long drive."

Steve piped up, perhaps a little too eagerly for Merri's taste, "Oh, it was nothing at all. I had to go down on business, so we just killed two birds with one stone."

Beulah locked on Steven, eyes sparkling, and moved toward him, now adjusting his flammable-looking tie and patting him on the chest. "You're such a gentleman." She gazed at him raptly. "Murray is so lucky to have you." Her eyes flashed for a millisecond to Merri, standing next to him, holding a gift bag.

Steven's cheek twitched nervously.

"My name is *Merri*." A rage of jealousy rose within her as face got beet red. "Here's the goddamn tea. Goodbye." She threw it at Beulah, grabbed an astonished Steven by the hand, and marched him out of the house.

Beulah, unruffled, just called out behind them, "Bye, Stevie. Don't be a stranger!"

Eighteen / Women of the Cloth

Jacquie O was ambling down the sidewalk in Tyee Lagoon's tiny downtown, pushing Frankie in a stroller and babbling to her about unicorns and puppies and other things. She stopped briefly and ogled a dress in the window, deciding to go inside and ask the price. As ever, she felt an overlay of guilt about shopping for clothes. She simply didn't need any, and anything new would instantly be covered in barf or flung food, but the dress just looked so pretty. *Oh, hell, it can't hurt to look ...*

Serena, kneeling behind a bench with binoculars resting on the top rung, trained them on Jacquie and tried to see the baby, *her baby*, in the stroller. Was she strapped in? Could Serena get her out quickly? Or should she just hip-check that bitch and run away with Baby still in the stroller?

■ ■ ■

Margaret Morrison and her husband, two steps behind her with his shoes wet from having washed the car for the sixth time this week, were on the march to the boutique where she bought the tartan fabric used to make garishly Scottish getups. It was called Women of the Cloth. She swivelled her head around like a surveillance camera. A motorcycle drove past, and she grimaced unhappily. *Noisy death traps. Pass a law against them.*

Even her own son railed at the poisonous level of control over all things in her world; if she could see it, she assumed command over it. He secretly referred to her as "the ol' Home Despot." As Scottish as she imagined herself to be, Mrs. Morrison had completely failed to appreciate the Scots' deep instinct to disobey the wants of tight-arsed, presumptuous gentry.

She spied a shocking amount of trash surrounding the ornate garbage can on the corner; disapproving, she thought about lodging a complaint, but was distracted by the tiny coffee shop that charged more than five dollars for some unnecessarily foreign-sounding faddish nonsense everyone insisted upon calling "cappuccino." *Why can't they just use the English term? Swarthy tea …*

Under no circumstance would Mrs. Morrison have considered cutting across the street to save time. Crosswalks exist for a reason. Marching past the block of buildings, beyond the walk-in clinic that used to be the town's only tobacco shop, she strode to the crossing with the park to her right. There she noted something irregular.

It was a woman, crouched behind a park bench, perhaps bird-watching through "spyglasses," but if so, her aim was off. It seemed more as if she were looking at the woman pushing a baby in a stroller. How odd. Margaret didn't like it but continued to the fabric shop with only one censorious look of suspicion flashed over her shoulder.

▬ ▬ ▬

"Yee-ouch!" *The price of that dress!* Jacquie laughed as she departed. She leaned over the back of the stroller and said to Frankie, "Never pay top dollar for a dress, sweetie. Save your money. You'll need it to support your boyfriend's guitar habit someday." She let out a cackle, wishing fervently that Frankie would meet a fine, young, mentally stable non-musician, with a growing career and maybe a pile of loot squirrelled away. *Send the kids to uni, go on a trip or two, and of course be presented with a small but tasteful collection of jewellery.* She smirked. The last few years with Tony had pushed her so far beyond jewellery that the memory of coveting bling now embarrassed her.

▬ ▬ ▬

Once she arrived at Women of the Cloth, Mrs. Morrison's order was taken with urgent speed. She was a regular, but they couldn't get her out of there fast enough. Her order was accompanied by the now worn-out admonition, "Remember the very handy acronym, which I invented myself ... WASH: *Weathered* Morrison, *Ancient* Morrison, *Society* Morrison, and *Hunting* Morrison." She never, ever forgot to mention that the tartan had first been recorded in an old Morrison family bible, circa 1747. God help the clerk who feigned interest, for they would be deluged with a mind-numbing lecture on Clan Morrison history, which felt so like torture that there had been suggestions in the past to report the old Scotch bag to Amal Clooney.

As she departed the boutique, Mrs. Morrison noted that the woman with the spyglasses had now moved and was partially hidden behind the Cenotaph monument, probably to get a better angle of view. This raised Margaret Morrison's hackles so stiffly that she decided to cross the road and expostulate with this *snoop*.

Mrs. Morrison had raised her voice enough for Jacquie, just exiting the dress shop, to hear her. She looked on curiously.

"You there! Excuse me, you there! You, behind the monument?" She was waving her hand in a strange manner, as if motioning for Serena to lie down.

Serena knew she was busted and turned tail. She was into the trees and gone within a moment or two, with Jacquie not clearly able to see her, the large war memorial blocking her view. All she could see were the words *Lest We Forget*.

■ ■ ■

Con-Con grimaced and drove to the Cenotaph, know-ing already that she was on her way to meet Margaret Morrison, her "best customer."

Old *Maggie* Morrison — *whatever you do, don't call her Maggie* — had summoned the RCMP so many times in the last few years that almost no one took her seriously anymore. In fact, Con-Con was the only member of the local detachment who had the patience to deal with her. It was as if Margaret Morrison now had a cop at her beck and call. Yet again, Con-Con had set out on what everyone delightedly called a "Tartan Tribulation Trip," or a "T3," the implication being that a painkiller was required to bear up to it. Her fellow Mounties dreaded the calls but loved to hear the stories about them afterward.

■ ■ ■

Cosmic Ray hit on a realization that he had not con-sidered. He was freeing himself of past baggage as a result of his passionate affair with Ronnie Balthazar. It was her influence that was urging him forward in his life. It joggled him somewhat, as he had resigned him-self to forever being at the periphery of society, dipping his toe in the pond of normality once in a while, but usually wading hip deep in things mystical, situations numinous, forces metaphysical.

Step one in freeing himself was to have an honest talk with Vicar about leaving the band. He wasn't into it anymore. He didn't want to cart around that big drum kit, ending up more of a furniture mover than a soulful artist with a universal mission. Not sure what had to come next, he was at least certain that membership in a "power triangle" art-rock trio, misfiled in the twenty-first century, was not it.

Ray borrowed Ronnie's truck again, this time to go and talk to Vicar. He entered the pub determined to give him the straight, unvarnished goods.

Nineteen / Quitters and Spies

Vicar saw Ray's face as he entered the Knickers and sensed what was coming. Ray would apologize for the tantrum, but quit, and he'd be left in search of another drummer. *Damn. They are hard to find out here in the sticks.*

"Hi, Ray!" Vicar welcomed him as pleasantly as he could.

"Tony, can we go somewhere and talk?"

So, it was going to be that direct. Tony felt his guard go up as he led the way to his little office, behind the bar.

"What's up, Ray?"

"I can't be in the band anymore." Ray said it as if he'd rehearsed it a hundred times. No hesitations, no hedging language, no "y'know"s, no reference to vibes, karma, herbal medicaments, kundalini, manifestation, or ectoplasm.

"Ray, it was my fault. I didn't do my diligence — didn't follow up with the guy to make sure everything was going to go smoothly. I promise you it will never happen again."

Diligence? Ray frowned and looked at the floor for a few long moments. Vicar was talking silly. Ray hesitated, a little sick at heart. Finally, he spoke. "Tony, you know I have always been your friend ..."

Vicar nodded yes.

"And we've done a lot of things t'gether, right?"

"Yup, lots of adventures!" Vicar was still hoping to spin the conversation into a happy one.

"So, I have to be honest. It's not just me. It's that the band is, is ... ah, kinda useless. Nobody wants to hear that old shit anymore. It's silly. An *embarrassment*." He accentuated the word. "We never seem to get through a whole set of our 'riginals ... We always end up covering ABBA or something cuz everyone is leaving. Remember when we wrote 'Tails of Tropical Fish Tanks'? We spent weeks on it and never played it once. We ended up doing Hootie and the Blowfish because you said that there had to be 'some reference to aquatic life'?" He used air quotes.

As Vicar sat there, feeling as if being pummelled, he still marvelled at Ray's rare exhibition of a cohesive statement.

Ray swallowed audibly and continued, "I don't know how else to say it, Tony. I don't have to leave the band. It's dead already." To show respect for his old friend, he found the jam to cough up the truth; he had never been so concise. "We weren't getting standing O's for being awesome. Everybody thinks it's *comedy*, brother."

Vicar sat in shock, knowing in one lightning bolt that Ray and Farley had been bit-part players: the band had always been *him*, the entire idea was about him, from him, made up out of whole cloth by *him*. If it was outmoded, or laughable, or *embarrassing*, it meant that *he* was those things. He believed preciously that *he was the music he played*. If that was truly the case, then this was not good news at all.

Vicar turned red, his hands went numb, and a surge of shame washed over him. The truth stung like a Portuguese man o' war. *Ray is right. The whole thing is idiotic.* How blind of him. How much of a fool had he been ...? The chance of a big break — something he had always secretly hoped for — was less than getting hit by lightning while accepting a cheque for a giant lottery jackpot just before a meteorite from the Oort cloud missed you by an inch. He was nothing more than a laughingstock. All that footage and internet buzz were barely disguised ridicule, served with a sprinkling of sympathy. He had been in denial. *Oh my God, I'm a singing juggler at Whoop-Up Days in striped pants.*

Ray watched Vicar redden, saw his shaking hands. He hurriedly tried to reassure him. "Tony, don't be mad. It's just past its time."

Vicar was far from "mad." He'd been feeling it, too, but admitting it to himself was akin to falling on the knife-like shards of a smashed mirror, watching himself get speared from a multitude of fractured angles as the glass penetrated his flesh and then his soul. He saw the regret on Ray's face, realized how hard it had been for him to just come out and say it — just tell the truth once and for all, and in complete sentences, to boot.

Vicar shrivelled in mortification and waved his hands at Ray as if to say *please stop*. He stumbled out of his office and headed to the parking lot, leaving Ray there by himself, wondering what to do.

Vicar fell into his Peugeot, started the tired old motor and drove home, limp, defeated, humiliated, and deep in dark thought.

■ ■ ■

Ronnie was deep in thought, too. For a while now, she had ridden Cosmic Ray like a rodeo clown rides a bronco and had begun to feel as if their fun was done.

She could not imagine introducing him to her parents — she knew that Mom would take one look at his shirt and call him a *ragamuffin*; she could never bring him to one of her many equestrian events — he'd be stumbling around in Birkenstocks, reading horses' auras, fellow ranchers dismissing him with a derisive snort. She couldn't imagine taking him on a trip to some fancy locale where he might need to dress for dinner and use the correct fork. *Good Lord, he might not even own socks.* She had certainly never seen them on his feet to date.

He was liking her a bit too much, and she didn't want to lead him on and then unnecessarily break his heart. He was sweet and his out-to-lunch pseudo-paranormal prattle had been entertaining at first — it had added an air of mystery to the whole thing that actually felt very similar to romance, but the kind you read about in a cheap paperback, not the kind that involves cohabitation, life insurance, and taking the trash to the road at five in the morning during a pelting rain. She chuckled. Now, if his astral travelling and flying saucers were real, she might rejig her thinking. She cackled at the mental image of a shirtless Cosmic Ray riding Pegasus, the winged horse, into the cargo hatch of a spaceship while her tight-assed mother, looking on from the distance, secretly got the vapours from his rock-hard abs.

Con-Con found Mrs. Morrison standing next to the Cenotaph, looking at her watch impatiently, as if she had expected every local copper to rush in, guns hot, over her nineteen-millionth complaint, this time possibly about *superfluous slang overused by our modern youth*.

"Good afternoon, Mrs. Morrison. What seems to be the trouble?" Con-Con attempted to be as respectful as possible but found it difficult to sound convincing.

"There was a woman right here, hiding, with field glasses, spying on the lass pushing the stroller." She pointed at the park bench.

"You mean binoculars, Mrs. Morrison? Are you certain she was 'spying'? Perhaps she was watching birds or just looking around? Could be a tourist, don't you think?"

"No, Constable," Mrs. Morrison said firmly. "I saw her when I headed there" — she pointed at the fabric store — "and then when I exited, she was still spying on the lass and her bairn, but from behind the Cenotaph." She walked the few steps toward it and touched it with her hand. "Her object of interest was most definitely the mother and child."

Mrs. Morrison always seemed to speak as if she were reciting Arthur Conan Doyle, and Con-Con was sure she was picturing her in a bobby's helmet. *Cue the pea-soup fog.*

She listened for a few moments, jotting notes in her little book to look as if she were dutiful. She had already chalked this up to Mrs. Morrison's new personal best in paranoia and conspiracy.

Intending to lead her toward a more believable conclusion, Con-Con said, "I am trying to imagine why someone would do that ..." She left it hanging, hoping to hear how nutty Mrs. Morrison's theory would be.

"Heaven only knows. It just seemed such peculiar behaviour."

There it was, Mrs. Morrison basically admitting that she was calling the police on someone who dared be "peculiar" in her presence. Con-Con tried not to smile as she remembered once having seen Margaret's son, Arthur, in full drag, replete with a three-foot-high feather headpiece, at the raging party where she and

Nancy had first met. *That* certainly would have been chalked up as peculiar.

"I'll write up a report. Can you describe her?" An official report would mollify Mrs. Morrison and give her something to gossip about.

She described the woman she had seen in the most general and unhelpful way. There wasn't a single distinguishing descriptor she could offer. "Brownish hair, medium height, medium build, nondescript clothes."

"And the mother and daughter you say she was surveilling? Can you give me a description of them?"

"Why, yes. Better than that. I believe it was the lass who runs the Knickers Pub. Miss O'Neil, and her waif."

Con-Con recoiled slightly at her judgmental choice of words, but then looked up from her notebook, her eyes suddenly sharp as she entertained a scary thought.

PART III

'Bout time for wine by now,
don't you think?

D ebbie and Dawna, the Extra-Large Mediums, walked down the hallway of the Hotel Valentine toward infamous room 222, where Larry Kaminski, formerly of Saskatoon, had died of food poisoning some fifty years before, and was said to reside in the hotel as a paranormal vestige.

With Valentine's help, Vicar and the children had walked safely through a wall of flames. This was the hearsay, but even Vicar himself could not refute it. He had been asked about it a thousand times, and he usually stayed silent, unable to fully believe what had transpired while knowing that it had.

With Vicar along to give them an introductory tour, he mentioned Kaminski's birthplace and then stood back and listened as Debbie and Dawna tried to pronounce *Saskatchewan*. "Sass-*katch*-EEE-wahn."

Hilarious. It would have made a brilliant password in the Second World War. *Not a Canuck. Open fire!*

"So, this is where you first saw 'Valentine'?"

"Umm, yeah. I saw something out of the corner of my eye in the closet over there." He pointed at the newly renovated, modern closet and remembered how much of a junky old room it had been back then.

"Can you describe the scene?"

Vicar gave the Coles Notes version, making sure to mention the falling valet pole and the rattling coat hangers.

"Oh yeah, after I fled — I was out of there like a shot — I heard something growl at me. Menacing, really frightening. I was scared to go up there for the longest time."

A tech crew was setting up cameras and kooky devices to measure telekinetic energy, like that was a thing, and some kind of horseshit laser-beam gewgaw to detect *entities*. Vicar was pretty sure they were going to detect one of the five ka-trillion bugs around Tyee Lagoon, always in search of someone's carelessly mislaid lunch.

He watched with great curiosity, hoping they'd get something on *camera* so that he could be more confident that what he'd seen was repeatable, not just in his own head; something that could be an unimpeachable witness to the weirdness. Camera footage, he could believe.

The sisters wandered around the hotel, from room to room, down the hall, into the lobby. It was night, of course. No lighting in the building save handheld flashlights. Vicar was *not* going to be responsible for one of them plummeting down the stairs to her death in the pitch dark. He had been clear about that and even called the insurance company, uncomfortably aware that he wouldn't have given a shit about liability a few years ago. *Call the insurance company?* Jesus, he was like a member of the Book Club now.

Vicar had opened up to this pair of TV celebrities with questionable qualifications and regretted it. His doubts increased as he watched them in action for a few minutes. The psychics would call out randomly, "Valentine, are you here? Can you hear us? Where are you, Valentine? Why are you hiding, why did you disappear ... or did you cross over?"

Really? Vicar snorted. Which question was this poor ghost supposed to answer?

He had a thought. "Hey, you guys," he interrupted. "What happens if you come across a ghost that doesn't speak English?"

They paused, clearly annoyed, and both said, simultaneously, "All ghosts speak English."

With that ludicrous response, Vicar felt sure that the whole schmeer was going to be utter hogwash. His mistrust about this pair, *damned flim-flam artists*, coalesced. Drily, he replied, "Ah, but of course."

■ ▬ ▬

The next morning, Con-Con dropped by unexpectedly.

"I have no solid facts, Jacquie. When Mrs. Morrison told me, I went up to yellow alert. I just think you ...

uh, *we*, should be extra cautious. I know she's free and out there somewhere. She is not at the last address we had. Could be anywhere. Keep everything locked at all times and call us immediately, even if you're just hearing weird sounds in the night." Con-Con stood in the doorway of Vicar and Jacquie's Tudor house and shuffled on the well-worn tile as she delivered her warning.

At the mere mention of Serena's name, Jacquie felt a punch to her gut that turned into a tightness in her shoulders and neck. Sleepless nights went hand in hand with that.

Vicar entered the house briskly, having seen the police cruiser in the driveway and assuming the worst. When Jacquie saw his worried face, she blurted out in emergency shorthand, "Serena ... *Here.*"

Vicar's mouth tightened and he turned to Con-Con. "In town? She's here for sure?"

"No, not for certain, Tony." Con-Con was informal with him — she had known him since she was a girl. "The description was vague, but the witness said the person was using binoculars to watch Jacquie and Frankie. Probably nothing, but I don't see why we all shouldn't use an abundance of caution until I can poke around a bit more."

"Who saw her?" Vicar wanted to know how reliable the sighting had been.

Con-Con looked at the floor, slightly uncomfortable. "It was Mrs. Morrison."

"... Ewww ... You realize she asked Jacquie to book an 'audience' with me to help select the gender of her grandchild, right?" He thought back when Jacquie had told him about it; he had thought she was shitting him. But nope, it was legit. Margaret Morrison was a full-on wing nut.

"Umm, yeah. I heard." Con-Con glanced at Jacquie, then moved on. "All the same, you'd better keep everything locked all the time."

Unnecessary advice, as Vicar had learned that harsh lesson with the hotel arson.

"Don't answer the door without knowing who's on the other side. She could have weapons, or maybe even confederates. Keep your phone ready and charged. And ..." She paused for effect. "If anyone manages to get in, just whang 'em with one of your guitars. If you have any left." She gave them a lopsided grin.

Vicar looked down at the floor in shame. A few years ago, he'd have been proud of his Townshend-esque performance.

Twenty-One / Camera Shy

I t was day two of filming for *The Extra-Large Mediums of Littleton.* The place was dull; psychically dead, they claimed.

"Suddenly I feel nothing, absolutely nada." Dawna had her head in her hands, feeling a stomach ache coming on.

Debbie nodded. "I know. So strangely inactive."

"Well, we might have to get creative. Otherwise, this is an awfully expensive sightseeing trip."

The costs were stratospheric for a travelling television production with staff, rentals, equipment.

A plan developed involving microfilament string and a plastic drinking cup. They would conduct an interview with "Valentine" the ghost, while one of their crew knelt nearby, controlling the responses of the apparently animated cup. They'd had to resort to that technique a couple of times in the past. It wasn't spectacular but it sorta worked and would get them over the hump. Quite a disappointment, given how much they had hoped for.

"Okay, are we rolling?"

"Rolling. Go ahead."

The jury-rigged cup — a production cost-saver if there ever was one — miraculously moved thanks to the production assistant tugging on the monofilament thread wrapped around its base. It jumped and jiggled as the sisters attempted to set up a yes/no answering system. Oblivious, they abandoned the system as they veered ridiculously into questions such as "Where are you from," or "How many years have you inhabited this hotel?" Even a haunted red Solo cup couldn't answer that with a one-wiggle answer.

They went at it for probably an hour, which would be boiled down to a segment forty-five seconds long that would, strangely, elicit no outraged criticism from fans. Because why would it? A ghost inhabiting a plastic cup — one that could communicate with humans *as phantasms hiding in cups are often wont to do* — did not elicit further in-depth investigation. It was just how these things were done.

Vicar, downstairs, alone in his office, glum and jumpy about the suspected Serena sighting, had gotten wind of the cup schtick and couldn't believe it.

A goddamn talking cup! Had he experienced such a bizarre thing, he'd have asked some pretty bloody detailed questions, dammit. But instead, the "psychics" dropped the questioning and wandered darkened hotel hallways — never, never with the perfectly functional lights on, cheap-ass flashlights probing the gloom. Their audience was curious, but only to a point, it seemed. After a time of aimless, chatty wandering pitch-black hallways, inevitably one of the sisters blurted, "Hey, a spectral entity just brushed against me." On to the next set-up.

The psychic sisters had tried to keep Vicar in the dark about what they had filmed — he was being quite a bitch about "keeping it real," as he called it. But it was awfully hard to keep a secret in the Hotel Valentine.

Debbie and Dawna leaned against the wall, snacking on massive muffins that were nothing more than thickly iced breakfast cake, and listened to Vicar's grievances.

Vicar complained, "I never said you could film magic-show illusions in here. I am trying to find out if there is truly something to this phenomenon or if I'm out of my damned mind."

"We sympathize, Tony, but you know these shows cost us a lot of money and we simply can't afford to go fishing in a dry hole. If there's nothing real, we have to go to Plan B … Sorry." Dawna, tired and suffering from a raging bout of indigestion, looked at him with some sympathy, but the sisters did not back down at all.

"I don't want you to continue. Please stop this charade. It's total garbage. It is so fake that no one could possibly believe it." He punctuated his statements with the back of his hand slapping the other open palm.

"Believe it or not. It's entertainment first, documentary second. Maybe third." The sisters were matter of fact.

Vicar glared at them, frustrated, aware now that he had gotten himself into another situation that could have been easily avoided. "I can't believe you'd descend to this level."

Neither of them bit at his remonstration. "Tony … You signed a contract with us. You gave up all rights to determine the tone and direction of the story. And your non-disclosure agreement prohibits talking about any of this. It's our tale now, and you can either honour our agreement or get lawyers involved."

Vicar immediately thought of tan-pantsed, golf-shirted Steven Leigh-*gal* trying to out-Aikido the big American TV network lawyers these two could muster, and blanched.

"You won't win, and it will cost you a fortune." Dawna's gaze was level and unblinking. It wasn't a threat. It was just a statement of fact, delivered with at least a small dose of kindness. This was the real world — *totally normal* where they operated. The tension of the discussion was sapping Dawna's energy; she looked around for a chair.

Vicar gritted his teeth in defeat, spun on his heel, and trudged down the steps of the hotel back to his little office in the pub, where he shut the door just a little too hard and flopped into his chair.

■ ■ ■

Powerless or not, Vicar was still steaming. He grumbled to Jacquie, "They're ginning up some fake crap to make it look like they're communicating with our ghost."

Jacquie wore a look of vindication. "I told you, Tony. You knew very well that they'd screw you around. You didn't think they'd come up here with their million-dollar circus and happily go away with sweet dick-all, did you?" She was curt, impatient about Vicar's lack of foresight.

He looked at the floor and realized how stupid he'd been. Or rather, how stupid he'd been *again*. The merry-go-round spun to the same tired result and the repetition was infuriating.

The Extra-Large Mediums would be within their rights to claim *anything* now. Zombies, unicorns, the Loch Ness monster, Farley elected president of Mensa … Vicar had signed away his own "moral rights," a funny clause in the contract that protected the Extra-Large Mediums from having someone like Vicar dictate what they could or could not claim. Christ almighty, they could make Valentine the Ghost into a singing S&M Himmler and he could do nothing at all to stop it. Vicar would be author only of his own shame and regret.

He looked up at Jacquie, desperate to justify himself, and then stopped. There was no defence. His decision had been shallow; he had been impulsive and had broken his own strict rule, so whatever the lurid result, he'd certainly have it coming.

Jacquie O drove down Sloop Road to the intersection with Gull Street and headed downhill toward the town centre. She glided past the Knickers and continued toward Ross Poutine's property on McCormack Lodge Lane, a long country road lined with huge parcels of forest and field, where the richest people now fell over each other to buy. It had been cheap like borscht in the late seventies. Poutine had bought ten acres of forest for eighteen thousand dollars back then. It was worth millions now. He was the quietest, most under-the-radar multi-millionaire there was. It was as if Ross Poutine was a real-life urban legend — the classic codger with thirty-year-old clothes, who didn't realize he was wealthy. Surely, *surely*, he could afford deodorant, though ...

She was oblivious to the shoreline off to her side, the beach wide and gravelly, mares' tails up high in the stratosphere on an otherwise sunny day. Instead, her thoughts wandered to Serena, at large and vying heavily to be in charge. It felt to Jacquie as if she were running from a quickly flooding tide, and the only way she could survive was to climb a tree while the deadly surge swirled below her, waiting, waiting, until she could hold on no more. It would eventually wash her away, never to be seen again. She felt powerless.

In the beginning, she had fought for Vicar, and he had fought for her, too. But taking things too far — for example, getting into another fist fight with Serena, taking the law into her own hands — might well result in Frankie being taken away from them. Their love for Frankie wasn't worth shit if someone at the ministry decided that they were a danger to her. They'd yank Frankie, boom, *just like that.* Jacquie swerved around the potholes at the corner of Gull and Dumfries.

She could only imagine how awful their relationship would be if Frankie was removed. It'd ruin them. Jacquie would forever be tattooed with grief, but Vicar would wither and die. Vicar had gone into a sulk when she'd chucked out his bulk chocolate macaroons, for God's sake — and they were at least a year old and turning white.

They were still only foster parents — shaky legal ground in this kind of discord. In the eyes of the law she feared they were little better than glorified babysitters. They loved Frankie as if she were their own and put all they had into taking care of her. Having Frankie had changed Jacquie's life and way of thinking, filling a hole in her heart that she had not realized was even there. Jacquie and Frankie and Vicar together, her "sweet trio," were now Jacquie's whole world.

Jacquie turned into the rutted mud track that was Ross Poutine's driveway and lurched over a giant, water-filled depression the size of a small pond, grunting "oomph" as her little car bottomed out with a boxy thump.

Would she call the cops if there was trouble? Sure. But it'd take them ages to get there, even if it was Con-Con going at warp eleven. This situation was a needle that she did not know how to thread.

Jacquie had surmounted so many things in her life — *but this was really an Everest of a problem*; a mountain to climb with a black abyss below.

Niggling in the back of her mind was the dream. *Beware the mother.* The ladder descending from the sky. She pushed away her worst fears and continued up the muddy trail.

▬ ▬ ▬

Jacquie watched on with admiration as Ross Poutine split firewood with his big, yellow-handled maul. He did it in a practised motion that he'd made thousands of times. The maul would come down — hard, but not too hard — crack open the nicely seasoned wood in one fell swoop and then he'd lean down, heaving the pieces into the bucket of his tractor with his left hand, his right holding onto the maul's shaft. He did it like a dance move — something she could appreciate. She had once complimented him on his technique, and he had dismissed her. "Aww, shit, anyone with disposable thumbs can buck up a little firewood, fer chrissakes." He'd cackled, once again oblivious — or, rather, *bolivious* — to his malapropism.

The split chunks of wood were soon driven to the doorway of his house or, more exactly, his archaic and bedraggled mobile home. Jacquie had set foot inside once and decided to never enter it again.

It was the ghastliest accommodation that she had ever seen, and her emotions led her to the edge of pity for him when she thought of it. The streets of Stalingrad during the Great Patriotic War were more appealing.

Everyone he knew begged him to build a little house. He simply wouldn't entertain such a lavish expenditure. It was so strange … He had a head-shaking blind spot about the state of his ancient mobile home. No way it was as bad as everyone said, he believed, although it was filthier than a Hastings Street salad bar.

Ann Tenna, his girlfriend now of several years, stood nearby, resplendent in her 1985 hairdo, acid-wash pants, and dollar-store perfume. Jacquie knew that even Ann could not bear the squalid hut and usually went no farther than the box of her pickup truck, where lawn chairs and a cooler full of food and drink seemed always to be fully stocked and close at hand.

The property upon which it sat had been paid off decades ago. Poutine knew that he could easily sell it for 1,500 percent more than he had paid, even as a piece of unimproved dirt. But he preferred to keep life simple; Jacquie had never encountered anyone so lacking pretense.

Poutine approached Jacquie in only a pair of unlaced cork boots and discoloured long underwear, with the top buttons opened to the waist. The pits were a crescent of sodden, yellowed wetness, as was the crack of his arse. The dank pong that wafted from him smelled like an army tent full of febrile gerbils.

Jacquie stood way, way back and raised her voice a little. "Do not hug me. Stand right there." She put her open palm out, in what she hoped was an unmistakable sign to halt. She surveyed his matted grey chest hair, dripping perspiration, and the scrawny crepe-like chicken skin hanging at his neck and abdomen. She adored the man, but sweaty and adorned in decrepit Flin-Flongerie, he might put her off food for weeks.

Ann Tenna came toward Jacquie, welcoming her, offering a cold beer.

"No thanks, Annie … I'm on the run." She pulled a folded poster out of her pocket. "Have you seen this woman in the Knickers?"

Ann shrugged. "Uh, no, I never seen anyone like that."

Jacquie clipped her reply, "Keep an eye out for her. She's the one who took me hostage."

"Oh, *that Serena chick*? I never knew what she looked like."

"Problem is that she uses disguises. She never looks the same way twice." Jacquie's voice lowered. "Annie, she is the devil. Call the cops *immediately* if she comes in. And then call me right afterward."

Ann Tenna glanced over at Ross Poutine. He crept toward the pair and Jacquie noticed.

She held out her hand again and yelped, "Stop!"

He stopped, still mostly oblivious to the rank honk that came off him. He said, "I know her, Annie. I toll ya all about it. I know th' crazy eyes. If she comes into my store, I'll bop her in the snout!"

Jacquie wasn't certain he'd "bop" her. He was a gentleman and would never strike a woman, no matter how much piss and vinegar she was spraying. But she could hope that he might temporarily stun her with his carcass-y aroma.

— — —

A few miles away, "that Serena chick" sat in a drab, cinder-brick motel and ruminated. She surveyed her clothing, which provided endless options for disguise and, she hoped, would keep everyone confused. She was so good at it that descriptions of her were as vague as Bigfoot illustrations in pulpy paperbacks.

Solo now, she was for a rare instance without her harem of men, all of whom invariably lusted after her; she had always been very bad news. With the snap of her fingers she had wrought havoc and vengeance on anyone who "hurt" her. Which is to say, anyone who impeded her way forward on the latest perilous adventure. Countless boys had fought over her, only to end up with bruised bodies, injured pride, and broken hearts. A few had ended up in hospital suffering "undisclosed" injuries. They often required a shot for lockjaw.

Of course, she had been a victim of childhood abuse and abandonment. It was practically a cliché, as predictable as winter following fall. Mercurial shifts in mood and a short attention span were countered by conjuring a customized, plush state of denial. There was no unknotting her life, so why even try?

Serena had learned how to manipulate men while she was still a teenager. She had never really held down a job but sold little pieces of her soul to buy whatever she needed. In fact, she had managed to graduate high school only through a "special arrangement" with the principal. It all seemed calculated but was not. With her awful family situation, movie-star good looks, and potent charisma, she never really had a chance. Different rules applied to her. She hadn't quite gotten away with murder yet, but give her time.

She never used her last name, De Medici — a perfect surname for a walking vendetta. No man had ever gotten the better of her — at least, not since she was a kid — but no man, save Tony Vicar, had ever treated her with authentic kindness or understanding. She was just too hypersexual to be viewed as a normal person by average Joes. She was certain that Tony Vicar was no average Joe — certain, beyond any doubt. He had been put here specifically for *her*. She had taken a long time to conclude this, but she was now irrevocably decided. He was for her; she was for him. She would make it so.

Serena fondled the giant hunting knife stuffed into her coat and emerged into the afternoon sunshine, off to do a little reconnaissance. As she closed the motel room door behind her and strode to the street, she was, quite literally, dressed to kill.

■ ■ ■

Farley was wandering toward the grocery store. He had seen a flyer that said they had ramen noodles on two for a buck, which was a *wicked* deal. He had finally figured out that they charged for grocery bags now, so he had brought his own. Well, sorta his own. Ronnie had given him a pink frilly bag she didn't need anymore that came from a ladies' gonch shop, where she bought her panties. He had asked her if she had a shopping bag he could borrow, and she dug it out of the cupboard.

Ronnie was giggling the whole time, and Ray was chuckling, too. But shit, it saved Farley five cents, so who cared? He tried not to think about Ronnie's underpants, what with Ray being her boyfriend now, but dear Lord it was tough. She was gorgeous and he had seen Ray banging her on top of the wash machine. He'd barely made it outta there without yelping.

She looked like a supermodel. Legs for days. Almost as gorgeous as Jacquie O, and that was saying something. He was still awash in puppy love for Jacquie and probably would be for the rest of his life.

Everything about her was soft and safe and … perfect. She smelled like a lady oughta. Just *per*-fect. She had given him a little peck at Christmas and he'd nearly died from the sweet taste of her fruity lip gloss, and her hair smelled like *heaven*. No matter what happened in his life, he knew he'd always hold a torch for her. Hell, if Vicar croaked, he'd *definitely* try to get called up from the minors.

Ronnie was a dish, too, but she wasn't as *soft*. Plus, she was way tall. She rode horses and prolly could weld. She knew how to switch out a 220-stove connection — he'd watched her do it. She and Jacquie were the hottest babes in town by far. Both of 'em had jobs and houses and cars … And sometimes helped him fill out forms.

Farley turned it all over again and again and tortured himself over his non-existent love life. He knew he had to find a girlfriend. Fuck, even Ray had found one and sometimes he din't even know what year it was.

Farley ambled ever closer to the grocery store and saw ahead of him, standing by a telephone pole, a hot chick. Like, waaaaay hot. *Who in the hell is that?*

As he approached, instantly as horny as a three-peckered Billy goat, she turned to him. She had not seen him wandering up the road and was slightly surprised.

Among his many charms, one could put at the top of the list "absent minded." Farley had absolutely no idea that he had met this gorgeous woman several times before. It was Serena, once again in a disguise, this time with auburn hair of medium length, big Italian sunglasses, and a jacket short enough to show off her legs and curvy bottom. He fought the lump in his throat. *Damn*, he never seemed to be able to talk to beautiful girls. Maybe *that* was his problem. *Yeah … It has to be that.*

He mustered up his confidence and thickly spat out an awkward, "Hi!" He tried to clear his throat to no avail. *Helluva start, Farley.*

Serena, all too aware of who Farley was, could see he did not recognize her. She was reassured that her latest disguise was effective, and decided to play a little, to get some intelligence out of him. She'd done it before, and he had been as willing as a child. She remained cautious, though, because she found it hard to accept that he could not identify her. *When he looks, what does he see?*

"Hi, sailor … Whatcha doin'?" She had decided, just to be safe, to use an accent to disguise her voice. She tried to sound British but ended up sounding more South Indian than anything else.

Farley was stone deaf to it. He just saw glowing beauty standing inches from him.

"Ulp." He choked and started to shuffle nervously like an eight-year-old about to get a needle.

"What's a handsome bloke like you doing wandering around on a workday?" She looked into his eyes and could see him summoning his courage.

"Uhh, umm, uh, I am goin' to the store to buy some Ichiban."

"Brillo! My favourite!"

"Really?" he enthused, acting as if he'd just found his soulmate.

"Yes, do you eat them as soup or just as noodles?"

"Huh? It's soup, right?" He was instantly nervous. What if he said the wrong thing?

"Oh no, love." As she said it, he flushed. "You can also drain out the water and just eat the noodles. Whisk in an egg and some green onion and it's a *scrummy* snack." She undulated her body while demonstrating her cooking method. This guy was going to fall over if she didn't watch it.

Farley's eyes were wide, and his mouth was smeared all over his face as if he'd dropped it under one of Ronnie's skittish horses. He couldn't muster a response and stood there dumbly.

Serena continued to take the lead. "You look like a bit of a pop stah, love ..."

"Ungh ... How did you know?" His emotions were now a bucket of water hurled onto the floor. Did he really have the look? Had she really noticed? *Is this for real?*

Cough, cough. Touch face unnecessarily. Cross arms. Uncross arms. Shuffle. Readjust toque. Shit, is this my good toque? *Fucksakes, Farley, say something.* "I play in a band ..."

Serena inhaled deeply and obviously, pretending to be impressed, maybe even turned on. "What band, hun?"

A strange warbling moan came out of him, then he hacked loudly. "H-H-*Hospital Fish.*" He nervously skipped over the part where they weren't together anymore, mistakenly believing that it'd matter to anyone on Earth. *I never did get that free pop from the Turbo ...*

She threw her head back and jutted out her ample bosom, looking like she was about to orgasm right then and there. Farley could have been one inch from being hit by a bus and would not have noticed. She moaned, "I *love* that group."

"You've seen us before?"

"Oh yes, baby. What was that guitar player's name?"

No, no. Don't talk about Tony. Talk about ME. ME. ME.

She could see the desperation on his face as he replied.

"Tony. Tony Vicar."

His tone had changed, so she decided to keep attention squarely on him.

"Yes, he's good, but I liked *you* the best, love. You're so dead sexy, the way you move, *mmmmm*."

Vicar had never believed him, but Farley knew the bobbing head move was going to be his signature. Briefly he imagined his melon bouncing up and down in time to the groove and this goddess getting all randy over him. Farley had tunnel vision now and thought he might vom. A good kind of vom.

"So, tell me *all* about the band, deah. Don't leave out any details." She reached out and with her index finger tugged at the kangaroo pocket on his grimy hoodie. He lurched an inch or two toward her and nearly lost his shit.

Farley spilled; he told her literally everything about the band, about Ray, about Vicar, about Jacquie, about Frankie, about the long, exhaustive adoption process,

their schedules, everyone's addresses, and, bizarre-
ly, about how some chick named Serena was hanging
around and was "super-sketch." He had once hit a member of her gang on the head with his bong and broken it.
That made him *super-bummed out*. She feigned a look of
concern and touched his hand. He twitched.

He also supplied a whole bunch of detail she did not
want to know, such as what kind of strings he used on
his stupid bass guitar. She also had to bear up to five
straight minutes about his toque collection and its watery destruction in "the flood." He referred to the disastrous event as if he was some ill-fated, be-toqued Noah.

Twenty-Three / Brave Hotchy-Coochie

The chairs in the pub started moving around as if manipulated by a multi-limbed poltergeist. Debbie and Dawna gasped, as rehearsed. The plan would be to replay the moving furniture in ever slower slo-mo about six times, using the bit as a major feature of the half-hour-long show.

"Guys, we're going to have to do that one again. Camera two accidentally caught Joe pulling the wire." The director pointed toward the young crew member holding the long, slim wire attached to the back leg of a chair, conveniently located on the smoother hardwood floor where it would slide easily.

"Well, shit … okay. But otherwise, did it work?"

"Yeah, the set-up is good. We just have to stay tight on the table and not swing around too much." He made a note and then turned back to his duties.

Debbie dashed toward the platter of pastries during the brief lull while Dawna stretched her aching lumbar. They tried again, failed, and had a stab at the simple gag a third time. By then, Debbie and Dawna were looking at the time and becoming impatient. This was day two of two, and they had to be done by sunrise.

"C'mon, guys," Debbie chided. "We have two hours left and we still have one more set-up to do."

Just as the sisters had feared, things were moving too slowly. Fire Hall Gordy, accompanied by his pal Hotchy-Coochie, sat on folding chairs at a discreet distance from the camera, in the dim corner, far enough away that they were not easy to see, and watched how the crew manufactured ghostly activity. They really shouldn't have been there, but the crew was under time pressure and forgot all about them.

Hotchy was delighted to be proven correct, as he had always known it was bullshit, but Gordy was the kind of guy who believed even in the veracity of wrestling broadcasts, so he was outraged.

"This whole thing is BS, Hotch." He was truly surprised. "They're makin' it up as they go."

Hotchy-Coochie put his finger up to his lips in a gentle shush — they had snuck in during a break and were lurking quietly in the dark. Hotchy-Coochie didn't want to miss a minute of the scam.

"Well, of course it's BS, Gordy," he murmured. "The TV show is nonsense — and the whole Vicar *thing* is just a marketing plan. A gimmick for the pub. He's world famous because of *campfire stories*."

Gordy looked at him glumly and muttered, "Hmmm. What a bummer. I really believed him, y'know."

"Uhh … I wanted to. But how would a half-assed guitar player like that suddenly become a swami? No way, Jose." He was disappointed but had to tip his hat to anyone with such a slick angle.

"I guess." Gordy had been hoping to be part of the first televised experience of ghostliness in the pub and hotel. It was not to be. He felt a stab of resentment toward Vicar. He was a liar. Gordy didn't like liars. He had spent a shite-load of loot at the pub, mostly cuz of Vicar's lies.

All the same, he still appeared a half-hour later, on camera at the sisters' direction, pretending to steer them clear of the dank cave-like sub-basement where the beer kegs lived. Even the high-output lighting brought along for the purpose couldn't fully cut the darkness, and he used his non-existent acting chops to recite a line the producer had fed him. "Come back — there might be rats in there!" Had he been even slightly more wooden in his delivery, someone might have chopped him up for kindling.

They stopped tape and tried to walk him through the line of dialogue, Debbie and Dawna very obviously glancing at their wristwatches. Gordy got a bit nervous and his voice got weird, kinda yodel-y, plus he found himself herking and jerking around like a kid trying to stay super still for the barber. In their eighth and final pass, they simply gave up and abandoned the idea, sending Fire Hall Gordy back to his folding chair, oddly unclear about the quality of his performance.

Hotchy-Coochie tried to hide his mirth but burst out snickering after a few moments.

"What?" Gordy was on the back foot.

Speaking through his suppressed laughter, Hotch coughed out, "My God, you're a natural. You and Pacino, Gordy. And with award season just around the corner, too!" He wiped his eyes and chuckled intermittently for the next ten minutes.

Gordy scowled and turned away.

By then, zero hour had passed, and the crew called it a day. Everyone was milling around, and Debbie said vaguely, "I sure wish we would have had a little more luck with Valentine the Ghost."

Hotchy-Coochie piped up from behind her. "I think you did purdy good, considering the whole thing is fake. There's no ghost. But there's lotsa free advertising."

Both Debbie and Dawna were certain he was wrong; they had sensed many odd things in the pub and hotel and had faith in their experience and psychic abilities. They avoided direct eye contact with him, wandering toward the snacks. Debbie glanced at Dawna, who was scrunching up her nose in distaste at Hotchy-Coochie. She had just gotten her first taste of his double-edged frenemy-flavoured charm.

Gordy put his hand on Hotchy's arm and said, "Hey, gimme a hand — I gotta readjust the leg. It's startin' to hurt now."

Hotchy stood and helped Gordy out of his awkward folding chair. They slowly moved to a little area of "pipe and drape," a crudely fashioned curtain behind which he could take off his jeans and jigger with the padding in the socket of his prosthetic.

The production crew had been very quick to set up, but they were incredibly fast tearing down. Cameras were unplugged and stowed within a couple of minutes, miles of cable were spooled and packed, and lighting was already coming down in a noisy dismount.

Gordy sat on the edge of a bench as Hotchy helped him with the straps that secured his leg to his thigh. Gordy's prosthetic removed, Hotchy wandered off, absently carrying the bulky prosthetic leg under his arm, to retrieve the little backpack that contained thicker pieces of padding. Neither of them could remember exactly where they'd left it.

Gordy said nothing but didn't enjoy seeing his leg departing without him — he imagined buggering off with Hotchy's dentures to show him how it felt. *Oh well . . .*

Debbie and Dawna, sipping soft drinks, stood in a circle with the producer and his assistant and spoke quietly as the room emptied of equipment. They were discussing how they'd salvage this failed on-location shoot. The tone of the talk was realistic, professional, yet tinged with disappointment; the psychic sisters had felt nearly certain that they'd come away with something spectacular from this location. They had not, and it was difficult to view the shoot as anything other than an expensive failure.

There came a rattling sound from the side of the room; no one paid attention, as the crew was taking down all the gear and it made quite a clatter as they packed it up. But Joe, the general factotum of the production team, was on his way in that direction and could see one tall, sturdy lighting stand rattling and shaking for no reason. It was on solid, level ground, there was no one near it, and it tremored as if being shaken by an invisible hand.

"... Guys? Guuuuuyyyys!" Joe drew everyone's attention to the strange phenomenon.

The camera operator slowly came toward Joe and then to a halt beside him. He looked at Joe, and then yelled over his shoulder, "Everybody! This light stand is moving!"

Now the whole crew approached the shaking stand, fascinated, but careful not to approach too quickly.

Dawna, who was beginning to feel rather unwell, was first to see him. The vision that appeared very suddenly was to her right, where no one else was currently looking; their attention was fixed on the light stand ahead. What she saw was a young man in a checked shirt, a ghostly figure that matched exactly the description of Valentine, the hotel's famous ghost. Dawna stood stock still, simply staring at the figure, who approached her slowly.

The racket from the lighting stand had ceased, and Debbie looked around for her sister, who was not beside her where she'd normally be but behind her and staring at, at, at ... a frickin' real-live *ghost*.

The rest of the crew was slower to catch on, still muttering in amazement at the poltergeistian activity they had just witnessed. Skeptical Hotchy, over in the far corner, got an eyeful of the vision and stopped dead in his tracks. His voice failed him, and his jaw flapped silently for a moment or two. He had to lean against the wall to steady himself as he gawked.

Debbie watched as the ghost drifted toward Dawna and stopped near her, looking at her impassively. Without taking her eyes off the action before her, Debbie put her hand on the shoulder of the guy nearest to her and silently drew his attention to Valentine, who continued to gaze at her sister.

Within a moment or two, everyone in the pub was aware of the presence and simply watched. Gordy, looking on from the opposite side of the room, blinked hard and kept blinking. There was no way this was happening right now. Yet it was. Something about this felt better — scary, but better: Vicar wasn't a liar after all.

For a few heartbeats, the shimmering, ghostly figure hovered with no one else even breathing. It scintillated and flashed as Dawna tried to take in every detail. She had never seen anything so incontrovertible in her paranormal investigative career. Same for Debbie, who was rooted to the floor twenty feet away, agog, undecided if she was delighted or frightened for her sister's safety.

The plaid-shirted phantasm slid closer and closer to Dawna until it was inches away. Her body prickled with a feeling of electricity, and the ghost smelled to her of petrichor and ozone, or something like it — like the smell of a humid evening when rain is spitting and lightning has unexpectedly struck.

Then, just as suddenly as it had come into view, Valentine the Ghost winked out, disappeared — just vanished. To Dawna it felt as if it had rolled up from the bottom, like an old-fashioned, spring-loaded window shade, and then, *zip*, it was gone. It happened in such a flash that she jolted, tossing her head back in surprise.

Hotchy saw the ghost, saw it move, saw it wink out, and made the practical decision to flee at his best speed — *To hell with this! I'm outta here!* He would live to wheedle another free pint, but right now did not give a solitary shit about his one-legged pal. A high wheezing sound emanated from him as he ran, full out, for the first time in years.

Oblivious to Hotchy's loud display of spinelessness, Dawna turned to her sister, who stood nearby, wearing a look of astonishment. Neither spoke for a few moments until Debbie gathered her wits and took note of an unusual development.

"Dawna ... Are you okay?" She was focused on her legs, which were now wet, the dampness spreading down her thighs, leaving a discoloured patch on her leggings.

"What?" Dawna had not noticed anything until that moment. "Oh, good Lord, I've peed myself. I didn't think I was *that* scared ..." She trailed off, embarrassed and mystified at this odd turn of events. She looked back up at her sister and shook her head in dismay.

At that moment, she was doubled over by an abdominal cramp that was by far the worst gas pain she had ever had, and God knew she had had her share of them. She gasped and reached out for a chair so she could steady herself. After a few moments it passed and she gasped out, "I think I went too heavy on the Bismarcks."

One of the crew members turned away, stifling a snicker.

Across the room, against the north wall, Fire Hall Gordy was peering around in the distance for his now-misplaced prosthetic. Craning his neck around, paying no attention to Dawna and her wet pants, he was a voice in the wilderness, calling out from the periphery, "Has anyone seen my leg? Can you see my leg? Hey! Help! Can you see my leg?"

The crew looked on in confusion. *See his leg?* Only the producer was aware that Gordy wore a prosthetic. At any rate, Dawna's condition was the priority. She again grabbed her abdomen and inhaled sharply, clearly in major discomfort.

At that point the crew surrounded her, guiding her to the ladies' room. "Are you going to be okay, Dawna?"

She nodded yes quickly and limped off to a toilet stall. Everyone else withdrew to the pub and looked at each other with concern. Eating all the pastries was SOP; crippling gastric distress was not. This was new.

Joe grimaced and said softly to his fellow crew, "I wonder if she's gonna give birth to the Anti-Christ." He furtively waved his hand in front of his nose and pretended to shudder. There were rueful chuckles, but they made sure Debbie hadn't heard anything.

Gordy was getting panicky now, cursing that chickenshit Hotchy-Coochie, wondering if he had taken the prosthetic leg with him as he ran away. What a frickin' numbnuts. *This is just too goddamn much!* He couldn't figure out why no one was helping him find his missing limb.

Dawna was perched on the toilet now, in agony, regretting every morsel of food she had ingested in the last month, seriously concerned that she was going to cleave herself in half with the vilest bowel movement in medical history. She thought she was about to crap out a bowling ball. There was something terribly wrong — she might have to chug a pint or two of stool softener if things didn't let loose soon.

There was an unfamiliar tearing, burning feeling in her pelvis and the fear began to rise within her. Given her shape, she couldn't really see what was going on down there, but she cautiously felt around and discovered something massive coming out of her ...

Dawna screamed a death shriek so intense that the men on the crew recoiled in alarm, and her sister came barrelling into the toilet like a battering ram to see what the hell was going on.

"Dawna, honey ... What is it? What is it?"

She blubbered, in a terrible state. "Something's coming out!"

Debbie stood erect for a second, thinking that, indeed, something *had to* come out, eventually. "Something? Are you constipated?"

"It's not poop, Debbie!"

"Oh God …"

Debbie muscled the toilet stall door open and leaned down to inspect the situation, fully expecting to see something prolapsed and revolting.

Debbie screamed like she'd just witnessed someone falling out of an airplane. "It's a head!"

"A head?" Dawna was dumbfounded.

Debbie gawked at her, astonished, and said, "Dawna … What the fuck did you eat?"

With great difficulty, Debbie and the entire crew half carried Dawna out to the main part of the Knickers Pub and laid her down on a large pile of scrims, black sheets of cloth, while someone summoned an ambulance.

Fire Hall Gordy managed to get up on his one remaining leg, his heinous old man underwear failing to cover his flopping bits, and hopped toward the emergency there before his eyes. He wasn't any good at public relations but had taken numerous first aid courses with the volunteers at the station and trained with them regularly. If there ever was an earthquake or a forest fire, first responders were going to be in short supply. He was qualified to muck in if needed.

"Hold on, I'm comin'," he called as he hopped pogo-like toward the heavily labouring Dawna. He had delivered two babies in his life, one of them in the toilet of the Turbo Station, and the other at the scene of a car accident. The mother had given birth while Fire Rescue was still struggling to pull out the driver of the other vehicle. Both events were a bit of a blur, but he knew it would all come back to him.

As he approached, his stump flapped up and down in a disquieting manner. Dawna was out of it and at that point would have accepted the medical assistance of an alien passerby from Andromeda. Debbie, on the other hand, squeaked in fright. Gordy didn't give a shit. He was all too aware that it wasn't pretty. But it was a fact of life.

"Gimme some room. I know how to do this." He said it with authority, and everyone obeyed.

Debbie began acting as a doula, a role not required and one for which she had literally no training, but she was desperate to be useful and look in control of the bizarre situation.

She kept repeating, "Breathe, Dawna."

Gordy, half lying on his side owing to his lack of one leg and already annoyed by her fussing, muttered, "Great job. Without you, she'd prolly forget."

Debbie stared daggers at him and then turned to her sister, asking, "How did this happen?"

Dawna, eyes closed and head back, croaked out, "It has to be the Haunted Meat-Packing Plant episode. The firemen. The two tall ones ..."

"Yeah?"

"Umm ... We had our very own sausage party near the wiener-stuffing machines."

"Oh." Debbie was unable to say more.

Joe from the crew overheard her and scrunched up his face in horror.

Debbie paused and looked away, finally responding, "*Both* of them?"

Dawna, pale and sweaty, still managed to grin a little and said, "Oh yeahhhhh … They wanted it. I wanted it. I had no idea they'd hit the bull's eye, though. I didn't know I was pregnant." She winced in pain.

Debbie was so thunderstruck by the conversation that she escalated her jiggering around to the entire area, as if tidying unnecessarily would somehow tidy her brain, which was now on overload at the thought of Dawna's X-Rated Night of the Living Knackwurst.

The baby was coming now, and Gordy had to manoeuvre himself into a better position while Debbie continued to fidget and mutter and get underfoot. Finally, he turned to her quickly and said, "I need you to do something."

"Yes?"

"I need you to either do this yourself or get the hell out of the way." Gordy turned his attention to the emerging baby. Goodtime Gordy had departed the scene; a first responder had stepped onto the stage.

Debbie, scalded, looked down at the action and realized that this guy knew what he was doing. She went quiet, drew back, and stopped fidgeting.

"Get ready to push when I tell you. This ain't gunna take too long." Her uterus contracted and he yelled, "*Push!*"

Dawna pushed.

"Almost there ... One more goodie and baby is here."

She nodded and took a deep breath.

"Okay, a mighty push now. *Push. Push. Push.*"

After three massive, heaving attempts, the baby's head finally slid out and Gordy pulled out the rest of him, quickly laying the newborn on Dawna's chest. She stared up at the lights on the ceiling, stunned and unable even to speak.

Debbie quietly cried and murmured how beautiful he was. The boys from the crew were balanced between admiration for the heroics of Gordy, wonder at the newborn arrival, and pure horror at what looked to them like a crime scene. Prepared to see ghosts, goblins, demons, and the living dead, they were shocked at a little bit of blood and goo.

The new baby cried as Gordy tasked the bystanders with fetching towels and blankets.

The Vicar's Knickers Pub, the very seat of the spirit of Valentine — the young man who had so tragically died here — was now also the site of a birth, its first ever. Valentine's ghostly arrival minutes before seemed to have signalled the advent of Dawna's new babe. The startling yet joyous event seemed, strangely and wonderfully, to close a long, mysterious circle.

▬ ▬ ▬

Vicar, unable to sleep and irked about the Extra-Large Mediums, came to the pub very early in order to putter around and supervise their departure. He was anxious to be rid of the pair of them and all their nonsensical claptrap; they couldn't leave a second too soon.

Parking the increasingly rattle-y Peugeot in his spot, he deliberately walked around to the front door of the Knickers so he could do a quick inspection of the building before starting his day. He'd often find discarded garbage or other junk on the sidewalk, occasionally an egg splattered on a window, and once even a young guy sleeping on the concrete who, when awoken, claimed to have been "excessively celebratory." He had still been drunk, acting like a tipsy professor — clearly his drunk schtick, extremely apologetic, but with booze breath out to there. He'd fumbled with his car keys; Vicar had gently taken them away and guided him toward one of the booths inside, where he could snooze for another hour or two.

But on this morning, as Vicar stood in front of the door and picked out the correct key, he spied a discarded prosthetic leg in the doorway to Hot Thoth. It lay there incongruously, an artifact so unlikely to be found randomly in the street that it stopped Vicar in his tracks as he yelped involuntarily. Cautiously he picked it up off the ground. Clearly, this was Gordy's after-market appendage.

It had lodged itself partly in cobwebs and leaves in the corner of the doorway. It was heavy, heavier than he had imagined. He looked around now, somewhat weirded out, and turned a full three-sixty, thinking suddenly that perhaps he ought not have touched it — spooked that this might be a crime scene, maybe. Had somebody abducted Gordy and left his leg behind? *Is this more of Ray's UFO bullshit?*

His brain spinning, Vicar decided his best move was to get indoors and make a few calls. He stepped into the pub and noticed the odd cluster of people kneeling around one of the psychic sisters lying supine on the floor. She appeared to be snuggling a newborn baby, swaddled in bar towels. Gordy hovered over her, leaning on one arm, minus one of his legs; it was in Vicar's arms.

Vicar, accustomed to wild happenings in this old joint, was flabbergasted all the same. Although it took a few moments, he managed to find his voice. He cleared his throat, and said drily, "Uh, Gordy ... If you were looking for your leg, I appear to have found it."

Gordy turned around and looked at Vicar, pointed his index finger at the newborn child lying on Dawna's chest and simply said, "Baby."

Vicar nodded, quite acutely in need of some context, and replied, "Yes. Baby?" *Well, I'll be goddamned.*

Twenty-Five / Here She Comes

Everyone in town was looking for Serena. Her conversation with out-to-lunch Farley had confirmed it. Every telephone pole seemed to have a Be on the Lookout handbill featuring her face and name, but she no longer feared being noticed. Her unnatural confidence had once again surged after her face-to-face test with Farley.

The remarkably aged and squinty population of Tyee Lagoon could not even *find* the BOLO posters that were plastered liberally around the downtown area — or, for that matter, the telephone poles they were taped to; their pranged-up rear bumpers were testament to that. And anyway, reading them would be impossible through those geriatric welding goggles.

Lucky for her, the currently untraceable car she was using was a "loan" from a lonely older man she had grifted some weeks ago to get some much-needed cash and, well, a car. It wasn't stolen — at least not yet. There was no way the old fool was getting it back, but he didn't know it. She just texted him every day and kept the hook set. When he started getting needy, she'd call and whisper sexy things to him until, until … She laughed — even the cellphone was his.

Serena knew she'd have to go to Vicar's house, where he lived with that bitch, Jacquie, and get her baby from there. Up until now, Jacquie was nowhere to be found. Serena hadn't seen her coming into town for groceries or out doing anything, really. She was clearly hiding at 411 Sloop Road. "Yeah, yeah, yeah, four-one-one, just like ya use ta call in-fro-mation on the phone." *Thank you, Farley.*

Once there, her half-assed surveillance had gone on for part of a day — Serena couldn't spend more time on it than that; she'd felt the pressure to do the deed and get out and hadn't the patience, anyway. Getting Vicar was another matter. She tossed it around in her head but still couldn't decide how best to play that one. Her mind was crowded with plans, scenarios, and fantasies. She had once broken into his house and waited for him nude … Maybe if she had been wearing an outfit, it might have worked.

She thought about it for a while. Serena's mind was a zoetrope of unmoored illusion.

No one had told Cosmic Ray to hide the ladder behind the shed; they hadn't even thought of it, and so he set it down against the house where Vicar had left it for him days before. Directly above his head were windows, the top one cracked open to allow the pleasant sea breeze inside for sleeping Frankie.

▬ ▬ ▬

In her car not far away, Serena jumped in her seat as she eyed the gift fairly laid at her feet. Her method of entry had been delivered to her on a silver platter and set down under the very window she'd need to get through. Her plan was coming together.

The baby's bedroom — *her baby*, that was; no, no, *hers and Vicar's* — was in a little attic or loft on the top floor. Serena did not know the interior layout but could tell, through binoculars, that there was also a room below the baby's that was probably for Vicar and that ugly slut, Jacquie.

The only way in that guaranteed direct access to the baby was to get up high and climb in from the outside. She would nix the lingerie plan and just snatch the baby and run, fully clothed.

▬ ▬ ▬

Later that evening, Jacquie puttered as Beulah cooked. Tony was bartending at the Knickers and wouldn't be home until late. She resigned herself to another night of listening to her mother's grating babble.

Twenty-Six / Extremely Improbable Giraffe

"This house, my God ... Three floors and a basement ... More stairs than Cologne Cathedral."

Jacquie sighed. *Not the stairs thing again.* "Mom, it was a free house. Am I supposed to complain to a dead lady about willing me a mansion, *gratis*, because *you* don't like the layout?"

"It's not safe for Frankie. She's going to fall and you're going to have a disaster on your hands." Beulah shook her head disapprovingly as she chopped vegetables. She was awfully confident with that knife, given how many glasses of "cooking wine'" she had ingested. She snipped at Jacquie, "Let's just hope she doesn't break her neck."

Let's hope I don't break your neck, thought Jacquie, darkly. *Maybe if you chop off your own finger, you'll have something new to piss and moan about.*

"This vegetable sprayer leaks everywhere. Can't Tony fix it?"

Jacquie rolled her eyes. If she wanted plumbing help, she'd be better off calling Ronnie. Had Beulah known how mechanically inept Tony was, she wouldn't have asked the question — but such knowledge would have opened yet another line of helpful observations from Mother about Daughter's *life choices*. It always came back to Jacquie's days as a stripper to pay her way through school. The twisted prudishness Beulah leaned so heavily upon was laughable … That woman was a trophy wife begging — yes, *begging* — for a man, or maybe several of them. Preferably a geriatric million-aire, but a young stallion would no doubt work until she found the super-rich nearly-dead. She might still have the energy to run them both. Jacquie realized she was being prudish herself. Mom had got away with a shit-ton not only because of her outrageous sense of humour, but also her good looks. She had been catnip to the boys and was doing later in life what she couldn't do when she was young.

Mom did love Tony, but this was another perfect opportunity to unload surplus grievances that were just gathering dust in a corner of her cobwebby brain. Beulah seemed to have a lifetime supply of them. It was cruel, but apparently nothing personal, as bizarre as that was.

Mother had a template; she only needed to plug in a target and a trivial complaint. Her toy-filled attic would complete the process, powering her squawky pie-hole to output oodles of gratuitous unpleasantness. The bitching would continue until either a fight erupted or everyone wandered away, leaving Beulah complaining to the walls about how neglected and lonely she was. *Talk about a blind spot ...*

"I swear, Mom, if you couldn't complain, you'd have literally nothing to say. No sound would come out." Jacquie realized she was paraphrasing something Tony had said in another context, years ago — a bit harsh, but in Mom's case, true.

She and Tony had really started to think alike.

— — —

Vicar was busy behind the bar — it was dinner time and the pints were flowing as fast as he could pull them. The regulars were all ensconced in their favourite places, and Chief Wheat was to his left, as usual, accompanied by Fire Hall Gordy, having a jolly laugh with Hotchy-Cootchie, whose arms were spread wide apart, no doubt estimating the size of the one that had got away — or maybe the thickness of the bullshit he was currently trowelling on. Vicar had now officially marked him down as a coward after hearing about his flight during the ghost sighting. Yet here he was, jolly as you please, acting as if everything was all hunky-dory. It seemed as if Gordy had forgiven him, although Vicar didn't think he would have if the shoe was on the other foot. *Ahem.*

The place was nearly full, and Beaner, behind him in the kitchen, was running around raising hell with the staff yet again, this time about the speed of french fry delivery. "Faster! Faster!" The barking emanating from the kitchen sounded like sound bites from a porn flick.

Since the flying frying pan, Beaner was almost petrified of being in there, and he took it out on everyone. Vicar imagined the Labour Relations Board citing the Knickers for Beaner's rotten behaviour, and Beaner blaming his terrible attitude on a poltergeist.

Vicar had really dragged him on the carpet when his wretched attitude backfired into a series of complaints and threats to report him "to the authorities." Vicar explained that he simply could not get away with screaming at the poor, bumbling, minimum-wage kids who helped in the kitchen. This was the twenty-first century. *We've spent the last forty years raising kids to have self-esteem — and then you get surprised that they won't take shit, Beaner?* Beaner had squinted and looked away, not certain what Vicar meant, but realizing he'd probably made a good point. *Whatevs.*

Vicar wondered about the evolution of Beaner, from mild-mannered into almost barbarous. When he'd met him, he'd seemed the gentlest, most retiring, sweet weirdo ever. More innocuous than Farley, who was practically a human puppy dog some days. Now Beaner was very brittle. Vicar suspected that his longing to insert himself into top billing of all the Vicar stories had made him stiff and defensive, like an unhappy middle brother; fragile, grasping, chronically feeling overlooked. His recent fright, courtesy of self-propelled airborne kitchen supplies, had made him only more chippy. Vicar decided that — given he could apparently never have control over the narrative of his own life anymore — he would ask Beaner to take on the role of spokesperson, with the caveat that Vicar never had to give stupid interviews again. Beaner was *already* proudly blabbing crap on a regular basis; this would make it official and maybe bring Beaner back around.

Harvey Kirck back from the dead was an interview Vicar would gladly get up early to do — and God knew there seemed to be enough of that "back from the dead" shit happening. But if he couldn't control his story, couldn't steer it into calm waters, fuck it. It was like trying to hold back the ocean with a spoon. His fans already contorted themselves into knots trying to make the bizarre legend add up, and never seemed to look for a simple explanation, but rather added more twists and turns. He'd met some of them, most of them lovely folks. But they had a willingness to believe, almost a desperate need to buy in, that he would never understand.

Vicar had to let some of this go, give the portfolio over to someone who was into it, whatever the motivation. Beaner, Vicar knew, would gladly take on all the ridiculous interviews, all the nonsensical nutbar news … He might as well let his imagination run wild, telling the world fairy tales about Tony Vicar, a man known to be capable of practically *anything*, laws of physics, thermodynamics, and common sense be damned.

The Extra-Large Mediums of Littleton had finally gotten their boffo performance and an amazing parting gift — Dawna's brand-new baby boy, the surprising re-sult of what the ambulance attendant had called a "cryp-tic pregnancy." Sounded spookier than the ghost, but the little gaffer was cute and healthy, and his birth seemed to have been heralded by the timely arrival of Valentine. Again, he had appeared when no one could record him for posterity. He certainly chose his moments; although camera shy, Valentine always seemed to arrive like the cavalry. Man, there was something about him and kids, wasn't there? This was, Vicar thought, one good thing about the last few weeks. There had been far too few.

"Evenin', c'mon in." Vicar was on autopilot.

The pair of patrons smiled and took off their coats.

Hotchy-Coochie came up to the self-serve, glanced over at Gordy, who was nodding his head and pointing into an empty pint glass, and said, "Three pints of your finest, Vicar!"

His standard over-the-top cheerfulness grated. Vicar simply nodded and replied, "'Kay."

"A little down in the mouth, there, Vicar?" Hotchy-Coochie was now treading in no man's land, inches from getting a snootful of the old, cranky Tony Vicar.

Vicar paused, glanced up, and then said with false cheer, "Oh no, I'm fine. Everything is wonderful. I'm sure I feel almost as good as you do."

"Thatta boy." Hotchy said it with a hint of condes-cension. As someone who seldom listened, he did not feel Vicar's barb.

Vicar had always found Hotchy to be just on the edge of palatability. Amusing if you could observe him from afar, but up close like a fly landing on your face as you slept. *Smartass* he could stomach in small quantities, *coward* he could not. At that moment, Vicar's distaste for him papered over the full-on running retreat he himself had made the first time he met Valentine the Ghost. He had been so frightened he almost wet himself. *Poor Gordy*, he thought, *forever saddled with this ass*. Gordy deserved better. His actions at the pub, delivering the baby sans one leg, were already the talk of Tyee Lagoon. Vicar was more than glad to share the limelight for a while.

Vicar's thoughts drifted back to Hotchy-Coochie. He just couldn't understand some people. He glanced up at him with resentment. *Some people just fuck around in life, charming but never amounting to much*. After a heartbeat he felt the jarring irony of his statement, thinking of his years playing music, living the dream, which had in truth been a low-income nightmare but with jolly costumes and preposterous hair. He swerved back to the present.

Toothless normalcy beckoned, directing him with an icy-cold grin toward the hamster wheel of responsibility. He gently stomped his foot in protest, hoping no one had taken notice, and deliberately changed tack. His thoughts swam around for a moment before grabbing onto *I'm very pleased with the mix of customers tonight*. It was like talking about the weather. To himself. *How dire*.

He glanced around the place a bit frightened that he might spy the face of Serena sitting out there somewhere, just waiting to stir up shit again, but, thank heaven, what he saw were two nicely dressed couples having dinner and drinks; young folks just pinting and kicking up their heels a little; a young couple, probably on some kind of romantic date, snuggled next to the giant inglenook, she wrapped in a blanket and he with his arm around her shoulders; and a table filled with regular working folk, ball caps and T-shirts, loud but cheerful and well liked by all. A perfect balance. *Thank God it's not full moon on a payday*, he thought. *That is when the dangerous jiggery-fuckery comes calling.* He did not have the wherewithal to wade into a fist fight. Thankfully, they were a rare occurrence. He glanced over at Chief Wheat at his customary spot at the end of the bar, his giant forearms easy to spot; his right hand, the size of a Virginia ham, casually held his pint. He made the fights go away, almost magically. A true gentleman and scholar, but highly dangerous if provoked.

With that, something caught Vicar's eye. It was a group drifting through the Knickers, having entered from the lobby door — or so he presumed, as they looked very out of place. He toggled off the taps, looked up and saw, as plain as day, the late Frankie Hall flanked by what appeared to be Valentine, the hotel's famous ghost, with his short, tousled hair and checked work shirt, and minus one argyle sock. The spectres waltzed past the long bar, surrounded by numerous forest creatures great and small, with, of all things, a damn giraffe taking up the rear.

He stopped dead and stared, open mouthed. Dazedly, he wondered how the giraffe was going to negotiate the light fixtures hanging down from the high ceiling. It passed through them like a shaft of sunlight. The ghostly Frankie Hall looked Vicar directly in the eye as she slid past. There were no sounds, and no one else appeared to see the apparitions. Mrs. Hall's eyes began to get bigger and bigger, and finally enlarged until they were bigger than her body, obscuring her form. Vicar saw within them an image of Jacquie sobbing, baby Frankie limp in her arms. Valentine had turned his ghostly attention to the vision she projected, staring at it with concern, and then locked eyes with Vicar.

Vicar felt a tidal surge of anxiety overtake him, his blood pressure launching upward, his lower back suddenly aching.

Glancing around for a moment, he barked huskily at Chief Wheat, "Hank, take over … I gotta go."

He ran at full speed back to the office to call home.

Unfazed but curious, Wheat stood up and said, "Aye, sir," and saluted Vicar's departing back, feeling delighted to be deputized as barman. He chuckled delightedly: *another dream coming true.* He drew a small tumbler of beer for himself and drank it — *just to be sure it is safe for human consumption, you know* — and let out a satisfied, raspy "Ahhh" as he thunked the now-empty glass onto the bar. He shouted over to Hotchy-Coochie, "There's nothing more delicious than free beer!"

Hotchy's eyes lit up as he made a beeline for the bar.

Twenty-Seven / Serena's Ladder

A cry erupted from upstairs — the sound of Frankie, who had been asleep in her crib, frightened badly. Jacquie furrowed her brow and hurried toward the steps, climbing them with more urgency than usual. *She must have had a bad dream.*

Then she heard a voice — a woman's voice — coming from Frankie's room. "Mommy's here, shush, shush ..."

With that, Jacquie broke into a full run. The telephone in the kitchen began to ring, sounding like a klaxon. Quickly switching off the stove, Beulah ignored the phone and trailed behind Jacquie, looking confused and spooked.

Storming up the short steps from the master bedroom to the little loft where Frankie slept, Jacquie saw her child's arm held by someone — *a kidnapper!* — who was trying to back down a ladder perched outside the window. She then recognized Serena, grinning at Frankie with all the motherly comfort of a clown peering out from a sewer grate. *Oh, little girl, would you like a balloon?*

The horror Jacquie felt at that moment was as tangible as a knife to the heart.

■ ▬ ▬

No answer. But Jacquie and Beulah had to be at home, he was sure of it. Frankie was stuffed up and cranky, so tonight was going to be shirtless Brad Pitt, fresh baguette, and Beulah's chicken soup. Vicar called Jacquie's cellphone number, pounding his fist on the desk as he waited for the interminable connection. She didn't pick up.

His apron flapping wildly in the breeze, Vicar grabbed his car keys and fled out the back door toward his ancient, beat-up Peugeot, listed as "rust" coloured on the registration form for good reason. Briefly caught up on the antlers of the moose head mounted to Beaner's Bottles (& Cans) truck, parked beside him, Vicar's now torn apron was discarded carelessly. His car door still hanging open, he cranked up the exhausted Cuisinart of a motor and wound it up to a hellish speed toward the house. Vicar was driving so fast that the tiniest error would leave him looking like a Sloppy Joe splashed on the dashboard, but he was responding to a situation he knew was the real thing.

Blowing a shift while turning at a hundred kilometres an hour onto a side street, he managed somehow to call Jacquie's cellphone. *No joy*. He thought of his front tires, which his mechanic had ruefully called *Lieutenant Kojak* and *Captain Picard*, and hoped they'd get him there without a blowout. He kept pounding toward the house at top speed. He knew that Frankie Hall never came to him unless things were going to get bad. Yeah, it was hocus-pocus, but he'd rather be laughed at than cried with.

■ ■ ■

Jacquie's butt was vibrating — someone was trying to call, but she took no notice. Frankie was bawling loudly, and Jacquie lunged toward her. Serena tried to yank Frankie away as Jacquie's fear and anger mixed into a terrifying rocket fuel.

"Let go of my baby!" she shrieked.

"It's *my baby*," Serena screamed back.

"Let go! Let go! Let go!" Jacquie screeched ferociously.

"It's *my* baby."

Even in the furious tug-of-war, Jacquie was aware that Serena was referring to Frankie as "it." This pissed her off.

Serena had nabbed Frankie and set her on her feet as she tried to exit feet first and back down the ladder. She was half-in and half-out of the bedroom now, balanced on her stomach like a see-saw, the ladder buffeting back and forth dangerously. If she could just get her feet on one rung, she could at least make a break.

Jacquie saw her grabbing for a huge, frightening knife sticking out of her jacket.

Urgently, she got her body between little Frankie and the escaping Serena. For the moment Frankie was protected, but Jacquie was determined to keep Serena from fleeing. She snaked out her arm and tried to grab Serena's hair, to haul her back inside. The move failed as a clip-on hair extension came off in her hand, briefly surprising her. Serena flailed on the rickety ladder and failed to get hold of the knife, which fell to the ground. The ridiculous thing was so long she couldn't even get it out properly.

Incongruously, the cellphone in Jacquie's back pocket began to ring again.

"Give the child to me, dear. She's safe with me. It's all right …"

Jacquie, her emotions ratcheted as high as they ever had been, was certain she was hearing the voice of the late Frankie Hall.

Serena had reached back inside with one arm, managed to grab little Frankie by the sleeve with the fingertips of her left hand, and was roughly dragging her closer in a desperate, last-ditch attempt to snag her firmly and flee. Jacquie, in turn, grabbed Frankie by the collar of her pyjama top and felt the snaps pop open. The babe was suddenly shirtless and free, and so Jacquie pushed her to the side, out of danger, toward the voice she had heard, to ensure she was out of Serena's grasp. She briefly glanced over to see Frankie Hall, arms open, ready to accept her namesake in an embrace. Jacquie was shocked but could not afford the time to stare at the impossible sight before her.

Off balance now and in a panic, Serena kicked the ladder over with a loud clatter as she flailed her legs frantically. She had hold of the flat, wide window frame with both hands, hanging on for dear life, but was no longer able to fight.

Beulah had followed up the stairs to investigate the alarming sounds of combat. Above her, at the top of the steps, she saw a young man in a checked shirt. He scintillated and flashed slightly as he held little Frankie's hand.

Beulah was terrified but raced into the fray with every milligram of courage she could muster. She had certainly imbibed enough of it. She intended to body-check this invader. She lowered her head to use as a ram, preparing herself to be repulsed and thrown back down the stairs to her death. Beulah glanced upward to stay on target, but the man had suddenly disappeared — just vanished. Baby Frankie stood stock still, shirtless and alone near the banister, looking on with confusion and fright. *Thank God she didn't fall down the stairs!* Beulah scooped her up and watched the action with alarm, not sure what else to do.

Jacquie could now see that Serena was barely hanging on and might fall at any second. She grabbed one forearm and tried to pull her up. Serena was making sounds of deep, animal-like fear now, as she faced imminent death. She looked up into Jacquie's eyes pleadingly, unable to even speak.

Jacquie held on with as much strength as she could, but she was running out of steam. She could not manage to haul Serena up far enough to manage a rescue, nor hold on to her much longer. The fingers of Serena's other hand began to slip off the window frame, so Jacquie grabbed on. She was now holding both Serena's hands in hers, one by the wrist, the other precariously by the fingers. Jacquie was losing it — she could feel her back giving way.

She rasped through gritted teeth, "Mom ... Mom ... The ladder ..."

Beulah hesitated for one second and then raced down the stairs as fast as she could, Frankie in her arms, toward the door that would get her to the life-saving ladder the fastest, all the while terrified that the mystery man from the top of the stairs might reappear.

Twenty-Eight / A Fall from Gracelessness

V icar skidded onto Sloop Road, toward the most dangerous driveway entrance in town, right there on the sharp corner that was almost a switchback. He could see the roofline of his house now; he was seconds out.

Serena was cogitating at a million miles an hour, trying to find a way to survive. She just hoped Jacquie could hold on for a few moments more.

Beulah had plopped a wailing Frankie down where she could see her through the window and ran as fast as she could to the ladder that lay on the lawn. It was so heavy, so long … She could barely move it.

At that moment, Vicar stormed in through the gate, looking up in utter horror at the scene that greeted him.

"Jack! Hold on!" Vicar grabbed the ladder from Beulah and tried frantically to hoist it up.

Serena heard the voice of Vicar and her fear transformed into a rush of victory. He'd save her, once again. *It was happening.*

She awkwardly twisted her neck enough to see Vicar below, wrestling the ladder, and then looked back up at Jacquie, her crazy eyes spinning, and growled, "I knew he'd come for me ... *Thanks for babysitting.*" She spat the last through tensely clenched teeth.

Jacquie felt Serena's words splatter like a spray of hydrochloric acid. Something about the way she had delivered them felt true. There was no longer a shred of doubt: her taunting words had snapped the situation into crystal clarity. Jacquie flashed on the memory of Mrs. Hall's warning in the dream and connected it to her presence here, now. *Beware the mother,* she had said.

Jacquie was certain now. *Oh God ... She* is *Frankie's birth mother.* That loathsome freak was willing to put everyone through hell — even her own child. It would never end. *This loveless monster is evil incarnate.* Serena was a succubus that had to be exorcised.

It all cascaded through her mind in an instant, a kaleidoscope of the worst things in the world combined: torture, slavery, war, brutality, Farley's checked Dacron pants, mother's liver and onions soaking in milk before frying, and then Serena's somehow beautiful yet murderous face in front of her. Everything. It was all just a malevolent ball of bilge and cruelty that must be chopped out to protect Frankie.

At that moment, Jacquie made the biggest decision of her life. It was a statement, a protest, and a solution, demonstrated by one simple act.

She released her grip and let Serena fall.

◼ ◼ ◼

Serena screamed in terror. Vicar perceived her fall in slow motion. He darted to safety as he shoved Beulah back out of danger, fixating on the colour of the Low Top Converse sneakers Serena wore, in an ironic Safety Orange.

The entire fall couldn't have taken more than a second, but it was an event that everyone present would remember for the rest of their lives. Most particularly, Vicar would remember the sickening, flat "pock" that resounded as Serena's skull hit the concrete sidewalk like an exploding melon.

For a few moments, Vicar, Jacquie, and Beulah just stood there, mouths agape, staring frozen at the grisly scene as if in tharn.

Jacquie was the first to come to life. From her emanated a moan of distress so intense it sounded non-human. Vicar looked up at the window to see her withdrawing indoors.

He embraced Beulah and put his body between Serena's remains and her line of sight. "Are you all right?" He was hiding her head in his shoulder.

Beulah pulled away from him, saying, "I'm, okay, I'm okay ..." It was clear from her pallor that she was not; it was also obvious that Serena was dead.

- - -

Jacquie couldn't remember how she'd gotten down the stairs to the scene of Serena's messy landing. The sight of a crushed skull and snapped neck was deeply shocking. Although physically numb, she could still feel fear and regret boiling inside her like a hot storm.

Face in her hands, she wept, "Oh my God, I've killed her, I've killed her …"

Vicar looked on, stunned, swaying trancelike from foot to foot, attempting to gather his resources.

Beulah grabbed Jacquie gently by the shoulders, herself in deep shock, and tried to look directly into her eyes.

Jacquie, in a panic, was repeating, "Mom, it's my fault … I dropped her … I killed her."

Beulah thought of Marv, dead on the rug in Saskatoon, little Jacquie above watching in utter horror. She responded firmly but quietly, "No you didn't, honey. Honey, look at me. *No, you didn't.*"

Their circle had closed.

Twenty-Nine / A Quintet of Trios

osmic Ray, a man who believed himself deeply connected to the universe, was blissfully unaware of
the drama happening at Vicar's house only a couple
of miles away. He was dealing with his own challenges.
Downcast, he muttered, "I knew it ... I could feel this
coming."

He looked down and away from Ronnie, who had
just dropped the bad news that she didn't think they
should see each other anymore.

"I like you, Ray, but our lives couldn't possibly be
more different. All we have in common is sex."

"I know." Ray was glum. "But you would understand
if you were just a little more open minded."

Ronnie paused and quickly thought about it. "Ray,
honey, you live in a world that is totally foreign to me.
The source of your whole way of thinking is, is ..." She
shrugged and trailed off.

"Uh, that's, that's the, uh, *idea*. We aren't going to grow up until we can see things from other viewpoints."

Ronnie felt a tug at her heart. When he said *we*, he meant the entire human species. Surely that was beyond the purview of a basement-suite-renting, reiki-enthusiast-slash-rock drummer. He was honestly trying to explain the deep feelings of his heart, but it was wasted breath. She had made up her mind and seldom changed it after a firm decision. She was just too cut and dried.

Cosmic Ray got up out of the wicker lawn chair and stepped out a short distance under the open sky, where he stood staring at the view for a while. Ronnie just sat quietly, feeling relieved but unkind.

Ray put his hands up toward the sky as if silently beseeching the heavens. He hummed a low, sustained note for a long time. The sun was sinking into the water and the colours were warm and inviting.

Ronnie didn't want to interrupt his moment of grief, or prayer, or whatever in the hell ceremony he was observing at that moment, but she really had to pee. She quietly rose to her feet and padded into the house.

Ray turned toward the east, his back toward the setting sun, and faced the darkening sky.

When Ronnie returned, she followed Ray's gaze. She seldom took notice of the stars, but tonight a handful of them sparkled diamond-like in the dusk. She remained quiet. To her surprise, three lights in rapidly shifting triangular formation glowed brighter than the rest of the pinpricks of light and emerged from the background. They appeared to be coming toward them. She stifled a gasp. Ronnie was aware that formations of moving stars were highly unusual. Impossible, in fact.

Closer and closer the lights approached for what might have been a minute, until they had a shape. Her stomach jumped — *Jesus Christ, they look exactly like flying saucers!* Flattish on the bottom and a curved lid on top, like the fancy paella pan Mom had.

She stayed silent with difficulty, but her curiosity trumped her anxiety.

The objects stopped just above the treeline to the east, inside the split-rail fence that marked the border of Ronnie's property, right over a stand of tall Douglas fir trees. They hovered. Other than bugs and some distant animal noises, there was absolutely no sound.

Ray finally lowered his arms, turned to face Ronnie. He tilted his head and raised his eyebrows as if to say *I told you so.*

Ronnie just stood rooted to the patio, wordless. *Did he slip me a roofie?* Her voice failed her. What manner of wizard was this strange man?

Ray wore a look of vindication as he approached and wrapped Ronnie in a gentle bear hug. He pecked her on the cheek. Strong, independent, pragmatic, and clear-headed Ronnie Balthazar went limp as a noodle.

▬ ▬ ▬

Con-Con got the call to respond to Vicar and Jacquie's house and felt her gut lurch. She knew — she could feel it; this had something to do with Serena.

Lights on but no siren, she took Sloop Road at a clip and looked as far ahead on her route as she could to provide maximum time to deal with elderly, meandering motorists certain to be in her path, desperate to get home before sundown. It was as if they were afraid of vampires emerging from the shadows.

There had been one instance, early on in her career, where she'd had to muck in to get some seniors home, after having helped them locate their parked car — which had only been around the corner of the ice rink. The pair were so flapped that the husband couldn't muster the jam to drive afterward.

Con-Con understood; just watching her mom try to pay with a debit card had been a real shock. She had been so sorely confused.

Charging down Sloop Road, she knew her day would come, too. Then, like the legendary lady of lore wearing purple, topped with a red hat, she would wander the streets in search of her mislaid umbrella, hoarding sugar packets, aghast at the thought of the out-of-doors after sunset, peering suspiciously out her window at passing pedestrians whom she would, of course, refer to as *those ruffians*.

Con-Con did a high-speed turn into Vicar's driveway and skidded to a stop next to his car. As she jumped out of the cruiser and donned her cap, a sight in the sky caught her eye … three lights, hovering in the distance.

Chinese lanterns, such a fire hazard. *That's the kind of shit people report as flying saucers.* A forest fire they did *not* need. She glanced for only a second.

At that moment, Vicar appeared before her, white as a ghost and shaking like the Cascadia fault, bidding her to follow; she forgot about floating lanterns in the sky when she saw Serena's lifeless remains oozing onto the sidewalk.

■ ■ ■

It was beautiful out on the water; one of those crisp fall days that come just before the skies open in November and reduce the landscape to a grey *bleh*. Steven and Merri really should have been headed back to the marina, where he would still be able to see well enough to moor the craft without *kanging* into another boat. But things had gone another direction.

Maybe it was the wine, or maybe the appies, but Steven was feeling his hidden inner stallion rising to the surface.

Merri, flirting and coquettish, felt a little flush from the delicious Merlot. She reached out and touched Steve's hand.

He looked at her and touched her back. Merri made a little squeak, followed as ever by a titter.

Things heated up and Steve started with the sexy talk. "It's a nice evening." An aircraft could be heard droning in the distance and the strengthening breeze whistled.

Merri heard only Steve's voice and whispered, "Yes."

He held her gaze for nearly an entire second. "A lovely end to a lovely day." *So hot.*

"Mmm ... Yes." She was short of breath.

"Might be a bit breezy tomorrow, though." He gazed at the sky. Oh, he knew *all* the sexy weather talk.

Merri tilted her head back and wantonly said, "Yes, slightly breezy."

Mustering courage he didn't know he still had, he leaned toward Merri and gently pressed his lips on hers, kissing her, or close — more like rubbed his face on hers, desperately out of practice, nervous as three cats. He then said almost brazenly, "It's getting a little cool out here ... from the wind." He glanced up at high cirrus wisps whisking across the early-evening sky.

Merri was dizzy, slightly faint, and desperately hoped he'd mention the barometric pressure. She leaned into him so he could plant another smooch, her body experiencing sensations she hadn't felt for decades, when she saw in the sky behind him three moving stars.

They hovered over land, not too terribly far away, and were shaped like heavenly Pyrex pie plates. She just knew it was a sign, a very good sign.

She reached out and gently laid her hand in his lap while he felt his inner anemometer start to spin. He gazed at the reddish western horizon and felt the wind snapping at his face as he observed chop on the water. He licked his finger and stuck it in the air, saying quietly, "Oh my, there's definitely going to be a blow tonight."

Gunnar Bering sat in the right-hand seat and simply enjoyed being in the sky. It had been several months since the plane crash, and he was hungry to fly again.

An old friend had taken him for an evening tour of the area; Gunnar thought he might be able to manoeuvre around a little once they were aloft. Just for fun, to speed his recovery a little.

The pair of pilots had planned an outbound trip that would take the form of a great half-circle from the airport, out across the water where the evening view would be most spectacular, with mainland lights on one side of them and the Island glittering beautifully on the other. He had made the trip so many times it felt as comfortable as walking his pooch around the block.

The airborne pair chatted as they flew in calm, darkening skies — chatted as much as pilots do, which is to say not much. The poetry was in the view, the smooth control, the majesty of flying, not in chatter.

As predicted, Gunnar was given control briefly. "I've got the aircraft," he said in the shorthand that now, in his precarious convalescence, meant a thousand things.

"Roger — your aircraft."

After a few silent minutes where they both simply enjoyed the soaring ride, Gunnar piped up, "Umm ... I am seeing something ahead. Two o'clock, low." He gazed downward.

"Me too. What are we looking at, though?"

"Do not know." He said it tersely, for clarity, and with a little hidden anxiety.

"Okay. Three objects. Luminescent. Now hovering over land."

"Drones, probably. But awfully big drones."

"No kidding. Very low altitude. Maybe five hundred feet?"

"Yep."

"I'll keep watching; you should make a report to ATC."

Gunnar called it in while his buddy tried to capture a pic of the objects on his mobile phone. The pic was useless, looking like a smeary blob of lights. Could have been a drunken shot of candles on a birthday cake. After a few minutes, they overflew the area, but the lights had vanished.

＿＿ ＿＿ ＿＿

Peering out the bay window of her home, located in what she incessantly referred to as the *highly desirable seaside subdivision of Sandringham Mews*, Mrs. Morrison saw three aircraft flying low near her house. She immediately bustled out to the front step, grabbing her ever-present opera glasses, which sat right inside the front door.

She could hear droning in the distance and saw three aircraft, flying far too low and far too close to the quiet zone around her house that she had unilaterally proclaimed in that moment. She could see them, *there*,

there. She pointed accusingly as she called to her husband to come see, aggrieved at yet another disturbance interrupting her bezique game with Arthur, who had trailed along behind his parents to the front yard. Only an hour ago there had been the dreadful shrieking of children in the neighbour's yard, the latest affront in her litany of petty irregularities.

Arthur looked up and saw three pinpoints of light, nothing more. Her husband, glasses on the kitchen counter, couldn't find the top step, never mind the offending aircraft. Margaret bustled indoors, grabbed her phone and called the police immediately.

The 911 operator took her report and promised to send someone out to investigate the matter, but of course every emergency vehicle from miles around Tyee Lagoon was busy dealing with a messy death at the house of Tony Vicar and Jacquie O at that very moment. No one ever came, and Mrs. Morrison was livid, beside herself with outrage. She had waited up until ten.

The next day she called the airport to complain, and intended to do so vociferously, but only managed to get an answer from the cafeteria there. The teenager stocking commercially baked muffins into a cooler from a large cardboard box listened for a moment and told her it had nothing to do with him.

Margaret would not be dissuaded and railed at him for a few moments more. "I am a member of the public and I deserve satisfaction!"

"Ma'am, I work in the cafeteria. I don't run operations."

"I demand you summon your superior!"

He thought about it for a second. *His superior?* The cook? The commissionaire who fussed about the four parking stalls? The night janitor? "Ma'am, at the moment I am my own superior."

"Then I expect you to take steps, forthwith."

Forthwith? What in the actual fuck did that even mean? *This one is as entitled as they come.*

He took a breath and barked out, "Get fucked, you old douche nugget." He rudely banged the phone down. He was not a Boomer, apparently.

Margaret Morrison, stunned and vaporous, dropped her phone on the floor in a loud clatter and leaned heavily on the counter, gasping like a fish.

Arthur looked at his father, who stood rooted, aware he was facing yet another storm that must be weathered. Arthur looked heavenward and said, "Dad, let's go for a fucking pint."

His father looked at the clock, which read 8:15 a.m. He shuffled to the door, put on his hat and turned back to Arthur. "Let's get tae fook outta herrrrre, lad."

The look on Margaret Morrison's face surely curled the wallpaper as they departed the highly desirable seaside subdivision of Sandringham Mews without a backward glance.

Thirty / Unknotted

Con-Con rubbed her eyes briefly and thought nostalgically of how boring Tyee Lagoon had been before the adventures with Vicar, the town's greatest celebrity. He seemed to drag in his wake every manner of emergency she could imagine, and a few she had not.

Fire and ambulance were dealing with Serena's remains. The whole long driveway was lined with emergency vehicles and flashing lights. Jacquie clung to Vicar, unable to stop crying. Con-Con tried to gather statements and piece the scenario together. Jacquie tried to recount the scene but was far too upset to get the story out without weeping uncontrollably. Beulah's babbling was disjointed and of no help. She was going on about how many stairs there were and about someone named "Marv." Head down, she babbled quietly. Con-Con decided to get everyone indoors, have Vicar — shaky as a leaf but at least quiet — make them a cup of tea, and she'd try again.

"Tony, can you shed any light on this situation?" Con-Con was trying to set an orderly tone; she needed to take gentle control.

Vicar cleared his throat and looked at her. "Well ... Uhh ... It all started with the animals walking through the Knickers. And Frankie Hall was leading them. And, umm, Valentine ... You know, the ghost. I knew there was trouble."

"Ho-ho-hold on," Con-Con stammered with disbelief. "Frankie Hall. The late Frankie Hall?" She held up her hand to demonstrate how short Frankie had been. "... With some other dead guy? And animals — in the pub?"

Vicar reluctantly described the ESP distress call.

"Yup. Even a giraffe. It walked right through the light fixtures."

"A giraffe?"

"Yup."

"In the pub?"

"Mmhmm."

"A ghost giraffe?"

"Yep."

"Like a tall, spotted African animal with the long neck kind of giraffe?"

"Yes. It seemed a little out of place, to be honest."

Con-Con blinked a couple of times, exhaled with exasperation, and jotted it down in her notebook. What in the world was the follow-up question supposed to be after Mr. Ghost Giraffe popped up in a witness statement? A shit-ton of mental gymnastics were going to be necessary … She thought of the looks of mirth on her fellow Mounties' faces. Omigod, it was going to be a sensation.

She looked at the framed picture of Frankie Hall on top of the nearby piano and remembered so many odd things about this situation, these people. Ghosts, disembodied voices from the heavens, long-dead visitors showing up randomly. It all had to be insanity. Or a cult. But she knew these people. They were so far from a cult that she had to dismiss that suspicion out of hand. And what about the millions of "fans" who followed him, almost religiously? Con-Con tried not to get distracted. She had a death to investigate.

But there was her partner Nancy's book — her big new project. Nancy had decided to try her hand at telling the story of Vicar and his exploits. She had, after all, sacrificed her writing career to follow Con-Con around from posting to posting, often in far-flung, remote places, for years at a time. This was a book that needed writing.

Con-Con had nearly all the skinny on the big emergencies that gathered around Vicar and Jacquie. With her knowledge and proximity, Nancy's book could end up being the definitive story of Vicar … *Hmm*. It would surely be a much-deserved reward for Nancy, who had given up everything to be with her.

After Con-Con's first tangle with Serena, she had thought about the long, multi-generational series of events that had led to her rotten situation and had influenced her personality so deeply. She had hoped that Serena could pick up that long string of her life and redirect it to lead to a better future; she knew Serena had been trying, in her own immature way. Her death was a tragedy.

And Vicar and company? Being a cop, Con-Con had studied various psychological phenomena. Mass hysteria, cults, brainwashing, hostages and their sympathetic syndromes: the gamut. One of them almost fit the bill, a strange and rare mental state called *bouffée délirante*, a "delusional flash," a contagious madness that can involve more than one person at the same time. She wondered if the so-called Vicar phenomenon might relate to it. But it had been going on for years. This was no mere *flash*.

So, Con-Con moved along to Jacquie's statement.

Jacquie haltingly explained the whole confrontation, the fight, the defenestration. Even in her shaken condition, she had been vague about dropping Serena. "I just couldn't hang on any longer," she had said, weeping. *That horrible woman*, a living nightmare with *their* baby, hers and Tony's, who forever ruined everything she touched. Finally, Serena's recklessness had become fatal.

As ever, Con-Con wore a mask of neutrality, hiding sympathy for her friend Jacquie's predicament, wondering how she herself would have reacted in a similar pickle. She and Nancy were considering having a baby, too.

Con-Con figured that Jacquie, at her deepest depths, had seen the awful future with a hale-and-hearty, incessantly threatening Serena nipping at their heels and did not hold with it. She did not blame Jacquie for what she had done — she had found the courage to cut the Gordian knot.

Thirty-One / Ashes of Defeat

A few days after Serena's messy death on his concrete sidewalk, Vicar headed to Balmer's Funeral Home, which was still visibly beaten up, showing the scars of the airplane crash; however, it was open for business and had been since only a day or two after Vicar's plane wreck. As the story went, the boss of the place, Michael "Mick" Balmer, was doing his best to "stay ahead of the dead." Awfully glib, but probably true.

As Vicar approached Balmer's, he looked at the point of impact on the side of the building and re-played the crash. It was just as scary now as it had been then. He was certain he'd bought it that time but, once again, he'd seemed to come out of it in pretty good shape. He no longer limped, although he had occasional phantom stabs of pain in his thigh. Every one of them reminded him of the terror that had ac-companied the crash.

Given the dismal mental condition he was in, he wasn't sure if his survival was a message of encouragement, to keep marching on, or a sign that he was being kept alive by forces unknown, as a heartless prank. It took all his energy to put on a pleasant face.

Vicar walked down the hallway, its carpeting covered in paper from a heavy roll, and found the office he was looking for. Its sign read *M. Balmer, Funeral Director*. He stared at the sign for a few seconds and then shook his head. He knocked.

"Come in, Mr. Vicar. I'm Mick Balmer." The funeral director extended one hand while motioning to a chair in front of his imposing desk.

Vicar sat down and was silent for a second. He finally opened up by saying, "Mr. Balmer, I am so sorry about all the damage I caused. Just so, so sorry." His regret was magnified by his depression, which was beginning to spiral. He could feel it; he knew his own patterns all too well.

"Well, it was a mechanical issue and Gunnar Bering pulled off quite the emergency landing … It's a miracle you both survived, I'm told. I was so sad to hear about his injuries."

Vicar sat up, slightly startled. "I haven't checked in on him for weeks. Do you know how he's coming along? He was hurting, there, for a while."

"Broken bones can heal, but who knows what kind of toll it took mentally."

Gunnar was a nice guy, and a highly skilled pilot, too. Vicar felt bleak at the thought of his pain.

Stay steady, Vicar; the surest way to find misery is to go looking for it. He thought briefly of Merri Crabtree's obstinate positivity. He wished he could summon her sometimes-maddening skill. Vicar suddenly wanted to get to the point of his visit and get the hell out of the funeral home.

"Mick, tell me … Did Serena De Medici have next of kin? Someone who would take care of her funeral expenses?" He felt nausea as he spoke her full name out loud. It felt strange on his tongue, almost as if saying it enough times might bring her back from the dead. He'd had quite enough of her.

Balmer paused and said, "Well, no … I suppose they'll continue looking for somebody, but she had no living family that anyone could locate. A pretty sad case."

"Yes, that's incredibly sad." Vicar was not surprised — he had been able to sense her loneliness in those brief, anxious moments he was face to face with her. She had been needy to the point of lethality. "No wonder she was so fucked up."

He grimaced at his choice of words, but Balmer didn't even take notice. One thing about running a funeral home is that you meet every kind of person the world has to offer. Everybody dies, and it turns out that everybody swears now and then, too.

"Well, then. I, uhh, I want to pay for it. Maybe you could cremate her remains and I'll find a nice place to sprinkle the ashes."

M. Balmer raised his eyebrows, pulled a form out of his desk drawer, and said simply, "All right, let's get started."

The box was heavy, although it contained only the remains of one young woman, cremated in a flimsy coffin of beaver board. She'd been ragingly beautiful, but terribly confused — misunderstood by everyone, including herself. Vicar held all of Serena, every last dusty vestige, inside a plastic bag within a cardboard box. He thought of a similar cardboard box into which Serena had put her own newborn baby on the night she'd abandoned her, and felt a pang at the pitiable symbolism.

Vicar carried her ashes to the same cliff that had served as the resting place of Mrs. Frankie Hall. He'd brought along an old scoop, once used for dispensing kibble, that had been in the drawer at the house, dipped it into the ashes, and murmured as he flung the dust out to sea, scoop by depressing scoop.

"*You coulda bin a contendah.* Such a shame, Serena." She had just wanted what she'd wanted and couldn't see how it hurt anyone else. A tragedy. "I'll remember when you were a sweet girl holding my hand, just wanting a nice boy to protect you." His mind's eye sped through a slideshow of the hostage-taking incident years ago when he had, somehow, convinced Serena to surrender to the police, without a fight — without even a whimper.

Vicar finished scooping, emptied out the bottom of the box with a tap of his hand, and was overcome by how pitiable her end was. *Some random guy tapping what's left of you out of a box that's headed to recycling tomorrow.* He suddenly felt empty, barren. He was a little surprised to feel tears running down his cheek, too. *The waste, oh God, the waste.*

He wiped the tears with his sleeve and felt the high strangeness of his situation. Had Serena used her ol' noodle and spoken with someone at the ministry, she'd have gotten custody of Frankie, just like that. He and Jacquie would have had to spend months and years, and maybe every cent they had, trying to prove she was unsuitable. And it probably wouldn't have worked. Her death was both a tragedy and a blessing. He was horrified at the thought, and strode back to the rusty Peugeot, determined that Serena's daughter — he hoped finally *his* daughter forevermore — would not have to walk the same path down which Serena had sprinted to a premature demise. She'd lived fast, all right, but in the end hadn't even left them with a good-lookin' corpse.

━ ━ ━

As he slowly putted back home, wondering how he'd explain why he'd felt the need to sprinkle Serena's ashes alone, Vicar's mind swirled. The events of the last couple of weeks were as much as he could take; his exhaustion went down to his very core. Mind churning, he steered the car on remote control, a homing instinct trundling him back to Jacquie and Frankie.

He felt the car judder and paid no heed; he came up the rise, shifted down to keep up his speed, and the old red Peugeot wheezed a couple of times and died.

Vicar rolled to the turnout that looked out to the Strait of Georgia and got out. He lifted the hood; the motor, in its death throes, smoked and hissed steam. He didn't have the first idea what might have gone wrong with it, and he couldn't have fixed it anyway. That burning oil smell could not be a good sign, that was all he knew. He turned and stared out to sea, the sky mostly clear, a fragrant breeze brushing past him, the glorious mountains of the mainland rising out of the water. He gazed at it for a few moments and then looked again at his dead car.

Five minutes ago, he had driven it to the water's edge to dispose of what remained of Serena, who was barely more than a girl, really, and whose tragic childhood had utterly ruined what could have been a limitless future. He felt regret that was rather fatherly. She had had that effect on Vicar, and he mused that she might even have been satisfied with that, had she not been such an un-guided emotional projectile.

He then thought of Jacquie, the love of his life, who had hidden her own heartbreaking childhood from him and would forever be ridden with guilt over Serena's de-mise. She would never forgive Serena and might not forgive herself. He felt a twinge of concern.

He thought of mother-in-law Beulah, a woman whose whole life had been a failed attempt to apologize, all the while wanting to be the centre of attention. And then he thought of his own mum.

Vicar glimpsed a shimmering, deeply buried mem-ory from his childhood of Mum trying, haltingly, to explain that his dad had left — simply abandoned them both. He hadn't even had the guts to tell them face to face. He'd left a note on the inside of a torn-open cigarette package that he'd probably dug out of the trash. Oh, God, the sheer agony Vicar's poor mum had had to endure. For a moment he shrivelled, as if it had been he himself who had done the dastardly deed. The paradoxical transference of those harsh feelings from father to son were what kept him from thinking about it very often. Vicar was guilty on his own father's behalf. What a cocked-up situation ... A gift that just kept on givin'.

He hadn't visited Mum the night she died because he'd been fucking around like an *eedjut* in his Elvis costume, another chapter in a lifetime of ostrich-like denial; like the true tit he was, he'd managed to jump dramatically off a stage and spear himself in the balls by impaling them upon an unseen microphone stand, rendering himself sterile, and missing her final moments. He wouldn't even go to the hospital for treatment, horrified at the thought of having to hold his dying mother's hand while simultaneously cupping his wounded sack. He'd decided instead to go home and writhe in agony, choosing physical pain over humiliation. He was awakened too early the very next morning by a call from the hospital, telling him Mum had suddenly slipped away. *Omigod, omigod, omigod* ... He should have been there, escorting her to the gates of the tunnel, right by her side till the end. A wave of shame washed over him; he contorted and grunted out the sound of deep pain.

Breathing deeply for a few moments to gather himself, Vicar countered that awful memory with a thought of baby Frankie, the miracle Valentine's Day present, the very heart of so much joy and a wonder to him, a man who could not have his own kids. Mum would have flipped for her, just *flipped*.

How had Frankie come to them? The swirl of highly unlikely events leading to her arrival brought him up short. How to protect Frankie in the cyclone of madness that constantly surrounded him? *How?*

He thought of Merri Crabtree, who had showered good vibes every single time she saw him, or Frankie, or Jacquie — or her discreet and well-mannered beau, Steven Leigh-gal — for no reason other than she was *all goodness all the time*. What kind of otherworldly talent was that? Her loving nature was a lesson waiting to be absorbed, but Vicar was such a slow learner.

He was ruefully aware that he had spent the better part of a lifetime afraid to be happy, for fear it'd be snatched away from him; it had happened countless times in the past. He was an offbeat dreamer, an optimist with little faith in the future — a technically difficult and pointless exercise, much like the bulk of his musical "career."

Ann Tenna, oh dear lord, Annie — she had made him laugh and laugh and laugh. What an unforgettable gift she had bestowed upon all of them. *Oh Jesus*, her hairdos alone. Someone should have been keeping a record of them for future generations.

And then he thought of Frankie Hall, who looked after him ... even after her death. Her presence had to be real. *It had to be.* He dearly hoped she was with him now, sliding around the continuum of time and space that Vicar also travelled, her hand out ready to steady. He knew he was mostly a boy in the skin of a man, whose life had been surrounded by women who had brought him in when they simply could have pushed him away, for better and for worse. He could not balance it, not quite yet.

Had a few breaks gone the other direction, he easily could have been the one in the carboard box. He might well have ended up living under a tarp in the bush, not in a beautiful home with a stunning girlfriend he would one day make his wife — if she'd have him.

His good fortune had started with Jacquie; he knew she was the catalyst, and her presence might have been sheer luck, but then it might have been one helluva subtle plan. After all these years, he still hadn't decided. Vicar felt it all, a pressure on his chest that squeezed emotions out of him like a sponge into a washtub.

The setting sun on the western horizon began to glow yellow, gold, and purple. Vicar, feeling emotions of fear, regret, love and passion, gratitude and grief, was suddenly verklempt as a mofo. He put his face in his hands and wept.

▬ ▬ ▬

Vicar had walked into the house, his eyes puffy and his face red as he went directly upstairs to the bedroom, barely saying a word. Jacquie followed him, knowing he was in a state of depression. Somehow, she put aside her own anxieties and quietly followed.

He disrobed as he walked and put on pyjama bottoms and a T-shirt, climbing into bed and staring toward the window.

"You okay, baby?" Jacquie's voice was soft, a little shaky. She found herself crawling away from her own blackness to help deal with his.

"My car died."

Jacquie did not answer. She knew he loved his Peugeot, but *really*.

A pause. "I scattered Serena's ashes."

Jacquie felt a start but did not comment. She just stroked his arm, with the silence of the room growing into a presence of its own. She did not understand his sympathy for that woman. It stung her, made her feel vulnerable, but she tried to understand.

She had her own dark concerns but could tell some of them were being borne by Tony, who lay in the bed as if mortally wounded, encircled by a cloud of swirling self-doubt. Yet, by some alchemy she did not understand, he still buttressed her.

Tony needed to be alone, to process everything, to get over it. She did not know if he'd ever be the same. She, herself, would be indelibly tattooed by Serena and her death.

Jacquie stood, about to leave, and Vicar quietly said, "You didn't murder her, Jack. You couldn't hold on anymore and she fell. That's how it went down ... *That's how.*" Vicar had set the narrative that would forever be the official story.

She looked at him with a compassion that was partly gratitude. He would cover her ass to his dying day, that sporadically noble, sweet slob ... And he was right: *She couldn't hold on anymore.*

With that, Tony Vicar turned onto his side and went into a silent state of isolation that would last for a long time.

Ronnie had picked up Jacquie and they had headed out to the Knickers, leaving Vicar behind. Even though he left all the lights on, and Jacquie had filled a bowl with candy, no kids came up the long dark driveway trick-or-treating. The place was as dark as his spirits. Frankie was asleep, snug as a bug.

He lay in bed and watched the episode of *Star Trek* where Spock talks to a rock with the mind-meld and thought how much it looked like the awful lasagna-like glop that Mom used to make in the electric frying pan. No wonder he had never really learned to provide for himself too much beyond TV dinners that tasted like tin and chemistry. *I miss Mum a lot, but her cooking ... my God.*

One of the bumper crop of random back hairs Vicar too often sprouted had ingrown or otherwise volcanofied. It looked exactly like the alien Horta on the TV screen. *If Nimoy were still alive, he'd be able to communicate with my zit.*

Vicar had spent the last couple of weeks feeling everything within him slump, like the proverbial cake left out in the rain. His world had now shrunk back down to where he'd been years ago — before the Accident, before Jacquie, back when he still reread the same *Mad* magazines with as much relish as he had when he was ten. When he lost his comb, for instance, he didn't want to go to the expense — and bother — of getting a new one, so he barely adjusted his hair for two straight years. No one appeared to notice. Luckily, he found a replacement on the sidewalk right near the old barbershop.

He had been a complete layabout sleepinski, frivolous and idle except for a vague dream of rock stardom. He remembered that no one gave a shit about him back in the day. But that was because *he* didn't give a shit about himself. He knew that now. Vicar lay wrapped in a cocoon of recollection; his Elvis costume was partially visible in his closet, its door slightly ajar.

He was restless now, uneasy, almost prickly. He couldn't just lie on the couch with the remote and a bowl of Hawkins Cheezies. His time in hiding had to end; he had rounded a corner and, despite his best intentions, had seen not the end of the road, but the beginning again. He had to force the issue … Life *had* to be more than endless circles, didn't it?

■ ■ ■

Kosmic Karaoke was in da house. Farley and Cosmic Ray stood on the riser they'd hauled into the Knickers and DJ'd as the crowd of semi-interested nincompoops in Hallowe'en costumes juddered drunkenly to the music. The ladies did the Calgary shuffle, with all the sex appeal of a prosciutto swinging from the rafters; the gents attempting the Courtenay tractor, steering a jolly pantomime serpentine, the tipsier ones shifting imaginary gears, intermittently strumming an air guitar, and blaring out the last lyric of every line, seldom correct but enthusiastic. It was all just so jarringly uncool. *Popping and locking*, to these people, had only to do with knuckles and tetanus.

The silly twat dressed as a horse decapitated himself on the bathroom door frame early on and at that point, the laughter really kicked in. All the ladies wanted their picture taken while dancing with the fool whose bottom was quadrupedal but who had a human head. It took only a cursory inspection to see that he had thoughtfully tacked on a truly massive sausage between the rear legs. By 11 p.m., a couple of girls had attempted to fellate the Italian snack food and come away with mouths full of salami. The guy, of course, pretended to be grievously wounded. Arthur Morrison was there, in drag, wearing Madonna's bustier, fashioned out of stainless-steel flour sifters, surrounded by a large crowd, all collapsing with laughter as he drunkenly gnawed on the *salame*. His mother would have quite literally died, and he did not give even one solitary shite.

The joke was replayed about eight thousand times, to escalating laughter by a long lineup of clowns. Unlike anywhere else, in Tyee Lagoon bad jokes *never* got old. This was going to be like a 1970s kegger. You could feel it in the air.

Ann Tenna, trying to goad Ross Poutine into dancing — something so unlikely that airborne swine might be used as a simile — looked over to see Con-Con in attendance at a social event for a change, not on duty. She was chatting amiably with Nancy, both snuggled in front of the blazing inglenook, smiling warmly to the people in their midst.

Ann eventually decided to dance with someone to make Ross Poutine jealous, just to coax him onto the dance floor, but it was to no avail. Poutine had once won a prize for the Boot-Scootin' Boogie, back when he had a bit more flex in his sacroiliac, and then decided to retire his crown. As Ann taunted, clad in a braided toreador pant made of Fortrel — *America's Fabric* — swathing a behemothic Tyee Lagoon arse, she wiggled at him while pulling a strange man by the hand toward the dance floor.

Poutine yelled to the guy with a jolly grin, "Enjoy, dere. You can take over d'payments." Then he howled like a horny wolf on a hilltop. He yucked it up and elbowed the guy sitting next to him.

Ann, her hair fashioned into long ringlets that looked like Vapona No Pest Strips, scrunched her face in outrage and flipped him the bird. Poutine barked back at her like a pooch with separation anxiety, then threw his head back, cackling. He leaned over to the confused guy next to him and said, "It's a doggie dog world, eh."

The guy, uncomprehending, just put on a baffled smile and nodded.

Ronnie was there, dressed as Wonder Woman, her long legs the star of the whole dance. From the stage, Cosmic Ray had trouble keeping his eyes on the DJ equipment. She looked so *fine*! The gorgeous cowgirl's eyes twinkled as she moved to the music with a sexy prance, occasionally looking up and winking at Ray.

Farley's be-toqued head bobbed in time with the tunes and he grinned absently at everyone passing by. To no one's surprise, he had gone outside a few minutes before to smoke a bomber the size of the Spruce Goose — along with a large, startlingly hirsute fantasy nurse, hopefully a man in a costume, 'cause otherwise that much fur on the back might portend an imminent wax shortage on the Island.

Farley grabbed the mike and started making a rambling dedication of a love song from a *dude* (the extra-furry fantasy nurse) to a *chick* (done up as Freddie Mercury, with a moustache cut from an Oldsmobile floor mat). He fucked up their names and couldn't be understood anyway. So, he started "rapping" and attempting to dance the "Dougie" — he had just learned it. Sadly, he looked more like an elderly woman trying to walk on a moving bus.

Cosmic Ray gently prised the mike from his hand and muttered apologetically, "Sorry. Song now."

Vicar's head rolled back and forth as he puzzled through his circular dilemma. His life *did* go in endless loops; the persistent repetition had always been front and centre, predictable as a November downpour. He partially sat up, leaned over, and grabbed a Kleenex, blowing his nose loudly. Looking at the used tissue, he mumbled, "Oh my God, I think that's my temporal lobe." For the first time in a couple of weeks, he laughed.

Vicar knew that he always spun a grand dream at the beginning of any undertaking, and always imagined the happy ending. *I have so much trouble seeing the middle.*

The accursed, unpredictable middle was where all the madness blindsided him, every damn time. The Fog of War obscured the road, and he ended up on his ass repeatedly, unable to manoeuvre. Vicar knew he was missing something — something that all life's winners instinctively grasped. Yes, yes, he had achieved much, maybe even more than he had dared ask for, but he sensed a tenuousness, a tippy-over, house-of-cards quality that warned him his life was probably collapsing, coming down around him at that very moment. But was it? Vicar couldn't even tell. He was too unbalanced to tell good from bad.

Vicar never bothered about pop-psychology *buzz-words*, as he called them. Silly things like *self-care*, *mindfulness*, *holistics*, or dire warnings about *co-dependence*. All complete horseshit. Psychobabble.

He did, however, consider that he might be full-on loony. Not a gentle term, but right in his wheelhouse. He lived in a world where stupid was not "misinformed," or "mistaken" — nope … stupid was stupid. Nuts was nuts. Puny was puny. *With your shield or on it, Vicar.* He absently toed a well-used sock that hung out of his shoe, tucked partly under the bed. It was exhausted, threadbare, and stinky. Why did he *keep* socks like that? It was symbolic of his life. Yes, yes. His life was an atrocious sock that needed to be heaved into a bin.

Secretly, Vicar would rather be slightly touched than the alternative, a purveyor of faux, Hollywoodized grief that was nothing but effing whining. God knew that with his profile, he could pull it off if he wanted to. But he wasn't going through all this merely for attention's sake. Celebrity heartache: not his thing. It was like Naugahyde. Not real, not even a good fake, unworthy of even a dashboard in a Soviet-era taxi. He'd been through too much to wring his hands over a pimple on a Kardashian, and if expected to sympathize, the veil would come down instantly.

Vicar got up, brushed orange dust off his T-shirt and wandered to the mirror. He looked at himself — bloated from a Cheezie overdose, unshaven, dishevelled, pasty. His left eye was glued shut, but he hadn't even been sleeping. He looked like an aerial view of the town dump. He was a guy who'd go to a park bench and just sit alone all day long, rocking back and forth, occasionally twitching and growling about chemtrails.

A not-very-discerning lady had once remarked, "Geez, you're *ee-centric*." Maybe he was. But, but, but … There was something else there, just beyond his fingertips.

Was all this his *fate*? A predestined end racing toward him as he sat, alone, confused, and oblivious? A train car that trundled along with no brakes, no navigation, no nothin'? How pathetic. In that case, the best you could do was use the frickin' *Force* to make your way, blindfolded, but confident as a sleepwalker — an *idiotic* sleepwalker. How many people live that kind of charmed life? Only liars with handsomely paid biographers had lives that read so smooth and predestined.

He breathed deeply. Looking down at the floor, he squeezed his eyes tightly and dug in, turning over the problem. The effort took probably an hour — a very long time to chew on a single question without interruption, and a near miracle for a man with such a flea-hopping mind. But miraculously, his effort finally brought him something. A flash of the truth; a small, vital perspective change. Frankie Hall's antique "Grandmother Clock" bonged in the other room. Jacquie had nicknamed it.

What Vicar realized was that life moved in the shape of a *helix*, not an endless circle. A corkscrew. It orbited the same centre, all right, but climbed and climbed upward. It was not a line, not a pencilled track on a map from "here" to "there." *He* was the mass around which everything else orbited. It *seemed* like it was a circular track, but that was just an illusion. He was not looking at things from the proper angle.

Vicar felt a jolt in his gut. The image seemed to illustrate the whole schmeer; the penny had dropped.

Where his epiphany came from, he wasn't sure, but he was fighting a kind of battle that nearly everyone had to face. *How does everyone else get through this?* His internal life had always been a such a roller-coaster.

He gazed at the tattered corner of the quilt and imagined the threads of his life anchored in his past and carrying messages into the future.

As *double*-helix strings of DNA shaped his biology, these other corkscrewing "threads" made up his story: a narrative that spiralled forever upward. It recounted a tale *for the record* — like that fancy French tapestry that showed the Norman invasion of Britain.

He blinked, attempting to clear his head of butterfly sneezes. Also, to unglue his eye.

Images cascaded; not all were dark or preciously angsty like a Pink Floyd album. *But they always had been before.* He saw Serena's face floating in his mind's eye. Her tragic end had left a mark on him. Vicar realized that they were more alike than he wanted to admit. Two wandering souls, one surrounded by love, the other by a lack of it. Serena's end had required no rocket science to predict.

Serena's past, her "threads," were beyond her capability to grasp; she just couldn't overcome her own history, her own corkscrew path. When threads are that badly tangled, you can't do it without someone else lending a hand. Serena never had help — not the kind of help she truly needed, anyway.

Vicar at least had been blanketed in kindness and support. He had been so incredibly lucky. Funny how good luck sometimes looked to its recipient like nothing more than a series of mountains to climb, one after another, work, work, worry, worry. *Vicar, sometimes you can't find your arse in broad daylight with both hands.*

He looked again at his Elvis costume, peeking out from behind the wardrobe door. Everybody had skeletons in their closets, and he had his. Some died trying to deal with theirs, failing to lay their ghosts; others channelled through various means: religion or incessant volunteering, maybe obsessive cat-ownership ... or maybe preposterous dreams of rock stardom. He took a moment to think about that.

He felt a little shaky to be so crystal clear, so, so ... *certain*, so able to put a line under it, but he had learned that, though the devil might be in the details, there's always *another level beneath the devil*. It wasn't all bad, it really wasn't. Just like the plane crash ... worst-case scenario, until you got the full story. Yeah, this could be the end, but it could just as well be a new beginning. Vicar felt that magical but very human sensation of everything in his mind doing a one-eighty for the better with a "click," propelled by one insight.

He sat back down on the edge of the bed, took a deep, bracing breath, and got on the blower to Merri

Crabtree. She and Steven — *ooh la la* — would watch Frankie for a few hours. She jumped at the chance. She always did.

And Vicar himself? He had a *dance* to attend.

Merri swooped into the house, relieved to find it empty of Beulah, who would have received her flintiest glare, reserved for war criminals, people who mistreat animals, and skinny bitches who flirt with her man. *I hope she's slim because of a tapeworm that slinks out her ass at night looking for cracker crumbs in the bed.* There was no accompanying giggle to that thought.

She saw that baby Frankie was zonked and came back into the kitchen. There, Steven gawked rather uncomfortably at Vicar, resplendent now as Elvis Presley, signature shades pushed up into his fake hairdo, a wig made of the finest human torch material — guaranteed to light even the darkest soft drink commercial. Elvis swaggered around Steven, a paragon of the straightest-and-narrowest, delighted with the news advising that Frankie's adoption paperwork was now being finalized and they could get it all over soon, perhaps in a week or two. Suddenly triumphant, Vicar strode around the kitchen, feeling as if he wanted to crow. Steven Leigh backed away from Elvis in a cautiously polite pirouette on the tile floor.

Merri had been unaware of the adoption good news — Steven never said a peep about his clients or their business. But once she caught wind of it, she did not back away from the prancing Elvis-like effigy before her; instead, she hugged Vicar tightly. It might have been a surprise to Steven, but she occasionally enjoyed Vicar's nonsense. She remembered her daughter announcing she was to become a grandmother and felt a surge of similar emotions. Vicar, already loaded for bear, would no doubt turn on his afterburners tonight. He would need his Tyee Lagoon Mafia to place him in the fart sack when he returned later. *Fart sack* — that was what Wally used to call it. *How off colour!* Giggle.

Vicar's pilot light was indeed lit, and his tank was clearly full. Merri snickered as she and Steven sent him off to the Knickers, looking like a heroic doofus. Her endlessly generous heart was full.

Striding out to the garage, Vicar wrestled an old toilet bowl into the back of his gargantuan 1974 Cadillac and used the seat belt to hold it into place.

■ ■ ■

Earlier that afternoon, Jacquie had not been into it; the house had been so sombre, and the mood had not been conducive to getting hyped for a costume party, but she simply had to get out of the place for a while. She couldn't bear another minute tippy-toeing around a hibernating Vicar and listening to Mother's non-stop gabbling. Jacquie had yet to find the piss-pot that Beulah *couldn't talk the handle offa*.

Mother had scandalously decided to accept a ride to the Hallowe'en dance with a pile of young men in a huge truck. She had met them at the pub and flirted outrageously. Knowing her name, Beulah, was not a very sexy one, she claimed instead that she was "Milfy O'Neil." She was an instant hit.

Her escorts arrived dressed as a six-pack of beer bottles, head to toe in brown body stockings, pie plates on their heads for bottle caps. She was a princess, high cut and costume bejewelled, toy tiara perched on her head, sexy stocking top fully visible on one side. She hiked up her gown to climb into the mammoth pickup while one of the lads boosted her bottom. She pretended to be shocked and made sure to linger just a moment too long as the young men burst out in raucous laughter.

— — —

Earlier that evening, Ronnie had been putting the final touches on her superhero makeup while chatting with Jacquie, who stood leaning on the bathroom door jamb, car keys jangling in her hand.

Jacquie was surprised. "You cannot be serious!"

Ronnie shook her head and replied, "I am dead serious, Jack. Three of them. Three flying saucers, right above my yard. He *called* them — he summoned *saucers*. No, no, honest ..."

Jacquie O tilted her head dubiously and said, "Had you been smoking something from an exotic Asian locale?" She was only half joking because Ray was known to have herbal entertainments available that no other person in the Western hemisphere could get hold of.

"Yeah, right." Ronnie topped out at fancy cocktails with umbrellas. "I swear there were three flying saucers there before my eyes, and Ray grinning like a goof. I know you don't believe it."

"So, one saucer each for the members of Hospital Fish? Are they finally coming to take them away to Rock 'n' Roll Heaven?" Her eyes twinkled as she stuck her finger in her ear like Gary Owens. "Reports just in say they have a helluva band."

Ronnie made a face and said with sarcasm, "No, it was the Father, the Son, and the Holy Ghost ... Why are you giving me such a hard time, anyway?" She cracked a lopsided grin. "You've got years of Vicar's ghost stories ... *and* a haunted hotel."

"I just realized, Ronnie." Jacquie looked down and off to the right. "I got interested in Tony after all that weird supernatural stuff he was doing. Like when he brought that lady back to life at the accident. I fought it — still do a little, but that's what sucked me in." She looked at Ronnie's beautiful reflection in the bathroom mirror. "Umm, it seems to me Ray might be doing the same thing to you."

Tony was showing how it was done, whether he was aware of it or not. Once again, he seemed to have a plan, but she could've sworn he was just bumbling through life like an electrically stimulated corpse some days. Jacquie twisted her face into a wry grin.

Ronnie paused a moment. *By God, Jacquie is right.* But was Ray following Vicar's example, or was this a case of non-random randomness, like two quick lottery wins in a row after a ten-year losing streak?

Their men, the boys, were surrounded, *orbited* by stuff so anomalous that you either had to buy in or bugger off. Ronnie had the same flash of realization that Jacquie had had years before.

Jacquie watched Ronnie's thoughts crawl over her face and then imagined poor Tony, too bummed to go to the dance, babysitting Frankie but possibly too depressed to even take care of himself. He spent far too much of his life waffling between delusions of rock 'n' roll power-trio glory and self-loathing. His best offerings came from deep in the marrow, but getting down there required such a tremendous, exhausting effort, and not just from him. He really was a chore some days.

She looked at Ronnie and muttered, "Welcome to the club. It's a very *peculiar* club, by the way."

■ ■ ■

Behind the wheel of the giant Caddy, Tony Vicar felt confidence thrumming through him. He had been dragooned into normalcy for so long that he had almost forgotten the expressive, unearthly power of *weird*. He had thrown open the door and embraced all the contrary madness within him. *Fuck normal.* Goddamn, it felt good. He revelled at the feeling of freedom; his dalliance with being in the reassuring, safe middle of the pack had been very educational but not much fun. Highly unsatisfying.

Normal just couldn't stick to him for very long! He exulted, savouring what was about to go down. Life without *weird* was like, like, uhh … a cult; the only thing worse than blindly following rules was to be part of a group whose members are blindly following rules together. *I will teach Frankie how to be weird, too.* He thought of his treasured, customized brand of weirdness and then stopped short. There could be a lotta pain in them thar weird hills. Maybe she should just watch from a safe distance.

After a four-minute drive, he nosed the giant Caddy into his parking spot at the Knickers, deliberately made a bit wider to allow for the huge sedan on occasions just like this one. He hauled out his musty-smelling fifty-year-old toilet bowl and hugged it in his arms, his sequined eagle cloak fluttering regally in trail.

The people in the entryway parted with a hush as he swept right past Noreen, who always took the tickets at dances. Her eyes were as big as saucers, as if she'd just seen a ghost.

Ray spied him in the vestibule, bulky commode in his arms, sequins dimly flashing under the energy-saver forty-watt bulb, and immediately pulled up *"Also Sprach*

Zarathustra," Richard Strauss's Elvis entry music. He faded down the song that had been playing and the low notes of the dramatic piece began to rumble.

Elvis strode toward Jacquie, who was leaning on a high-backed stool just at the end of the bar, at that moment scandalized by her horn-dog mother, who stood surrounded by a retinue of young, hard-bodied yeomen, batting her eyes like a cartoon doe. Jacquie had a horrifying vision that their giant pickup truck might be the site of an extremely gross granny orgy in a couple of hours. She shuddered and then overheard, "Just Beefeater on ice, handsome ... I've brought my own bottle of Dubonnet. Did you know that's what the Queen used to drink?"

Jacquie looked at the ornately framed photograph of Queen Elizabeth hanging on the north wall and shrugged apologetically.

Elvis gingerly set the toilet on the dance floor and grabbed Jacquie around the waist, kissing her forcefully — a sex god's unemployed understudy, temporarily working at the Factory Outlet mall, a tidge out of practice. Her cheeks flushed. Their front teeth clacked together awkwardly and in her sultriest manner she checked for dental damage. He decided he'd tell Jacquie the good news about Frankie later, when they could have a private moment, and strode away, throwing a Memphis-flavoured "Thankyouverymuch" over his shoulder.

Elvis marched to the little riser cum stage, stared down Farley and Cosmic Ray like a gunfighter just for the theatrics, and put the toilet down front and centre where everyone could see it. In time with the music, he insolently grabbed one of the mikes, took down his stretchy Elvis *trou* and sat on the toilet, like a perfectly timed dance routine.

Ray, fully onboard, cued up a song to follow the dramatic intro, and it began to play. James Burton twanged, Ronnie Tutt double-kicked, Kathy Westmoreland sang coloratura from way up in the musical nosebleed seats, and J.D. Sumner shook way on down to the basement. Elvis and his naked arse had re-entered the building!

He began to sing — terribly. Sounded like shit, as usual; absolute crap. Apparently, This Time, the Lord Had Given Him a Mountain … The Lord really ought to have given him Auto-Tune. But he was back.

Sure, it was only the Knickers, but he could see it all, looking down from above now, clearly, contentedly, happily. He did not flail around willy-nilly, looking for guidance, special pleading, a pathetic copy-cat. He was beyond that now — he knew his own story; he felt his own compass pointing true north. What was to come, uncertain, but Vicar finally had his hand on the tiller. Leaving the safety of his old familiar harbour, he prepared to sail, and sang like a humpback whale serenading his sweetheart ten thousand miles away.

The crowd surged around him. As he approached the big money note in the outro, they were his, all his, even the *man called horse* dancing to the song, his salami dick swaying curiously, twirling in triplets to the groove. At that moment Tony Vicar was ten feet tall, bullet proof, and proudly preposterous, as Earth and heaven intended it to be. Jumping to his feet, quickly pulling up his pants with his free hand, he took a deep breath, hit the big finale note, and stood bestride Tyee Lagoon like a colossal Spandex God ...

Fade to black.

End

Acknowledgements

As has always been and always will be, I thank Pete McCormack for a lifetime of brillo advice, friendship, and commiseration. He is a treasure. I am his drummer.

I thank O.C. O'Cennide, who, early on, put my dialogue to the smell test. Captain Sig Sort aided me greatly by helping with airplane-y bits and UFO reports made by pilots. He also lets me steer sometimes.

Shannon Whibbs brought a lot of love and heart to this, all while fighting through personal loss — a trouper's trouper, she is. Erin Pinksen was uncommonly kind and patient and really made things work when I despaired. Vicky Bell came up big in the last round of edits, pushing things to a much higher level than I could have done myself.

Ani Kyd Wolff, TV producer, leather-bedecked rock star, and ball of energy is onto the next phase of

Tony Vicar already. Colin Rivers, literary agent: Quite a nice young man. No, really. *Way* nicer than people say.

Cindy Labonte-Smith, author and former grade four classmate, who can speak extemporaneously until *all* the cows come home, exhausted. My role is to distract her and point out the shiny thing on the lawn. She always lends a huge hand, and I thank her for her friendship.

Gage Hibbins, an understudy *Impossiblist*, surely related to The Man They Call Reveen, at least in spirit. Watch for this young man; he is coming to remind us that young people *rock*. JJ Martin, Jeremy John Dunton: gifted authors themselves, and supporters who put their money where their mouths are. They are bright guys and superb gents. Patricia and Zdravy, my grateful thanks.

Thanks to Robert King-Brown, who taught me to properly write a sentence — a lesson my editors frequently point out that I have forgotten — and who encouraged my love of our language while forbidding me to ever whistle in his presence. He was an oasis.

My wife, Merm, swears she was my ghostwriter on this book. Indeed, I can "see your yeg." I thank her for listening to my countless edits and tweaks, thank her for the title, and the colour she wisely chose for the cover. "Purple," I said. "Eggplant," she replied, aghast, pitying the colourless world in which I live.

Olly, Sparky, Louie — a trio more swingin' than Nat Cole's. Without these three unhinged yard apes, I'm just an old fart complaining about the rising price of bananas. Long may you rule at the apex of the Who's Who in our zoo.

To my daughters-in-law: What the hell were you thinking? To my sons: I promise to become incontinent in my final days, leaving the cleanup to you. I might even start wearing a onesie.

As always, I thank the great big Spirit of the West family and revel exultantly in the adventures of the second generation. I await the third gen with anticipation.

And finally, thank you to all the readers of Vicar and his nutty ball club. You have been wonderfully kind and supportive. It means the world to me.

VRD

About the Author

Vince R. Ditrich is a twitchy, half-deaf, recovering musician, greying, confused, prone to barking at his uncooperative celery blower — like that will help — and convinced he's hilarious, though family opinions vary. His 30-plus-year stint as a member of Canadian musical group Spirit of the West has left him tired of travel and suspicious of airport food, but savvy enough to put socks, underwear, a spare shirt, and antacids into his carry-on. Unless you are Dos Equis's "Most Interesting Man in the World," he will probably not chat during the flight. He has become, for all intents and purposes, a flinty old turd.

He does like *some* things … vintage cars, history, photography, a good pint or a delicious cocktail, the

VINCE R. DITRICH

smell of books, Mom & Pop shops, classic suits, dimly lit lounges, soft pants, the French onion soup at 15 Park Bistro in Osoyoos, B.C., and Hawkins Cheezies — humankind's most pleasing snack.

Vince lives in a tiny little town on Vancouver Island where any traffic is such an anomaly that he and his wife, Merm, rush to the window to point and gawk.

He is also author of *The Liquor Vicar* and *The Vicar's Knickers*.